THE FIRST CUT

A DCI DANNY FLINT BOOK

TREVOR NEGUS

INKUBATOR
BOOKS

Published by Inkubator Books
www.inkubatorbooks.com

Copyright © 2024 by Trevor Negus

Trevor Negus has asserted his right to be identified as the author of this work.

ISBN (eBook): 978-1-83756-386-9
ISBN (Paperback): 978-1-83756-387-6

THE FIRST CUT is a work of fiction. People, places, events, and situations are the product of the author's imagination. Any resemblance to actual persons, living or dead is entirely coincidental.

PROLOGUE

10.00 a.m., 7 March 1964
The Divine Shepherd Private Clinic, Marlborough Road,
Nottingham

The woman sat in the car staring out at the imposing red-brick house. The building was hidden from the nearby road by high conifer hedges and now that the heavy wooden gates had closed behind the car, the woman's sense of foreboding increased even more.

Sensing her unease, the priest who had driven the car into the small car park switched the engine off and said as if to reassure her, 'Try not to worry. The nuns who work here are all fully trained midwives. They'll take good care of you and your infant.'

He glanced down at the woman's stomach, heavy with child, and continued, 'You know you're doing the right thing.

Your husband made it perfectly clear to you that he wouldn't entertain the prospect of raising another man's child.'

The woman brushed a tear from her eye and nodded as the priest continued his barbed appraisal of her predicament. 'You had your sinful dalliance, sister. Your pregnancy is testament to that. Your husband is prepared to forgive you, and you should be thankful for small mercies. Many men would have kicked you and your bastard child out.'

The woman had heard enough and hissed, 'That's enough, Father. I know I've sinned, that adultery is a sin, but I couldn't countenance an abortion. If I'm going to save my marriage and respect the vows I made on my wedding day, this is my only option. It doesn't mean I'm happy with the situation.'

The priest raised an eyebrow and said spitefully, 'Nobody's happy with the situation. I think you meant to say respect the vows you haven't already broken. The only way you can save your marriage is by giving up this child for adoption, as we have agreed.'

The woman looked down into the footwell of the car, fighting against a strong urge to run away, to get as far away from that house, that priest, as possible. Her right hand gripped the small overnight bag so tightly that her knuckles turned white.

Without saying another word, she opened the door and heaved herself out of the passenger seat. The priest quickly left his seat too and walked beside her up the two stone steps to the double oak doors.

He rang the ornate bell, and the door was opened almost immediately by a young nun.

The priest said, 'I'm Father Hennessey. I telephoned your Mother Superior earlier, she's expecting us.'

'We were expecting you an hour ago, Father. Is everything all right?'

The priest tutted and said, 'The young lady here had expressed a certain reluctance to go through with the arrangements, but we're here now and she realises she's doing the right thing, both for her and the child.'

There was genuine compassion in the eyes of the young nun as she said to the woman, 'Try not to worry. We'll look after you and your baby.'

She took the woman's overnight bag from her, supporting her as they walked. 'Come with me,' she said softly. 'We've a lovely room ready for you. Father Hennessey can wait in the Mother Superior's office. You won't have to see, or hear, him anymore, not while you're here.'

Accepting her fate, the young woman walked alongside the nun down a dark, wood-panelled corridor. She knew she would never get to hold the baby she was about to give birth to. The adoption agency that worked in tandem with the Divine Shepherd private clinic would already have parents lined up, eagerly awaiting the arrival of their adopted infant.

What could she do?

When she discovered she was pregnant, the result of a fumbled one-night stand after a solitary night out, it was obvious to her who the father was. Her husband had been working away for six months. There was no way the child was his. She knew it and so did he.

Her husband had been enraged when she first told him she was pregnant, but he dearly loved his wife and wanted their marriage to work, so he had asked her, for the sake of their marriage, to have an abortion. As a devout Catholic that had never been an option for her, and she steadfastly refused.

As her pregnancy started to show, her husband insisted she move away from the family home, and stay with his sister in Norfolk until the time came for her to have the baby.

This meant the pregnancy was an extremely lonely and traumatic experience. She had been stuck in a house where nobody cared about, or even spoke, to her.

While she was away her husband had sought advice from his local priest. It had been Father Hennessey who suggested that, rather than his wife go through the sinful anguish of an abortion, the unwanted child be delivered and put straight up for adoption. He had assured the husband that he could arrange everything for a small donation to the church and that nobody local need know that his wife had ever been pregnant.

Once he had paid the not-so-small donation, her husband had driven to Norfolk and informed his wife what he'd arranged and that if she wanted to save their marriage, she would agree to the adoption and sign the papers.

Feeling trapped and desperate to be away from the loveless house in Norfolk, she had readily signed the papers which agreed for her baby to be adopted.

She still loved her husband and didn't want a single act of drunken madness to ruin her marriage, and her life.

Now as she settled herself into the spartan room at the private clinic, she knew her living nightmare was coming to an end. In a week's time she would be able to return home and continue her married life, with a man she genuinely loved.

All she had to do now was convince herself she could live a happy and contented life, one that would never acknowledge the existence of her firstborn.

1

1.00 a.m., 10 January 1991
Nottingham City Centre

Mark Bradbury cringed as another round of guffaws issued forth from the four men he was drinking with. Their boorish, immature behaviour in the bar of the hotel they were staying in had been irritating Mark for a while, so he made the decision to leave them to it and venture out into Nottingham city centre alone.

It wasn't just the men's behaviour and inane jokes that he had found boring. Now in his late twenties, Mark hated his job as a salesman and, although his salary was generous, he yearned for a more fulfilling life. He had an Oxford University degree in business studies and could speak several languages fluently, including Cantonese. This made him a prized asset for the multinational company that employed him, as they were keen to further expand their already substantial business links with China.

He was at the hotel in Nottingham for yet another business seminar, that no longer held his interest. It had been a long week, and he was looking forward to going home to Leicester in the morning.

As he walked into the city centre looking for a nightclub, or a bar that was still open, he thought about the application he had recently completed and the possibility of an exciting career change.

He was hoping to start a career in the security service. After his initial approach, he had been encouraged by the apparent desperate need for fluent Cantonese speakers within the service. He knew the application and vetting process was complex, extremely thorough and would take a long time, but he was hopeful he would qualify and be able to make the change he craved so much.

He didn't really know Nottingham city centre and after wandering aimlessly around the almost deserted streets for thirty minutes he still hadn't found any clubs or bars that looked inviting, so he decided to return to the hotel and turn in.

He had a rough idea what direction he needed to go to make his way back to the hotel. He turned a corner and found himself at the side of a churchyard, next to St Mary's church and near to the Shire Hall, two imposing buildings he did recognise. The street lighting here was poor, and he began to feel a sense of unease. He wasn't overly worried as he knew he could handle himself. He'd been a keen student of karate ever since childhood and kept himself very fit.

He heard a scuffling noise behind him and turned to see a man smoking a cigarette standing about five yards behind him. The man didn't approach or say anything, so Mark turned intending to walk away. As he did so, he was confronted by a second man standing directly in front of him.

This man had long dreadlocks and was much bigger than Mark. He stared at Mark and hissed, 'Give me your wallet, or I'll cut you.'

For the first time Mark saw the knife in the man's right hand. The blade was slim and about four inches in length. It was a knife designed for fighting.

Mark took a pace back and stammered, 'I don't want any trouble. I haven't got a wallet, just a few quid in my pocket. You can have that.'

The man smiled, revealing a gold glint in his teeth, and said, 'Don't try and play me, man. Give me your wallet, now!'

Mark was about to turn and make a run for it when he remembered the second man standing behind him blocking any escape route.

Feeling backed into a corner, in that moment he decided to defend himself, knife or no knife, and he said, 'No chance.'

Without a second's hesitation, the knifeman rushed forward lunging the blade towards Mark's stomach. It was the move Mark had been expecting and he managed to parry the thrust by grabbing the blade of the knife. He felt the searing pain as the sharp blade sliced through the flesh on the palm of his right hand and he instantly released his grip.

The knifeman stepped back a pace and then rushed forward again. This time Mark deftly sidestepped and, using the knifeman's own momentum, he punched the man on his cheek.

Although it was only a glancing blow, it was forceful enough to cause the big man to spin off balance and fall heavily onto his back. There was a loud crack as his head whipped back and hit the kerb edge.

The knife he had been holding clattered along the pavement and ended up at Mark's feet. He quickly picked the blade up and sprinted away from the two men. As he ran, the streets became brighter and better lit. He turned a corner and could see a main road in the distance. He sprinted hard, directly across the main road narrowly missing being hit by a passing car. The driver of which sounded the car's horn angrily.

Having ran across the road he continued until he saw a right turn. He turned the corner and recognised where he was. He knew this road led to St Peter's Square. Glancing over his shoulder he was relieved to see he wasn't being chased.

Looking down he was shocked that he was still holding the would-be mugger's bloodied knife in his left hand. Scanning the street, he saw a drain in the road directly in front of him. He bent down and slipped the knife into the drain, hearing it splash in the water below. He then inspected the damage done to his right hand where he had grabbed the attacker's blade.

There was a three-inch cut across his palm. It wasn't painful but it was bleeding heavily. He took a handkerchief from his pocket and wrapped it tightly around the wound to stem the bleeding. Once he had stemmed the flow of blood he began to walk briskly back to his hotel. He knew it was less than a ten-minute walk from the square.

Once he was back in his hotel room, he would be able to take care of his hand properly. The wound was quite deep and bleeding heavily, but he didn't think it would require stitches. He knew if he involved the police, the incident may have a detrimental effect on his pending career change.

He slipped into the hotel foyer and using the stairs, not the lift, he made his way back to his room.

He had no thoughts about the two muggers, just a huge sense of relief that he had managed to come out of what had been a dangerous situation relatively unscathed. As he inspected the wound in good light, he could now see that the cut wasn't too bad. He would need to keep an eye out for any possible infection over the next few days, but he was happy enough not to go immediately to the hospital. After ten more minutes of direct pressure the bleeding had almost stopped and, although it was very sore, he thought it would heal well enough.

It had been an adrenaline-filled but unfortunate end to a very boring week.

2

3.30 a.m., 10 January 1991
Western Avenue, Mansfield, Nottinghamshire

Craig Stevens cursed under his breath. The effects of the copious amount of alcohol he had consumed had well and truly worn off and he was dismayed to see that his wife had locked the large wrought-iron gates that afforded the only access to his house.

He now had a choice of either trying to find somewhere else to crash for what was left of the night or climbing the gate or high stone wall to get into his house.

He was silently raging. How dare she effectively lock him out of his own house.

Finding somewhere else to stay wasn't really an option, so he started to try and climb the slippery gates. After several attempts he managed to reach the top and clamber over, intending to drop to the floor.

Manoeuvring his grip on the top spike, he suddenly lost his footing and fell to the floor. The sharp point of the spike sliced through the palm of his right hand as he fell. The fall initially knocked the wind from him and, at first, he didn't realise the damage he had done to his hand.

Cursing loudly, he staggered to the front door of his house and began beating on the door, 'Open up, you cow!'

As he banged on the wooden door, he saw the blood spatter from his injured hand and realised that he was cut and losing blood.

He shouted again, 'Open the door! I'm bleeding to death out here!'

A light appeared behind the door, and he heard the key being turned and bolts being drawn back.

As the door was opened, he pushed by his long-suffering wife and shouted, 'See what you've done!'

He shoved his hand in her face showing her the deep laceration, before slapping her across the cheek with the same damaged hand. It wasn't a heavy blow, but it left his blood smeared on her cheek.

As she backed away from him, he raged, 'Why did you lock the fucking gates? You knew I'd be home late tonight.'

In a frightened voice she whispered, 'I get worried here on my own. I waited until three o'clock before I locked the gates. I didn't think you were coming home. I know what you're like when you've been drinking in Nottingham.'

As he wrapped a tea towel around his injured hand, he snarled, 'And what's that supposed to mean, you know what I'm like? Are you trying to wind me up?'

In a desperate attempt to placate her angry husband, she said quietly, 'I didn't mean anything. Let me help you with that.'

She began to wrap the tea towel tighter around his injured hand trying to stem the bleeding.

She could see it was a deep cut and would need the attention of a doctor.

'You should go to the hospital. It needs stitching.'

'Bloody marvellous. That's all I need. The perfect end to the perfect bloody night. This is all your fault, you stupid bitch.'

She tried to back away, knowing what was coming next. She managed to half dodge the first blow, but the second punch found its mark and knocked her to the floor. As she curled into a ball, he aimed several kicks at the back of her head before storming into the kitchen, leaving her groaning in a pitiful, broken heap.

He grabbed the key for the padlock that secured the gates and stormed out of the house, spitefully kicking her again as he stepped over her in the hallway.

Slamming the door behind him, he unlocked the gates and started walking to the hospital, cursing as he wondered how long he would be stuck there waiting to be seen.

3

5.00 a.m., 10 January 1991
Woolmer Road, The Meadows, Nottingham

It was the longest amount of time he'd ever had off while serving as a police officer and now, as he drove through the almost deserted streets of Nottingham, DCI Danny Flint wondered how easy it would be to get straight back into the pressure cooker environment of the Major Crime Investigation Unit.

Any notion of easing himself in gently on his first day back had disappeared when he'd received the telephone call at four o'clock that morning from the police control room informing him that a body had been discovered in the Meadows area and that it looked like murder.

Danny parked his car on Woolmer Road and surveyed the scene. Several police vehicles were already parked on the narrow street. He could see DI Rob Buxton standing next to the white forensic tent that he knew would be covering the body of the deceased.

Woolmer Road had terraced housing on both sides. There were no front yards and the front doors of the properties opened directly onto the pavement. Parked cars lined both sides of the narrow street. Danny was aware that the Meadows district was one of the city's hotspots for vehicle crime. Vehicles were stolen from this area most nights, as gangs of joyriders and car thieves prowled the poorly lit streets.

This would be the first murder investigation he had led since his long period of annual leave following the arrest of Jan Miller and the shooting of PC Sanderson at the caravan near Dunstanburgh in Northumberland.

He hadn't realised just how much he'd needed the rest until the second week of the six-week break.

He had spent the first week at home, reading books, watching TV and just spending time with his wife Sue and four-year-old daughter Hayley.

He had managed to persuade Sue to take time off from work, and on the spur of the moment had booked the family a long holiday in Lanzarote for some much-needed winter sun.

He had come back feeling refreshed and relaxed and knowing he was ready to get back to work. After all the stress and fallout from the Guy Royal murder inquiry it was a break he had desperately needed.

Pushing thoughts of the recent holiday to the back of his mind, he took a deep breath, got out of his car and walked across the street to the tent.

Rob smiled and held out his hand. 'Welcome back, boss. How was the holiday?'

Gripping his friend's hand in a warm handshake, Danny replied, 'Just what the doctor ordered, mate. What have we got?'

'Dead man is Lionel Wickes. He's originally from Jamaica and we think he was seventy-three years old. He lived alone at sixty-two Woolmer Road. No next of kin that we know about yet.'

'Circumstances?'

'From what we've gathered from neighbours so far, it appears some lowlife was stealing Mr Wickes' car. He's confronted them to try and prevent his pride and joy being taken.'

'Anybody see what happened?'

'No. But plenty heard the commotion. Apparently, it's a regular occurrence in this area. Cars are always being nicked and people are edgy.'

'Okay. Let's have a look.'

Rob held the tent flap open for Danny to duck inside before following him. There was a white arc light inside the tent that lit everything harshly, making Danny squint against the glare.

Lionel Wickes was lying face down and Danny could see the massive wound on the right side of his head. The man's eyes were wide open and staring lifelessly at the tarmac of the road. It looked like he'd died instantly. He was dressed in pyjamas and a dressing gown and still had carpet slippers on his feet.

Danny squatted beside the dead man and said, 'Any idea what caused the injury?'

Rob replied, 'Tim recovered a bloodstained length of scaffold pole, which was on the floor beside Mr Wickes. It looks like he's been hit with that.'

Looking closer, Danny couldn't see any other obvious injuries.

'So, just the one blow to the head?'

'Could be, but we won't know until the post-mortem proper.'

'Do you think he was confronting one thief and was surprised by a second?'

Rob shrugged. 'It's possible; there could have been two, or it could be just one nasty bastard who didn't like the idea of being fronted up by an old man.'

'Any idea what time the pathologist will be here?'

'Should be here any moment. I put the call in at the same time as I requested you be called out. You'll be pleased to hear it's Seamus Carter attending.'

Danny nodded thoughtfully before saying, 'Okay. Show me his car.'

The two detectives stepped out of the tent and Danny took a moment for his eyes to readjust to the dark. It wouldn't be dawn for at least another three hours and the street lighting was dull.

Danny shivered against the blast of cold air and was pleased he had remembered to grab his overcoat. Thrusting his hands in his pockets, he said, 'Which one's his?'

Rob pointed to a bronze-coloured Ford Fiesta, situated two vehicles away from the forensic tent.

Danny could see Tim Appleby and other scenes of crime staff standing around the car.

As he walked towards the car, Danny saw that the front passenger window was smashed, and an attempt had been made to force the ignition casing.

He turned to Rob. 'That explains the scaffold pole. The thief has attempted to scaff the ignition to get it going.'

Rob nodded in agreement. 'Those were my thoughts. Just use the scaffold pole to smash the ignition casing and hot wire the car.'

Danny made eye contact with Tim and said, 'Morning, Tim. Have you arranged for a full lift of the vehicle?'

'Morning, boss. The vehicle examiners are on their way. The forensic bay at headquarters is empty and we'll lift the vehicle back there before we start going over it properly. I've had a cursory look inside and there's nothing obvious that could have been dropped by an offender.'

'Where did you recover the length of scaffold pole?'

'Right next to the old man. Whoever hit him, dropped it immediately and ran.'

Danny looked at Rob. 'Any ideas where the scaffold pole came from?'

'Not yet, but I've got people looking in the area. Some of these car thieves bring their own.'

'The way the window's been smashed it must have made a hell of a din, and nobody saw a thing?'

'Not that we've found yet, but it's still early days and there are a lot of people still to talk to.'

A dark blue Volvo pulled into a space opposite the forensic tent and Danny watched as Seamus Carter heaved his enormous bulk from the driver's seat.

He strode purposefully across the road and with a beaming smile he boomed, 'So, the boss man has finally returned. Good to see you, Danny, I hope you're feeling rested.'

'I'm all good, Seamus. Are you on your own today?'

'Not entirely. Brigitte will be joining us later at the mortuary for the post-mortem. She had a late night and was unable to attend this morning. She passed her final exams and will be moving on to pastures new shortly, so she was out celebrating. Though why the prospect of not working with me in the future should be a cause for celebration is beyond me. Anyway. What have we got?'

Once again Danny stepped inside the tent, but this time stood back allowing Seamus to examine the deceased.

After a few minutes, the big Irishman said, 'Well, it's obvious what the cause of death is here. That head injury is catastrophic. Do we have the weapon?'

Danny said, 'A short length of scaffold pole.'

'Yeah. That would do it right enough, but whoever wielded it used a hell of a lot of force. A blow struck with that amount of force was only ever designed to kill and not stun. This is somebody who's no stranger to this level of violence. Either they've killed before, or they've been trained how to.'

Danny said, 'I couldn't see any other obvious injuries.'

Seamus leaned forward to have a closer look. 'I'm not sure, but there could be some bruising on his hands. I'll know better when we get him back to the mortuary. In the meantime, I'll bag his hands, so we don't lose anything. It's possible that he defended himself and there could be traces of the killer on them.'

'What time do you think you'll be ready for the post-mortem?'

'Things shouldn't take too long here. I'll book the City Hospital mortuary for eleven o'clock.'

'Okay. Thanks, Seamus. Good to see you.'

'You too – and try to take it easy now you're back. I know you're busy right now, but I could do with having a chat about a personal matter when you get a minute.'

A puzzled look on his face, Danny asked, 'Personal?'

'Nothing to worry about, Danny. It will keep.'

'Okay. You know you can call me any time, right?'

'Will do and thanks.'

Danny was intrigued but didn't want to push his friend. He had worked, and been friends, with the big Irishman long enough to know that Seamus would talk to him when he was ready.

He stepped out of the tent and took a deep breath. He'd just taken the longest period off in his entire police service and it already felt like he'd never been away.

'Boss.' Rob approached him with a concerned look on his face. 'We've got another one.'

'What?'

'A road cleaner has just found a body near to the Shire Hall in the city centre. The uniform officers in attendance are saying it looks like another murder.'

'Okay. Get onto the control room and tell them to call out Tina and Andy to travel to that scene. We can't risk any cross-contamination of scenes. I'll go home, get changed and join them there as soon as I can.'

Rob spoke into his radio. 'DI Buxton to control. Call out DI Cartwright and DS Wills to attend the Shire Hall scene as soon as possible. Make sure uniform officers preserve the scene until they arrive. Over.'

'Thanks, Rob. I'm going to need you to assess the amount of house-to-house enquiries that will need doing here, and what personnel we're going to need. Just looking at this street I'm thinking we're going to need the assistance of the Special Operations Unit. I also want you to dedicate somebody to scoping for any possible CCTV cameras. It's unlikely in such a residential area but you never know.'

'I'm on it, boss.'

Danny turned to Tim and said, 'You'll need to arrange for other staff to attend this new scene at the Shire Hall in the city. Is that going to cause you any problems?'

'No problem. I'll get that sorted.'

'Thanks, Tim'

As Danny walked back to his car, he reflected on the thoughts he'd had as he drove to the Meadows earlier.

He'd wondered then how much time he would need to settle back into work.

Well, with two potential murders to investigate within hours of starting back, there would be no easing his way back in.

He was back, and that was that.

4

5.15 a.m., 10 January 1991
King's Mill Reservoir Sailing Club, Mansfield,
Nottinghamshire

At fourteen years old, Jamie Mullins was out of control. He was trouble with a capital T.

His parents were both drunks who had no idea where their wayward son was at any given time, or what he was doing. As a result, Jamie was constantly in trouble with the police and rarely attended school.

He naturally gravitated towards youths and young men who were also out looking for trouble. His two best friends were Paul Rowland, who was a year older and who lived two doors down from him on the notoriously rough Ravensdale estate in Mansfield. The third member of their little gang was Reggie Glover.

Nineteen-year-old Glover was effectively the leader of

the gang. He had recently spent two years in a young offender institute for a serious assault and the two younger youths idolised him. They were constantly trying to impress the man who had recently served prison time.

The three of them had spent the night patrolling the streets of Mansfield, looking for anything they could steal. Their latest enterprise was to check garden sheds and, if they found one unlocked, or far enough away from the house to break into without disturbing anyone, they would steal any power tools found inside to sell on at car boot sales.

Paul Rowland was carrying the old leather grip bag that now contained the fruits of their labours: two electric drills and an electric sander.

The last shed they had targeted was too close to the house and the noise they made forcing the padlock had disturbed the householder. The three youths had been compelled to run, dropping another drill as they escaped from its irate owner.

They had fled into the darkness offered by the footpath that surrounded King's Mill Reservoir. As they got their breath back, they started to giggle at their narrow escape.

Reggie said, 'Did you see that fat old fucker trying to chase us? I thought he was going to have a fucking heart attack.'

Jamie started to laugh and was rewarded with a hefty clip round the ear.

He yelled, 'What the fuck was that for?'

'For dropping that Black and Decker, you little numpty.'

Jamie scowled and muttered, 'Fuck off,' under his breath.

As they slowly walked along the footpath, they saw the outbuildings of the sailing club that operated on the reservoir.

Reggie hissed, 'Jamie, check the doors and windows.'

Jamie instantly scuttled off towards the buildings, returning moments later saying, 'Everywhere's locked. Do you want me to force one of the windows and climb in?'

Reggie was dismissive. 'Nah. No point. There's nothing worth stealing in there, mate. Unless you want to walk round wearing a bright yellow life jacket?'

He started to giggle at his own joke, and the two younger boys quickly started to laugh along with him.

They walked into the car park of the sailing club, where they could see three cars that had been left overnight.

Reggie said, 'One each. Come on, boys.'

The three split up and each approached one of the vehicles.

Jamie walked towards the one parked furthest away and was excited to see that it was a Ford Sierra RS Cosworth. One thing Jamie did know about was cars, and he knew this little beauty was rapid.

Using the sleeve of his bomber jacket to cover his hand, he tried the driver's door.

He quietly whooped with delight and hissed to the other two, 'This one's open.'

He then got his lighter out, flicked it on and inspected the lock on the driver's door. It had already been forced, that's why it was insecure: it had been nicked once before.

As Reggie approached, he let out a low whistle. 'Bloody hell! It's a Cossie.'

Jamie smiled broadly and said, 'And it's been nicked. The lock's been forced already.'

Paul Rowland peered in through the front passenger window and exclaimed, 'There's a fucking screwdriver still wedged in the ignition.'

Reggie opened the driver's door and said, 'Time for some fun, boys.'

As the two younger boys got in the car, Reggie twisted the screwdriver and grinned when the engine fired into life.

He slipped the car into first gear and slowly drove the car out of the car park.

When they reached the road, he flicked the lights on and yelled, 'Yes! It's got nearly a full tank. We're going to have some serious fun with this bad boy!'

With that, he revved the engine loudly and let out the clutch. The car accelerated powerfully and reached high speeds in quick time. It was all Reggie could do to control the car.

As they sped towards the motorway, he hissed, 'You two keep your eyes peeled for the cops. If they see this motor being driven around, they're bound to try and stop it, then we'll be fucked.'

'Where are you going, Reggie?' asked Paul as he gripped the top of his seatbelt.

'I thought we'd see what this baby can do on the motorway.'

'You're not going to crash, are you?'

Reggie laughed hysterically. 'Course not. I'm a great driver. This clutch is right sharp though and takes a bit of getting used to.'

Jamie yelled, 'Fucking hell!' as the car hit a speed bump and nearly took off.

As Reggie slowed to join the motorway, Jamie said, 'Are we going to sell it, Reggie? It's got to be worth a stack of money.'

'No chance. Who's going to buy this off me? Nah. We'll

just have some fun with it. I know an abandoned garage where we can keep it stashed.'

Paul said, 'Can we all have a go at driving?'

'Can you drive?'

'Fuck off, Reggie, course we can.'

Reggie replied, 'Well then. We'll take it in turns. Now hold tight. I'm going to floor the bastard!'

He pressed his foot hard down on the accelerator, causing the engine, that was still in third gear, to scream in protest. He pushed the clutch down and rammed the gear stick into fourth crunching the gears as he did so, before letting the clutch up too quickly. The car lurched forward and accelerated wildly again, the rear end fishtailing a little as it sped along the deserted motorway.

The two younger boys were terrified but daren't say a word.

After ten minutes Reggie finally eased back on the speed and used the first exit, to turn around and head northbound, back to Mansfield. As soon as he rejoined the motorway, he floored the vehicle again, touching speeds well over a hundred miles an hour.

Having left the motorway for the last time, Reggie drove the car slowly towards Mansfield and into the warren of streets that made up the Ladybrook estate. At the top of Brick Kiln Lane, they found the row of derelict garages.

Reggie stopped outside the garage at the end of the row and said, 'This is the one. Jump out and open the door.'

Jamie immediately got out and tried to lift the up-and-over garage door. Because of his short stature, he couldn't raise the door high enough for it to stay open.

Reggie laughed and said to Paul, 'Look at the fucking

dwarf. Go and help him, for fuck's sake. We'll be sat here all night.'

With the high-powered car safely stashed in the garage, the three of them looked in awe at their new-found toy. The rapidly cooling engine was still ticking loudly in protest at the inexpert way it had been driven.

Reggie said, 'I'll get a padlock for the garage this morning, so we can lock it up properly. We're going to have some real fun with this bad boy.'

Paul insisted, 'And we can all have a drive?'

'Stop whittling. You'll both get a turn. Jamie might need some blocks for the pedals though.'

Jamie hissed, 'Fuck off, Reggie.'

5

6.15 a.m., 10 January 1991
Kayes Walk, Nottingham

Danny stood next to Tina Cartwright and Andy Wills. All three were trying to make sense of the position of the body that had been found in the churchyard off Kayes Walk.

The churchyard was surrounded by iron railings except for this part, where the railings had been removed for repair.

The dead man was lying on his back, his arms by his sides. His eyes were half open, and his lips had pared back exposing his teeth. Three gold crowns were prominent on his lower incisors. His left leg was bent and folded beneath his right.

A black man with long dreadlocks, he appeared to be aged between his mid-twenties and early thirties.

His clothing was casual. Nike trainers, black jeans, a navy

blue zip-up sweatshirt beneath a black fleece jacket. There
was a blue baseball cap, with the white New York motif on
the front, on the ground about two feet from his head.

Danny said, 'You've been here longer than me, Tina. Do
you think he was killed elsewhere, making this a deposition
site?'

The experienced detective inspector shook her head. 'I
don't think so. I think that whatever took place, happened
right here. When you get closer in you can see blood on the
kerb edge next to his head. My first thoughts were that he's
been dropped here, you can see the bruising to the side of
his face, and that he's cracked his head on the kerb.'

Andy Wills nodded in agreement. 'That's a real possibility. Could be a street fight that's gone tragically wrong. The
classic "one punch" scenario. This possibility is backed up by
all the blood we've found leading away from the scene. It's
obviously not the deceased's blood.'

'What blood?'

'There's a trail of blood that leads from here to Weekday
Cross, then across the road onto Albert Street where it stops.'

Danny paused, deep in thought. 'Any identification on
the body?'

Tina said, 'Nothing. But one of the uniform cops who
was first on the scene said he thought it could be a man
named Randall Clements. He's never personally dealt with
Clements, but his photograph regularly features on intelligence bulletins issued to the city centre beat cops, as the
robbery squad suspect him of carrying out knifepoint
robberies.'

'Does Clements have any previous convictions?'

Andy Wills replied, 'He's got a long list – for violence and
robbery.'

'That's where we begin then. Andy, once we've confirmed the identification from his fingerprints, I want you to make enquiries with the robbery squad as soon as possible. I want chapter and verse on Randall Clements. It could be that what we have here is a failed knifepoint robbery and we have somebody else who's seriously injured somewhere. Make sure we pass out a message to all hospitals in the area to be on the lookout for injuries that could have been caused by a bladed weapon. Has the area been searched thoroughly for weapons yet?'

'Not yet, boss.'

'Get onto the control room. I want a section of the Special Operations Unit here as soon as possible; they need to do a fingertip search of this area. It's going to start getting busy soon, so we need this doing urgently.'

Andy walked away speaking on the radio as he did so.

Danny looked at Tina and said, 'Do we have an ETA for the pathologist?'

'She should be here in the next ten minutes. Because Seamus was already at the Meadows scene, the control room had to call out the next pathologist on the list. Dr Margaret Tanner should be arriving any time.'

Andy returned and said, 'Officers from the Special Operations Unit are being called out and will be here within the next half hour.'

'Okay. Ask the uniform cops manning the cordon to extend it outwards by fifty yards. Let's not risk some member of the public finding a weapon before we do.'

'I'm on it, boss.'

Tina said, 'Dr Tanner's here, boss.'

Danny turned and saw Margaret Tanner walking towards them. She said, 'Good morning, chief inspector, I'm sorry for the delay. I've got to be honest, the callout came as a bit of a shock to the system this morning, as I knew Seamus was first on call today. You must be having a busy morning.'

Danny half smiled. 'You could say that. Let me show you what we've got.'

Dr Tanner followed Danny into the churchyard until the body came into view. She said, 'I'll take it here from here, detective. There's no point in all of us clambering over the scene and surrounding area.'

Danny waited with Tina while the pathologist carefully carried out a preliminary examination of the body. He watched as she removed plastic bags from her leather case and placed a bag over the hands of the deceased.

After twenty minutes she stood up and walked back to the two detectives. 'My best guess would be that he died sometime in the early hours of this morning. The cause of death looks to be a large fracture to the skull, probably caused by his head striking the kerb edge next to the body.'

'So, he died where he fell?' said Danny.

'Definitely. The kerb has quite a sharp edge, so the fracture is long and wide. I expect I'll find massive trauma to the brain when I carry out the post-mortem.'

'Any other injuries? I saw you bagging the hands.'

'Apart from a bruise on his cheekbone, there are no other major injuries I could see, but that doesn't mean I won't find something else during the post-mortem examination later. I've bagged the hands as a precaution, as there are traces of blood on them that could be his but could also be the offender's.'

Danny pointed towards Andy Wills, who had returned after extending the cordon, and said, 'That's interesting. DS

Wills here has found a blood trail leading away from the body. Is there any way that could be from the deceased?'

The pathologist quickly shook her head. 'Definitely not. As soon as the deceased's head hit that kerb edge it would have been all over for him. He wouldn't have been able to move and probably died instantly.'

'So, the blood we've found must have come from someone else?'

'Yes.'

The pathologist looked directly at Andy and said, 'Can you show me this blood trail, detective?'

Danny and Tina followed as Andy walked with Dr Tanner until they were back on Kayes Walk.

Andy said, 'The trail starts here and leads all the way to Weekday Cross, then across the road and down onto Albert Street. The trail then goes along Albert Street towards St Peter's Square, where it abruptly stops. You can see by the amount of blood that it must be a serious wound.'

As she followed the detective along the trail of blood droplets onto Albert Street, the experienced pathologist stopped occasionally.

At the point where the blood trail stopped, she paused and slowly shook her head, saying to Andy Wills, 'You said earlier you thought this person had suffered a serious wound.'

Andy replied, 'Based on the amount of blood, yes.'

Speaking now to all three detectives, the pathologist said, 'I'm confident it will only be a superficial wound, for two reasons. Firstly, the blood is in droplets, not spurts. Secondly, contrary to what you might think, this is not a great deal of blood. I think the trail stops here because your offender realises they've been cut and have stopped to somehow dress the wound and stop the bleeding. I don't think this person is in imminent danger of death from this injury, but they may need medical attention. Have you contacted all the hospitals?'

Danny replied, 'Yes. That's all been done. What time do you think you'll be ready for the post-mortem?'

'I understand that Seamus Carter has booked the mortuary for eleven o'clock. I can follow him at two thirty for this post-mortem, if that makes life any easier, detective?'

'That's fine. Tina will organise the removal of the body. Did you want to stay and supervise that process?'

'Yes. I always like to make sure nothing has been missed when the body is moved.'

As Danny walked with the pathologist and his two detectives back to the scene at Kayes Walk, his head was spinning.

He knew he had to compartmentalise the two investigations and not get the enquiries needed on each one confused. The only thing the two cases had in common was the time the bodies were discovered.

He needed to separate what needed to be done in each investigation and not lose sight of that.

He had the feeling it was going to be a very long day.

6

11.00 a.m., 10 January 1991
City Hospital Mortuary, Nottingham

It was a stark, sterile place with an overpowering smell of strong disinfectant and glaring white lights.

The thought of spending the next four or five hours here at the mortuary at the City Hospital filled Danny with a sense of dread. He had always hated attending post-mortems, but he knew it was a vital part of the investigative process and something that had to be done.

For once he had arrived early. He wanted to speak to Rob Buxton about progress at the Meadows scene, prior to the start of the post-mortem.

Danny waited outside the room where the actual examination would take place. Through the small glass pane at the top of the door he could see the mortuary technician preparing the body of Lionel Wickes. The old man had been undressed and now looked even more frail and defenceless than he had out on the street wearing his pyjamas and dressing gown.

DC Jeff Williams, who was the exhibits officer for the investigation, took the clothing from the technician and bagged and labelled each separate item.

Also in the room were two scenes of crime technicians busy setting up a video camera and loading film into a camera for stills.

Seeing the deceased now, how vulnerable he was, Danny felt a surge of anger course through his body. It was all so needless. The offender could quite easily have pushed this old man over and fled the scene. There was no need to cause the catastrophic head injury that had ended the pensioner's life.

Danny muttered to himself, 'All for a bloody car.'

Footsteps in the corridor pulled him away from his thoughts and he turned to see Rob Buxton walking towards him.

Rob smiled. 'It's not like you to be early for one of these.'

'I know and I've got them back to back this morning. The second post-mortem is straight after this one.'

'Bloody hell. Welcome back to the MCIU, boss.'

'Anything happen at the scene after I left?'

'We've located a witness who can formally identify the deceased.'

'Who?'

'One of the neighbours has given Phil Baxter the name and a telephone number for a niece who lives in Birmingham.'

'Have we made contact yet?'

'The details have been passed to West Midlands police to

make the initial contact. Once that's done, I'll make the arrangements for her to travel here and formally identify her uncle's body.'

'Are there no relatives any closer?'

'From what we've gathered from his neighbours, this woman is his only surviving relative.'

'Okay. Anything else?'

'I think we've located where the scaffold pole may have come from.'

'Go on.'

'Jane Pope was doing the CCTV survey when she found a house on a neighbouring street that had scaffold erected. There was a builder's skip outside that had a couple of offcuts from longer scaffold poles. I've had a look at the length of pole recovered at the scene and they look similar.'

'Scaffold firms don't usually dump poles.'

'True. But I've known it in the past where some buildings need a bespoke length cutting. Then the offcut is just dumped.'

'Get in touch with the scaffold firm and see if we can get some sort of identification on the pole we've recovered. If it's from there it at least gives us a direction of travel for the offender or offenders. Did you manage to start the house-to-house enquiries?'

'Rachel's still at the scene. She's working with Sergeant Archer from the Special Operations Unit preparing the nearby streets for mastering.'

'Okay. I'll need to address that at the main briefing and see how far into the estate we're going to extend.'

'Did Sergeant Archer indicate how long we've got his section for?'

'That's the good news. At least a week.'

'Excellent.'

A door further along the corridor opened and Danny could see Seamus Carter and his assistant Brigitte approaching them. Both were already gowned up and Seamus said, 'We'll be starting in a couple of minutes, if you two want to grab some gowns and get ready.'

Without saying a word, the two detectives followed the pathologist into the room and took two of the bottle green scrubs from the rack, slipping the gowns on over the top of their suits.

Danny stood next to Rob on one side of the stainless-steel table and braced himself for the first of the two post-mortems.

Seamus spoke into a Dictaphone as he described the body in front of him. Once that was done, he turned to Danny and said, 'As there are no other significant injuries, I'll start the examination at the deceased's head and concentrate on the injury to the skull.'

Brigitte handed Seamus a scalpel and the burly Irishman deftly made the incisions that would allow him to peel the scalp away from the skull. The bright white lights exposed the creamy white bone of the skull and the enormous fracture was all too obvious.

Seamus took the short length of scaffold pole, still in the plastic exhibit bag, from DC Williams and held it next to the fracture, slowly nodding to himself.

As he worked, Seamus said, 'You can see the huge fracture of the skull. The scaffold pole fits the indentation made in the skull perfectly. Brigitte will get an exact measurement of the dimensions, but I'm happy this is the instrument used to inflict this injury. I'll examine the brain closely in a second, but this single blow was responsible for the death of this man.'

As Brigitte handed the electric cranial saw to the pathologist, Danny involuntarily took a small step backwards. Just the noise of that instrument made his heart beat a little faster.

He gritted his teeth and continued to watch as the pathologist performed his grisly but necessary task, deftly removing the skull cap to expose the brain beneath.

With the brain now fully exposed, Seamus said, 'As you can see the damage to the brain immediately below the fracture is widespread and devastating. I expect this poor fellow was dead before he hit the ground.'

Danny nodded, saying nothing. It was the result he had been expecting ever since he'd seen the dead man lying on that cold, dark street in his pyjamas and dressing gown.

He felt that surge of anger once again, but this time he knew he could harness it to drive him on to find the person responsible.

He watched as the pathologist continued the full post-mortem examination, hearing the cameras of the scenes of crime technicians whirr as they made a photographic and video record of the post-mortem.

Just over an hour and a half later, Seamus stepped back from the table, his work complete.

He looked at Danny and asked, 'Do you have any questions?'

Danny said, 'At the scene you mentioned possible bruising to his hands. Can you clarify that now?'

'There are marks and some discolouration to the knuckles on both hands. I don't think they're defence wounds. It's possible that as he fell his hands involuntarily took the full weight of his fall, but I wouldn't swear by that. Bit of a mystery, I'm afraid. Sorry.'

'Any other significant injuries or things that could have contributed to his death?'

Seamus shook his head and said an emphatic 'No' before continuing. 'Although this man looked frail, he was in rude health. His muscle condition was good, and his lungs and heart were both in a good state. For his age, he was a very healthy man.'

'Okay. How soon can you let me have your full written report?'

'I'll have it ready for you in two days' time. I've already got a stack of paperwork to get through, so that's the earliest I can get it to you.'

'No problem. Thanks, Seamus. Don't forget to call me when you're ready.'

Danny then spoke to Brigitte, 'Congratulations on passing your final exams. How soon will you be leaving us?'

Brigitte smiled shyly and said, 'Thank you, sir. I've been offered a post back in Dublin, but I won't be starting there for another two months.'

'That's great. Well done you.'

Brigitte said nothing, just smiled.

7

4.30 p.m., 10 January 1991
Woodville Surgery, Oadby, Leicestershire

'A nd how did this happen?'
Mark Bradbury kept his eyes fixed on his
injured hand and the lie came easier than he'd
expected. 'I was holding a glass when I stumbled. It smashed
in my hand and sliced my palm open. I wasn't going to
bother you, but it's starting to feel sore and looks a bit red
around the cut.'

Dr Aldread touched the area of redness Mark had
referred to and he involuntarily winced and pulled his hand
away.

Whether the GP believed what he was being told, he
didn't say or show.

All he said was, 'I'm glad you came to see me. There's the
start of an infection that will need a course of antibiotics to

shift. You've been very fortunate in that I can't detect any ligament damage. It does need stitching though, or it will take much longer to heal and could be open to further infections.'

'Can you do that today? Only I've a flight booked tomorrow morning, and I'll be out of the country on business all next week.'

'Just a second.'

The doctor picked up the phone and dialled an internal number. A brief conversation took place before he said, 'That's great. I'll send him straight in. Thanks, Donna.'

He replaced the phone and said, 'You're in luck. The practice nurse hasn't gone home yet and she's happy to stay and get that stitched for you. Are you going to be okay to travel – that hand is going to be sore for some time?

Mark stood up and said, 'I'll be fine. I travel light when I'm away on business.'

As the doctor scribbled out the prescription for the antibiotics, he said, 'Will you have time in the morning to pick up these tablets?'

'My flight isn't until eleven thirty, so I'll call in at the chemist before I leave for the airport.'

'Good. Make sure you take the entire course, keep the wound clean and you shouldn't have any further trouble. If you go next door, Donna will give it a proper clean and stitch it for you.'

As Mark took the prescription, the doctor said, 'Be more careful. If that cut had been a little deeper, you could have permanently lost some of the use in that hand.'

Mark smiled. 'Don't worry, doctor. I'll be taking more water with my whisky from now on. Thanks for seeing me so quickly.'

8

5.00 p.m., 10 January 1991
City Hospital Mortuary, Nottingham

Danny waited patiently in the examination room at the City Hospital mortuary. He was watching as two scenes of crime technicians set up a video camera next to the still fully clothed body of Randall Clements.

Tina walked in, followed by DC Nigel Singleton, who would be acting as exhibits officer for the Clements investigation.

She said, 'Sorry we're late. Clements was identified by his mother about forty minutes ago and I had to take her home.'

'How was she?'

'As you would expect, totally distraught. Her sister was waiting at the house when we got there, so she's not alone.'

Danny nodded. 'That's good. The mortuary technician

told me that there had been a positive identification when he brought the body in earlier. He's been waiting for Nigel to arrive, so he can hand Clements' clothes over as he undresses him.'

'The traffic was a nightmare, boss,' DC Singleton apologised. 'I'll crack on.'

Carrying a bundle of large exhibit bags, Nigel Singleton walked across to the technician, who immediately started to undress the body, handing each individual item to the detective, who then bagged it and attached an exhibit label to each paper bag.

Danny made eye contact with Tina and said, 'Anything new from the crime scene?'

'Special Ops are still searching the area where the body was found, and the areas surrounding the trail of blood. They hadn't found a weapon by the time I left to come here, but they're being extremely methodical. They're lifting every drain cover they pass and doing a full search of the drains.'

'That's good. Did you manage to isolate the scene from the public?'

'It was a bit of a nightmare, but the uniform cops did a cracking job.'

Before Danny could comment further, the door to the examination room opened and the diminutive Dr Tanner walked in. Her round spectacles were perched on the tip of her nose giving her an owlish appearance.

She walked directly over to the now naked body of Randall Clements and began making a series of written notes. Not for her, the Dictaphone; she preferred a pen and notepad.

Satisfied that she had seen and noted everything, she turned to Danny and said, 'I'm ready to make a start. Do you want to step a little closer please, so you can observe properly?'

Danny and Tina took a couple of paces nearer to the stainless-steel table.

Unlike Seamus Carter, Margaret Tanner never uttered a word throughout her examination. Every now and then she would pause and write copious notes on her notepad before continuing.

Danny found it fascinating to witness how differently the two pathologists worked. He continued to watch as Dr Tanner examined the head wound. She asked the scenes of crime technicians to take close-up photographs as she systematically exposed the injury. Firstly, she placed a measure against the cut to the scalp, then the actual fracture of the skull and finally the considerable damage to the brain tissue below.

She also requested close-up shots of the bruise on the dead man's cheek and of the blood staining on both hands.

A series of swabs were taken of the blood staining on the hands before she continued with the rest of the post-mortem.

Only when she had finished her work, did she look directly at Danny and say, 'It's as we expected. Cause of death was undoubtably the head injury caused when his skull hit the kerb edge. He was perfectly healthy otherwise. The heart was fine and in a condition befitting his age. There is some residue in the lungs that would suggest he liked a cigarette. The other major organs are all in a condition I would expect to see for a man of that age.'

'What did you make of the bruise on the cheekbone?'

'It looks like a punch. You can see the smaller individual bruises where the knuckles have connected with the thin tissue covering the cheekbone. The photographs will evidence what I'm saying.'

'Would it have been delivered with enough force to knock him over?'

'Hard to say definitively, but it was certainly delivered with some power. It would be pure conjecture for me to say whether it would have been enough to knock him down. It's possible.'

'I saw you taking swabs of the hands?'

'Yes. That's quite interesting. There are no cuts on the hands or anywhere near the hands that would explain how that blood got there, which leads me to surmise that the blood isn't from Randall Clements.' She paused before continuing, 'I fully expect it to match your mystery blood droplets, as found at the scene and on the pavement leading from the scene.'

Danny nodded before saying, 'Anything else I should know?'

'That's it. The cause of death is the head injury caused when he struck the kerb edge. You'll have my full written report in the next forty-eight hours.'

'Okay. Thanks, Dr Tanner.'

Danny looked at Tina and said, 'Pretty much as we expected. I want everybody back at the office by seven o'clock for a briefing. Can you contact Rob and let him know to make sure his staff are there too, please?'

'No problem, boss. I'll see you there. I'm just going to help Nigel get all the exhibits back to the office.'

As he walked through the hospital to the car park, Danny was deep in thought. He wanted to get back to Mansfield as soon as possible. He needed time alone in his office, before the briefing, to make notes on what needed doing on each investigation.

He had already made his mind up to split the staff available, to work each investigation. This would cause inevitable staffing issues and would mean longer hours for everyone. Some detectives wouldn't be happy, but others would relish the overtime.

As he had predicted, it had already been a long day, but strangely he didn't feel tired. There was a certain exhilaration coursing through him as he now confronted not one murder to solve, but two.

9

7.00 p.m., 10 January 1991
MCIU Offices, Mansfield, Nottinghamshire

A pall of cigarette smoke hung in the air of the briefing room at the MCIU offices. There was a low murmuring among the gathered detectives as they discussed what had already been an eventful day. They all knew that endless days and heavy workloads would be the norm from now on, as they investigated two suspicious deaths.

As Danny walked in followed by Tina and Rob, the room fell silent.

Danny addressed the room. 'Not the first day back I had envisaged, and I know it's been quite the day already, so I'll keep this brief and to the point. Save any questions you may have until the end of the briefing.' He paused to ensure he had everyone's attention before continuing. 'I intend to split the MCIU in two halves for the duration of these enquiries. Obviously, if we get a breakthrough and one case is solved more quickly that will change.'

He allowed another natural pause before saying, 'Working the Lionel Wickes investigation will be DI Buxton, DS Moore and DCs Williams, Paine, Baxter, Pope and Jefferies.' He looked for Fran Jefferies and said, 'I'll need you to dip in and out of the investigation only when you have free time from your office manager duties. It will be vital you maintain your role here whenever you can.'

Fran Jefferies nodded. 'Understood.'

'DI Buxton will see you individually after the briefing to give each of you your individual tasks. The main thrust of this inquiry will be to follow up any intelligence or leads we get from the house-to-house work being carried out by the Special Operations Unit. I expect this will keep you all extremely busy as there's a vast number of houses to cover in that area. I also want a full background check on the deceased. For now, we know very little about Lionel Wickes. We can't automatically assume this is a car theft that's gone tragically wrong; there could be much more to this than meets the eye, so let's get digging.'

Danny paused again and looked for Rachel Moore. 'Rachel, I know you've been busy all day with Sergeant Archer preparing the ground for the house-to-house enquiries. Tomorrow, I want you to devote all your attention to the current car crime being committed in the Meadows area. I want to know if Division have already targeted any prolific offenders. If they have, do they have any suspects?'

'Will do, sir.'

Danny nodded, then spoke to Tim Donnelly. 'Do you have any forensic updates for us?'

The scenes of crime supervisor addressed the room. 'We recovered what the pathologist believes is the murder weapon from the scene. It's a short length of scaffold pole taken from a skip a couple of streets away from the scene.'

'Has that been confirmed now?'

DC Phil Baxter replied, 'I contacted the scaffold firm working on the house where the skip is located. I've shown the manager the scaffold offcut we recovered, and he confirmed it is one they dumped in the skip a couple of days ago. He's agreed to remove any other offcuts, not realising the use they had for car thieves.'

'Thanks, Phil. Back to you, Tim.'

'There are no marks of any value on the scaffold pole, so either the offender was wearing gloves or took the time to wipe the weapon clean – after it was used on Mr Wickes.'

'Was any blood found on the weapon?'

'Swabs have been taken of bloodstains found and these will be compared with the victim's blood as soon as possible.'

'Anything forensically from inside the victim's vehicle?'

'Nothing obvious, but we've taken fibre tapings just in case the offender sat in the vehicle prior to being confronted by the victim.'

Danny turned to Rob and asked, 'Have the details of the formal identification been arranged?'

'Janice Hayes, the deceased's niece, is travelling by train from Birmingham tomorrow morning. She's arriving at Midland Station at eleven fifteen. I've kept myself clear at that time, so I can meet her and take her to the City Hospital myself.'

'If I'm back from my meeting with the chief superintendent at headquarters in time, I'll come with you.'

'Okay, boss.'

'Any questions?'

Simon Paine said, 'You've already mentioned what a vast area the house-to-house enquiry is going to cover. This will generate a lot of leads that will all need to be logged and then followed through. Just logging the calls will be time-consuming, without following up on the enquiries generated as well. Is there any chance of supplementing our manpower with extra staff?'

Danny was prepared for this inevitable question. 'Firstly, I've had telephone conversations with the divisional commanders covering the city centre and the Meadows areas. They've both agreed to supply manpower to cover the incident rooms needed for both investigations. This will free up the MCIU to concentrate solely on working the investigations, and not the time-consuming taking and logging of calls. Secondly, I intend to raise the issue of more staff for the MCIU with Chief Superintendent Slater tomorrow morning. In the meantime, we do what we always do. We work methodically and thoroughly. I don't want anything sacrificed on the altar of speed. Investigations like this, as we all know, are about quality of work not quantity. The devil is often in the detail, and I don't want anything that could help find the killer or killers of this old man being missed. Is that understood?'

There was a general murmur among the gathered detectives as that message hit home.

Danny paused to emphasise the point then said, 'Working the Randall Clements investigation will be DI Cartwright, DS Wills and DCs Lorimar, Singh, Singleton, Blake and Bailey.' Then, after a quick look around the room to ensure he had everyone's attention, Danny said, 'The post-mortem confirmed that Clements died because of the injury he sustained when his head hit a kerb edge. He also has facial bruising that indicates he was punched prior to his death. This means we could be investigating a murder or manslaughter; we don't have enough detail to make any assumptions yet. What is clear is that there is another person involved and our top priority must be identifying and locating that person.'

Danny took a deep breath, looking around at his officers for a longer pause before continuing, 'The Randall Clements inquiry will take on a different dynamic to the Lionel Wickes investigation. There's no house-to-house work to carry out, so this will be all about the victimology. We already know that Randall Clements had a long criminal history. I want that history fully researched. I want a good liaison established with the city centre robbery squad. Do they hold any current intelligence on Clements? Is he a suspect in any outstanding robbery enquiries? What do we know about his criminal acquaintances? Has he committed offences with other people in the past?'

He took a beat to let that message sink in then said, 'I also want enquiries made with the local bars and clubs in that area of the city. Let's see if we can locate any witnesses. People who may have seen Clements on the night he died. Anybody who may have witnessed an altercation between Clements and someone else.'

Next, Danny directly faced Tim Donnelly and said, 'What have your teams found at the scene?'

'There's some good news. Just before we came into this debrief, I was contacted by the scene manager, who informed me Special Ops officers have recovered a knife from a drain on St Peter's Square. This weapon may not be linked to the death of Clements, but it will be fast tracked to see if there are traces of either Clements' blood, or the offender's blood on it. The bad news is that it had been submerged in water, so any blood traces may have been washed off.'

'Some good news at least. Keep me informed on the blood situation and I want to see a photograph of the knife as soon as possible.'

'I'll get a photo to you, but it's been described as a slim blade, approximately four inches in length. Similar in shape to a flick knife.'

'Thanks, Tim. Anything else from the scene?'

The scenes of crime supervisor shook his head. 'Only the blood trail. We've taken plenty of samples of the blood droplets for comparison.'

'Okay, good work.'

Now Danny turned to Tina. 'Have we had any reports yet from the city centre hospitals regarding possible blade injuries?'

'Every hospital within the city, and on the outskirts, have been given the alert and there's nothing to report thus far.'

'Okay. Make it a force-wide alert to all stations. I want every officer to be aware of this incident, and that we're actively seeking somebody who may have a recent injury caused by a blade, or other sharp object. Let's get that done as soon as possible.'

'I'll make sure it's done for tonight's night shift briefings and will make sure that it's repeated for all day shifts on tomorrow.'

'Thanks.' Danny's serious gaze held the attention of each member of his team. 'It's imperative we locate this person as they may be seriously injured. I don't necessarily agree with everything Dr Tanner said. This person could be steadily losing blood and could be in danger. We don't know if they are a victim or an offender yet, and we need to locate them as a top priority. Does anybody have any questions?'

DC Lorimar said, 'It's not a question, boss. Before I transferred onto the MCIU, I spent three years working on the city centre robbery squad and I still have a lot of contacts there. If DI Cartwright agrees, I'd like to take on the role of liaison with them for this investigation.'

Danny glanced at Tina, who nodded and said, 'Sounds like a round peg in a round hole to me. Come and see me after the briefing, Glen, so we can discuss what I want from the robbery squad.'

Glen said, 'Will do, ma'am.'

Danny added, 'Rob, Tina, I need five minutes of your time before you talk to your teams. I want to get a press appeal out on both inquiries ready for tomorrow morning's TV and radio breakfast news and I want your input before I draft it.'

Now, he addressed the entire team. 'Once you've been given your individual assignments by your supervisors, finish up what you need to do tonight then get off home. I want everyone back on duty at seven o'clock tomorrow morning. The coming shifts are going to be long ones, with a lot of overtime, so advise your loved ones accordingly. I'll see you all tomorrow.'

10

10.00 a.m., 11 January 1991
Police Headquarters, Nottinghamshire

I t was the first time in almost three months that Danny had made the familiar journey to see the head of CID at police headquarters. The update meetings were a regular feature of Danny's working life, but it wasn't a part of his role he enjoyed.

His working relationship with Detective Chief Superintendent Mark Slater was much less strained than it had been with his predecessor Adrian Potter, so it was with an open mind that he made his way along the corridor to Slater's office.

He knocked once and waited.

The voice from within shouted, 'Come in.'

A smiling Mark Slater was standing, waiting for Danny

as he walked in. 'Good morning, Danny. How was the holiday?'

Danny relaxed instantly and said, 'It was good, thanks. I hadn't realised just how much I needed the break.'

'I could see you were under a lot of pressure before you took the time off. How are you feeling now?'

'I'm refreshed and ready to start work, which is just as well after the day we had yesterday.'

Slater indicated for Danny to take a seat and said, 'I saw the reports as they came in. I can't believe you've walked straight back into two suspicious deaths on your first day back. Do you have any updates for me?'

'It's early days but I can run through what we've got so far and what direction I want the two investigations to proceed.'

'That's good. We both know the chief constable will be quizzing me later, so perhaps start with the death of Lionel Wickes.'

'Lionel Wickes was a seventy-three-year-old pensioner, who lived alone in the Meadows area. His niece is travelling from Birmingham this morning to make the formal identification, but his next-door neighbour has already informally identified Mr Wickes. They've been friends and neighbours for twenty years.'

'Are you satisfied this is a murder investigation?'

'One hundred per cent. From what we've established so far, it appears that Mr Wickes disturbed a car thief, or thieves, as they were in the process of stealing his Ford Fiesta, which had been parked directly outside his house. He confronted the offender, who then used the same length of scaffold pole he was using to steal the car to strike Mr Wickes a fatal blow on the side of his head. That's what caused his death. The pathologist is happy that we've recovered the murder weapon and has stated that far more force than was necessary to merely incapacitate the old man was used. He's of the opinion that the blow was intended to kill the old man.'

Slater stroked his chin, deep in thought, before saying, 'Plans for the investigation?'

'It's going to be time-intensive house-to-house work, as it's all residential in that area. I've already arranged for the Special Operations Unit to undertake that part of the investigation.'

'That's good. And I see you've persuaded the divisional commanders to provide the staff needed for the incident rooms. Just for future reference, you should come to me to make that request. I'm the same rank as the divisional heads, so I can argue your case more effectively. No harm done on this occasion.'

'I'll bear that in mind, sir. The other two major strands of the investigation will be a thorough researching of the victim. Right now, we know very little about Lionel Wickes. Apart from this niece from Birmingham, we don't think there are any other living relatives.'

'And the second strand?'

'I'll be focusing on car crime in the Meadows area. Offenders who are known to us, any informants who give information and intelligence about the gangs of car thieves operating in the area. That kind of thing.'

'You said his car was a Ford Fiesta; that's not really the sort of car that organised gangs would be targeting. Isn't this more likely to be a kid looking for a night's joyriding?'

Danny flinched – he despised that expression; there was nothing joyful about young teenagers stealing cars and crashing them, causing damage, injury and on the worst occasions death.

He bit his tongue and said, 'That's obviously something we'll be bearing in mind and I'm sure the divisional CID will have their own list of teenage suspects responsible for car crime in their area.'

'Okay. Tell me about Randall Clements. Is this going to be a murder investigation as well?'

'I've got to treat it as such, until I know all the circumstances. Clements died after sustaining a severe head injury. He was punched in the face and knocked down. As he fell, he struck his head on a kerb edge and died.'

'So, the classic one-punch manslaughter case.'

'Possibly, but I need to keep an open mind. Clements has a long history of committing street robberies, where weapons have been used. We located a trail of blood leading from the scene, that couldn't possibly have come from Clements. It's quite possible this was a knifepoint robbery – committed by Clements – that has gone wrong, and the victim of that robbery has sustained a serious knife wound.'

'Have you recovered a weapon?'

'Late last night the Special Operations Unit recovered a knife from a drain near to the blood trail. I'm currently awaiting forensic test results on that weapon to try and establish if there's any blood on it, and if there is whether it matches Clements' blood, or the blood from the trail leaving the scene.'

'I see. Not so straightforward then.'

'I've put an alert out to all hospitals in the area to be on the lookout for any potential knife wounds, and I've also put out a force-wide alert to all officers to be on the lookout for anybody they come across who has a recent injury caused by a blade.'

'I saw the media appeal you put out for both incidents this morning. It was good; I'm impressed. Hopefully it will turn some witnesses up. What other enquiries have you got planned for the Clements investigation?'

'I intend to focus on the night-time economy to see if we can locate any witnesses who may have seen Clements on the night he died, and on the street robbery angle. I'll work closely with the city centre robbery squad and hopefully find some acquaintances of Clements who may know what happened that night.'

'Sounds like you've got everything in hand. Is there anything you need me to do?'

'Out of necessity, I've had to split the MCIU in two halves to cover each investigation. Even with the assistance being offered by the special ops teams and division, it still leaves me woefully short on manpower.'

'That's something I can help you with. Even if the two suspicious deaths hadn't occurred yesterday, I was going to mention this at our meeting today. I now have an agreement with the heads of CID on the four divisions to release one detective from each division for a six-month attachment to the MCIU. The idea being it will enable them to gain valuable experience in how major inquiries are investigated.'

'Yes, we spoke about this before I went on annual leave. It's a good idea.'

'What I can do is take those four detectives all at the same time, instead of one after the other. If you have four extra detectives, it will help alleviate your staffing issues and will still provide these detectives with a great learning expe-

rience. Do you think the MCIU would be able to accommo-
date such an influx of new faces?'

'As I said before when you first mooted this idea, if they
come with the right attitude and a strong work ethic, they
will fit in fine.'

'In that case, I'll get that organised today. I expect you'll
have them ready to start work on the MCIU within the next
couple of days, depending on their current individual
workloads.'

'Thank you, sir.'

'I've told you before, Danny, when it's just the two of us
talking, you can dispense with the "sir". Mark suits me fine.'

'Thank you. The extra staff will make a huge difference
and it might keep the overtime costs down as well.'

Slater half smiled and said, 'Ah yes. We must do all we
can to keep the dreaded costs down, mustn't we? It's good to
have you back at the helm. Keep me informed of any
progress, Danny.'

Danny knew the meeting was now over, so he stood to
leave. 'Will do,' he said, 'and thanks, Mark.'

11

The journey from Nottingham Midland railway station to the City Hospital had been made in a respectful silence.

After waiting patiently on the platform for the eleven o'clock train arriving from Birmingham New Street, Rob Buxton had successfully met Janice Hayes.

Janice was a smart-looking woman, in her mid to late sixties. She had spotted Rob at the same time as the experienced detective had spotted her. After introducing himself and having a brief, polite exchange, Rob had escorted Janice to his car ready for the short drive across the city to the hospital.

Now as they both walked towards the hospital's main

doors, Rob noticed that Janice had tensed up and her steps were faltering a little.

He said, 'There's no rush, Janice. You can take as much time as you need to do this. I understand it's not a pleasant task you've been asked to do, and I'm happy to go at your pace.'

'I'm sorry, detective. I'm just a little nervous, that's all. It's not about confronting death, though. I was a nurse on a busy surgical ward for most of my working life, I've witnessed a lot of death and injury.'

She paused before continuing, 'What I'm concerned about is whether I'll be able to recognise my uncle Lionel. You must understand, it's over twenty years since I last saw him. Although he was my father's younger brother, there was quite an age gap between them and the two men never really got on. The last time I saw him was at my grandmother's funeral. None of us thought Lionel would turn up for the funeral. Can you imagine being so estranged from your family that you don't attend your own mother's funeral?'

Rob shook his head. 'I've got to be honest; I can't imagine that. But he obviously did attend the funeral.'

'Yes, he did. He walked into the chapel after the coffin had arrived and sat on his own, on a pew at the very back of the congregation. He never spoke a word to anybody there. He paid his own private respects then left directly after the cremation. He never even went back to my father's house for the wake, he just disappeared. That was the last time I saw Lionel.'

'Does he still have any other surviving relatives?'

'None in the UK, that's for sure. He may have some distant relations still alive back in Jamaica, but I couldn't be sure. Apart from my own husband and daughter, I'm the last. Neither my husband nor my daughter have ever met Lionel.'

'Try not to worry, Janice. All you can do is have a look and see if you can identify this man as your uncle.'

'And if I can't?'

'That's something for me to worry about, Janice. Are you ready now?'

She reached into the handbag she was clutching to retrieve a tissue. She dabbed her eyes and nodded. 'I'm ready.'

Ten minutes later, Rob stood next to Janice as the mortuary technician wheeled the trolley carrying Lionel Wickes' body into the viewing room. The body was covered with a clean white linen sheet.

As the technician stood by, ready to pull back the sheet over the face, Rob asked, 'Are you ready, Janice?'

She nodded before saying quietly, 'I'm ready.'

Rob nodded towards the technician who deftly revealed the head and face of the deceased.

Janice let out an involuntary gasp. The marks from the post-mortem were evident and the wound that had killed him was also in plain sight.

She took a moment to compose herself before nodding and saying, 'That's my uncle, Lionel Wickes. I can see he's already had a post-mortem examination. Are you going to catch the man who killed him, detective?'

'We'll be working tirelessly to do that, Janice.' Rob then turned to the technician and said, 'Thank you.'

As the body of Lionel Wickes was covered and taken away, Rob helped a shaky Janice out of the observation room.

As they walked through the hospital, Rob said, 'Why

don't I get you a nice cup of strong, sweet tea from the hospital café. I'm going to need to take a quick statement from you, so we might as well do it here, rather than at the police station. What time's your train back to Birmingham?'

'A cup of tea would be perfect, thank you. I've an open ticket for the train but I think there's one leaving at half past two this afternoon.'

'Let's find the café then. I'll get the statement and make sure you're back at the railway station in plenty of time.'

'Will you keep me informed about what's happening? I'll have to arrange for his funeral and sort his affairs out later, as I'm the only relative he has left.'

'I'll do that. We searched his house when we were looking for a next of kin, but we didn't find a will, or any insurance policies, but it's possible we missed something. As you're his next of kin, you're entitled to come to his house to sort out his belongings. I'll give you my direct telephone number, just give me a call and I'll arrange that for you.'

'Thank you, detective. You've been very kind. I do hope you and your colleagues can find the person who did this. Lionel was a strange, reclusive man, but this isn't how he deserved to meet his maker.'

12

11.45 a.m., 11 January 1991
Central Police Station, Nottingham

Linda Squires was feeling nervous as she waited in the foyer. The main police station for Nottingham city centre was an imposing building and seeing the officers entering and leaving the busy station heightened her sense of unease.

She had always been supportive of the police but had been in two minds about coming forward. Hearing the press appeal on the local radio for a second time that morning had convinced her that what she had seen could be important.

The young woman working behind the front counter now made eye contact with Linda and asked, 'Can I help you?'

Having reached the point of no return, Linda spluttered,

'I think I saw something that could be connected with that murder yesterday.'

The counter clerk patiently said, 'First things first. Can you give me your name and address, please?'

Linda provided the young woman with her contact details then said, 'It's probably not important.'

Having noted the details, the counter clerk said, 'We had two incidents yesterday that have been the subject of press appeals. Which one do you think you can help with?'

'It will be the incident in the city centre. I saw a man running across Weekday Cross, around one o'clock in the morning yesterday.'

'That would be the morning of the tenth. What was it about that man's actions that made you suspicious?'

'Yes, the tenth. Because he just ran across the road like a lunatic. He didn't bother to look at all. I had to brake hard to avoid hitting him. Luckily, I hadn't got a fare in my cab, or they would have been thrown all over the place.'

'So, this man ran straight out into the road, without looking?'

'Yes. Even when I blared the horn at him, he didn't look up. He just continued running flat out.'

'Anything else?'

'This bit I can't be sure of because it all happened in the blink of an eye. I think he may have been carrying a knife.'

The counter clerk's interest had been evident from the start of the conversation, but now her attention spiked even higher.

Keeping a calm tone in her voice she said, 'Can you take a seat, please? I'm going to ask one of my CID colleagues to come and talk to you.'

'Okay. Will I be here long?'

'You shouldn't be,' the clerk reassured her. 'Please, just take a seat.'

DC Glen Lorimar from the MCIU was in the CID office collecting all the outstanding crime reports for recent street robberies when the clerk walked in. As soon as she mentioned the taxi driver in reception who had information about the murder near the Shire Hall, he said, 'I'll go and talk to her.'

Taking the woman into one of the interview rooms next to the foyer, Glen introduced himself, 'I'm DC Lorimar from the Major Crime Investigation Unit. I'm one of the officers investigating the incident near the Shire Hall on the tenth.'

He glanced down at the sheet of paper containing the woman's details before saying, 'Thanks for coming in, Mrs Squires. I understand you may have information that could help us.'

Linda Squires said, 'It's like I told the lady before. This man ran right out in front of my taxi, as I drove down Weekday Cross. He was running like his life depended on it, really sprinting flat out. It was all I could do to miss him. I really had to brake hard.'

'Can you describe this man?'

'Not really. Other than he was white and quite smartly dressed. I think he had either a dark suit on or a jacket and trousers.'

'Any idea of an age?'

'The way he was running, he wasn't an old man, but he wasn't a kid either. I'm sorry, I'm not being much use, am I?'

'I appreciate this must have all happened in a flash. Please, take your time and try to remember anything you can about this man.'

'I said something to the clerk before, but I don't know if I should mention it now, because I'm just not sure.'

'Not sure about what?'

'I think the man was carrying a knife in his hand.'

'Why do you think it was a knife?'

'As he continued running across the road after I'd braked to miss him, I saw something glint in his hand. That's all it was, something glinted off the bright streetlights there.'

'And your first thought was, he's holding a knife?'

Linda Squires nodded and then with a note of conviction in her voice added, 'Yes. And the more I think about it now, the more certain I am that's what it was.'

'Mrs Squires, this could be extremely important. I need to take a written statement from you about what you've seen. Are you okay for time?'

Glancing at her watch, she said, 'Not really, it's almost twelve thirty and I need to pick my daughter up from her nursery school at one.'

Lorimer nodded. 'I've got your home address here. Would you mind if I came to your house this afternoon to take the statement? That way you can collect your daughter and I won't have to rush with the statement. It's important that I get as much detail about this man as possible.'

'I've no problem with that,' Linda said. 'I just need to be at the school on time, to pick my daughter up.'

'Okay. I'll be at your house for two o'clock.'

Glen Lorimar watched as Linda Squires left the police station. He felt elated that he'd been at the police station when she decided to walk in to give her information. Although he had been on the MCIU for several years, it always felt good to uncover a nugget of information that effectively broke a case. He knew that this woman's information could do just that.

He looked around for a telephone to update DI Cartwright. He knew she would be expecting him back with the street robbery crime reports and she would also want to hear about what could be a significant breakthrough.

13

Danny had just finished the first major debrief of both inquiries and had asked to see his two detective inspectors before they left for home.

As Tina and Rob sat down, Danny said, 'I know this is a brand-new inquiry, but I was hoping for a bit more progress today than what I've witnessed in that debrief. We all know how vital the first twenty-four hours are.'

He paused before saying, 'I'll start with you, Rob. I know that the main thrust of your investigation will be the extensive house-to-house enquiries that have now commenced, but there should be a lot more progress researching the background of the deceased. To say not one of your team has found an acquaintance of Lionel Wickes is a little disappointing. The man wasn't a hermit, he must have had interests, hobbies. Somebody will have information about the man that could prove crucial. I want you to stress to your team the importance of this work. We can't afford to sit back and expect the house to house to deliver up our killer. I need your team to start thinking proactively.'

He paused, deep in thought before continuing.

'I want you to draw up a list of prolific car thieves, who we know operate in the Meadows area. Task your team with getting a few of them in. I want you to shake the proverbial tree and see what drops out. Understood?'

Rob said, 'Yes, boss. I'll get on it tonight and have a list of targets ready for tomorrow morning.'

'Good. In the meantime, I'll put out another press release, asking for anybody who knew Lionel Wickes to come forward and speak to us. It might not work, but somebody may come forward.'

Danny turned his attention to DI Cartwright. 'You've had a bit of luck with that taxi driver coming forward. I've read the statement taken by Glen Lorimar. He's done a good job, but I was hoping for a more detailed description of the man she saw. What do you intend doing with the information she's provided?'

Tina said, 'I said the same thing about detail to Glen, when he first gave me the statement. He said it was all the witness could remember, as it happened in a flash. One second, this man was directly in front of her car, causing her to take emergency action to avoid a collision – and the next he'd gone. I've already forwarded the description, such as it is, to all the hospitals to supplement the previous request made for any knife injuries to be reported to the police immediately.'

She paused before adding, 'Before I go home tonight, I'll

ensure that the description is also added to every police briefing in the force. It will go out as a supplement to the request we made earlier for vigilance when dealing with the public. Paying attention to anybody displaying an injury, old or new.'

'That's good and I hear what you're saying about the description. I know it could fit half the male population of the country, but it's all we've got.' He looked down at his notes and then said, 'I haven't spoken to Tim Donnelly since this morning. Has he given you any update on the forensic testing of the knife recovered from the drain?'

Tina shook her head. 'Nothing yet. I spoke to him prior to the debriefing, and he promised me that he'll keep chasing the results and will let me have them as soon as he does.'

'Okay. I do appreciate that both investigations are at a very early stage, but we all know that unless we continue to push and make progress, they could both very quickly stagnate. Keep at your teams. Let's drive them forward.'

As the two detective inspectors stood to leave, Danny added, 'On a more positive note, you'll both be getting two more detectives to work on the cases from tomorrow morning. They'll be here on a six-month attachment from the divisional CID. It's the brainchild of Chief Superintendent Slater; he wants divisional detectives to experience the work we do on the MCIU. It was going to be one detective at a time from each division in turn, but because of our current lack of manpower he decided to bring all four in at once.'

'Well, we could certainly use the extra pairs of hands,' Rob said with a shrug. 'Do we know who's coming yet?'

'I'm placing DC Martin Shaw and DC Steve White onto the Lionel Wickes investigation. I expect you and Rachel to mentor their progress, and to make sure they fit into the team well.'

Danny turned to Tina and said, 'You'll be getting DC Ray Holden and DC Lisa Bettridge to work on the Randall Clements investigation. I expect the same from you and Andy. Let's make them feel welcome and let's get the best out of them while they're here.'

'No problem,' Tina said. 'I'm sure they'll fit in just fine.'

14

8.00 a.m., 12 January 1991
MCIU Offices, Mansfield, Nottinghamshire

Danny had taken his coat off and was about to start reading the first report of the day when there was a knock on his office door. This surprised him because all his detectives knew of his open-door policy. They knew they could walk in anytime.

He shouted, 'Come in. Don't hang about outside.'

The door opened and Seamus Carter walked in carrying a manila folder. 'I knew you'd be in early, so rather than send it via the internal mail I thought I'd drop off the post-mortem report for Lionel Wickes in person.'

'Grab a seat, Seamus. Have you found something new that wasn't mentioned on the day?'

'No. It's pretty much as it was. Nothing out of the ordinary to report.'

It was clear to Danny that something was troubling the big man so he said, 'Nobody else will be coming in for at least thirty minutes, so if your visit this morning is to do with what you mentioned the other day, now would be a good time to have a chat.'

A broad smile spread across the pathologist's face, and he said, 'Don't worry, Danny, it's good news. While you were on leave, I got engaged.'

Danny sat back in his chair; this was the last thing he expected to hear. He had always considered Seamus to be a confirmed bachelor.

The smile widened even more, and Seamus laughed as he said, 'I can see by the look on your face that you're as shocked as I am. I still can't believe I proposed, and even more shocked that she said yes. It's all a bit mad, isn't it?'

'First of all, congratulations,' Danny said, leaning across to shake his colleague's hand. 'Second of all, spill! Who is she? Where did you meet? Do I know her?'

'Thank you.' Seamus beamed. 'Her name is Gemma Coleridge. We met in October last year. Do you remember I went on a course to Canada then?'

'Vaguely. Mainly because I had the dubious pleasure of meeting Dr Margaret Tanner for the first time.'

'That course was all about sourcing medical equipment. I was cursing at the time because admin isn't my thing at all. Anyway, after the first week, I was bored and ended up sitting on my own in the bar of the hotel, when I see this extremely smart woman walk in. She was on her own, went straight to the bartender and ordered a double Irish whiskey. I said to her, "It sounds like someone's had a bad day, cheers." She smiled and told me that she was on the same seminar and was also bored rigid by it all.'

'Go on.'

'We got chatting and it turns out she was from a health trust in Kent. We hit it off straight away and I had a wonderful few weeks in her company.'

'So, what happened when you got back to England?'

'Obviously we kept in touch and things went from strength to strength. She's a wonderful woman and a similar age to me, so we're both ready to settle down now, after years of being driven by our careers.'

'This is great news. I'm delighted for you.' Danny leaned forward. 'But what did you need to talk to me about?'

'I finally popped the question because she's about to start a new role as an administrator for the Nottinghamshire Health Authority. Her new office will be at the Queen's Medical Centre in Nottingham.' He paused before saying, 'Apart from my good self, she doesn't know anybody here. I thought it would be nice if I could introduce her to Sue. As a fellow medical professional, they will have something in common anyway, but I just know that Sue and Gemma will get on famously.'

'I still can't quite believe all this.' Danny smiled. I'm so happy for you – and of course I'll introduce Sue to Gemma. I'll sort something out when it's a little less hectic here. Why don't the four of us all go out for a bite to eat, and take it from there?'

Seamus stood, extended his hand and said, 'That sounds like a plan.'

The two men shook hands again and Danny said, 'I look forward to meeting Gemma very soon. Take care.'

The big Irishman started to open the door then realised he was still holding the post-mortem report. He grinned. 'I'd better leave this with you, Danny. Cheers now.'

15

11.30 p.m., 12 January 1991
Mansfield, Nottinghamshire

It had been nearly three days since Craig Stevens had badly cut his hand climbing over his garden gate after a drunken night out. Although he'd been to the hospital on the night it happened, where he'd had the wound cleaned and stitched, he had neglected it ever since.

The same dirty bandage was still covering the wound and he hadn't bothered to clean the area around the twenty-two stitches that had been inserted in the palm of his injured hand.

He had thrown the packet of antibiotics he'd been given in the bin as soon as he left the hospital, after the doctor told him he couldn't drink while he was taking them.

As a result, his hand had become infected and was now extremely painful to touch. The pain, on top of the several pints of strong lager he had downed at the pub, had put him in a foul mood.

This mood was made even worse when, as he staggered home, he tripped over a kerb edge and fell heavily. He managed to put his hands out before his face collided with the pavement, but that sent the pain in his injured hand off the scale.

He cursed loudly as he sat up. He remained sitting on the kerb for a few minutes nursing his injured hand, willing the throbbing to stop.

As he sat there, he thought about how he'd cut his hand. If that stupid bitch of a wife hadn't put the padlock on the gate this would never have happened.

He got to his feet and started to stagger home again. With each faltering step he took, the pain increased. By the time he got to his front door the pain was almost unbearable and he knew exactly whose fault it was.

Right now, he had one thing on his mind. And that was to make his wife pay for locking him out of his own home and causing this fucking awful injury. How dare she.

He closed and locked the front door, then bellowed, 'Bitch! Get your fat arse down these stairs.'

When there was no answer, he knew exactly where she would be hiding.

The stupid cow had no imagination. She would be where she always was, whimpering in the bathroom. The only room in the house with a lock on the door.

As he clumped heavily up the stairs, he imagined her cowering behind the bathroom door, knowing this was all her fault. He knew she would be expecting the beating he was about to give her.

If she thought the lock on the bathroom door would save her, she was badly mistaken.

His size ten boots would soon put paid to that flimsy bolt, and those same boots would give her the good kicking she deserved.

16

12.15 a.m., 13 January 1991
20 Western Avenue, Mansfield, Nottinghamshire

As PC Jamie Collins got out of the police patrol car, he could hear the screams and shouts coming from inside the semi-detached house. Neighbours had called the police, reporting a violent domestic dispute taking place.

The concerned neighbour had informed the police dispatcher that the man who lived there was a violent, nasty drunk, who he suspected beat his wife as well as yelling dog's abuse at her.

With over ten years' experience as a patrol cop, Jamie Collins had never had any time for men who physically or emotionally abused their wives, and hearing the screams emanating from inside the house only reinforced those feelings of contempt.

He strode purposefully through the open metal gates and began pounding on the front door with his clenched fist.

After thirty seconds of continuous pounding, the noise inside the house stopped and he heard heavy footsteps approaching.

A key was turned in the lock and the door opened a fraction.

Jamie could see a man's face through the gap. 'Open the door, now!' he said forcefully.

The man blustered. 'Everything's fine, officer. We've just had a bit of a row, that's all. You know how it is.'

'If that's the case you won't mind letting me in,' Jamie insisted. 'That way we can have a little chat about the noise.'

Very slowly the man opened the door. 'I don't mind at all,' he slurred. 'My wife's gone to bed now. She was screaming at me for getting pissed again, that's all.'

As soon as he was afforded access, Jamie pushed past the obviously intoxicated husband and started to make his way up the stairs, ignoring the bellows of complaint that followed him. He needed to see the physical condition of the man's wife for himself, before he determined what action to take.

He found the woman slumped, half conscious on the floor of the bathroom. He could see that the door had been kicked open. The force used had broken off the small bolt that usually locked the door.

He bent down and said to the dazed woman, 'I'm a police officer. What's happened?'

Through bruised and bloodied lips, she shakily replied, 'It's my husband, Craig. He's been drinking. This always happens when he's had too much.'

'Are you saying your husband has assaulted you tonight?'

The woman nodded cautiously, but said in a trembling voice, 'It's fine. It was my fault. I'll be okay.'

Jamie took a long look at the dazed woman. He could see fresh bruises, as well as older ones, on her face and neck.

He said, 'You don't have to put up with this. I can see you've sustained injuries, and I suspect your husband has caused those injuries, so I'll be arresting him and taking him to the police station. As soon as I've got him locked up, I'll come back, and we can talk through your options then. Okay?'

The woman simply whispered, 'Thank you.'

Jamie walked back down the stairs and said to the drunken man, 'What's your name?'

'Craig Stevens. Who the hell do you think you are? Waltzing in my house and going where you bloody well please. Nobody said you could go upstairs.'

'And that's your wife upstairs in the bathroom, is it?'

'Yes. That's Tricia. Has she told you we're all right?'

'Yeah. She told me.'

Jamie paused before taking hold of Craig Stevens by the arm and turning him, using a little more force than was required, until his face was pressed hard against the wall. As he put handcuffs on the man, he said, 'Craig Stevens, I'm arresting you on suspicion of causing actual bodily harm to your wife Tricia Stevens.'

Craig Stevens put up a token struggle, before calmly saying, 'You can take me in, but she'll never make a statement against me. You're wasting your time, copper.'

Jamie smiled grimly as he manhandled Stevens towards his patrol car. 'Maybe so, but it's my time to waste. Now move it.'

17

12.45 a.m., 13 January 1991
Mansfield Police Station, Nottinghamshire

The custody sergeant on duty had noted the injury to Craig Stevens' right hand, as PC Jamie Collins was booking him into custody.

He pointed to the dirty bandage and asked, 'What have you done to your hand?'

Stevens slurred his reply. 'I cut it on the gates at home the other night. The gates were locked, so I had to climb over them. It's fucking killing me, and these bloody handcuffs aren't helping.'

'Are you going to behave yourself if we take the cuffs off?'

'Of course. I haven't kicked off so far, have I?'

With a nod of his head, the sergeant indicated for Jamie Collins to remove the handcuffs, then said, 'Is it seriously causing you pain?'

As the cuffs were removed, Stevens gingerly touched his injured hand, nodded and said, 'It feels like it's on fire.'

'Okay. As soon as I've finished booking you in, I'll arrange for a police surgeon to come out and check your hand. Have you changed the bandage at all?'

Stevens shook his head. 'Nah. This is the one the hospital put on the other night.'

Ten minutes later the booking-in process had been completed and Stevens was placed in a holding cell.

Jamie Collins returned to the custody desk and said, 'How long before the police surgeon arrives?'

The custody sergeant replied, 'I've just come off the phone to the control room. The duty police surgeon's being called out and should be here within the hour. Don't worry about the time, your prisoner's far too drunk to interview yet anyway. Go back and see the victim and see if you can persuade her to make a witness statement about the assault.'

'Will do, sarge. There was something on the briefing tonight about looking out for anybody with a potential knife injury. The MCIU need to be notified.'

'Don't be too hasty, Jamie. Let's see what the police surgeon says about the injury first. He's claiming that he got it on the gates at his house, so when you go back and talk to his wife, see if she can confirm if that's what happened.'

18

2.15 a.m., 13 January 1991
20 Western Avenue, Mansfield, Nottinghamshire

I t had taken a lot of persuasion, but Jamie had finally managed to talk Tricia Stevens into making a full written statement about the assault she had suffered that night at the hands, and feet, of her husband.

As she signed the statement with a trembling hand, she asked quietly, 'Will Craig be let out in the morning?'

'I'll do my best to get him remanded in custody as he's a potential danger to you, but the sergeant will ultimately make that decision.'

He could see the look of fear that immediately flashed across the woman's features, and he said hurriedly, 'It may not come to that. Craig may have to be spoken to about something else before any of that happens, so try not to worry.'

'Spoken to about what?'

'Detectives have asked us to look out for anybody with a bad cut after a serious incident in Nottingham a few days ago, where a man was killed.' He held her gaze, as he continued. 'When did Craig injure his hand?'

She was thoughtful for a few moments before saying, 'He cut it the other night. He'd been out drinking all day in Nottingham and when he got home in the early hours, he had marks on his face and that cut to his hand.'

'Exactly what night?'

He sensed her counting back through the days before she said, 'He went out drinking on the ninth but didn't get home until the early hours of the tenth.'

'Did he tell you how it happened?'

'He didn't say anything,' Tricia lied. 'Whenever he goes on a drinking session in Nottingham, he likes to get pissed and start fights. He often comes home with injuries. I didn't really take much notice. I did have a look at his hand as it was bleeding quite badly. I told him he should get it stitched at the hospital.'

'Did he go to the hospital?'

'Yeah. He walked to King's Mill Hospital; it's not that far from here. He didn't get home until about nine o'clock that morning. The last couple of days he's done nothing but complain about how much it's hurting.'

'And he said nothing about how it had happened?'

She shook her head, looked down at the floor and mumbled, 'Not to me.'

'Okay,' Jamie said gently. 'Do you have anyone who can come and stay with you?'

'No. All my family live in Ireland. I don't know anyone around here; the neighbours keep their distance.'

'Do you have anywhere you can go, if Craig does get released?'

Again, she shook her head and said, 'Do you think that's likely? He'll go mad if he knows I've made a statement.'

'If that looks like it's happening, I'll make sure you know before he's released. There are hostels you can go to, where you'll be safe. I can help arrange that for you. You shouldn't have to put up with his violence any longer.'

The woman, obviously still fretful about what might happen, nodded.

As he looked at the sad, lonely expression on her face, PC Collins felt a strong sense of responsibility. 'I'll help you all the way,' he assured her. 'He's beaten you for the last time. How's the pain now?'

The woman winced and said, 'Honestly? My back's killing me. He laid into me when I was on the floor, with those heavy boots on. I think he's damaged something.'

'Come on. I'm taking you to the hospital. That needs checking out.'

'It does hurt bad. I'll grab a coat.'

Jamie walked out of the house. As he waited for Tricia Stevens to make her way gingerly down the drive, he shone his torch on the path near the large metal gates with the spiked railings. There was no sign of any blood on the concrete, but it had been raining heavily for the last two days. There was no way he could prove or disprove Craig Stevens' account of how he had sustained the injury to his right hand.

As he helped Tricia Stevens into his car, Jamie thought if Stevens had cut his hand on the gates, then surely, he would have mentioned that to his unfortunate wife.

19

8.00 a.m., 13 January 1991
MCIU Offices, Mansfield, Nottinghamshire

Tina Cartwright and Andy Wills were both waiting outside Danny's office when he arrived.

As he walked into his office, he said, 'This looks ominous, what's happened?'

They followed him in, and Tina said, 'We've had a notification from Mansfield this morning. A man by the name of Craig Stevens was arrested for assaulting his wife last night. He has a wound on the palm of his right hand that could, according to the examining police surgeon, be a knife wound.'

'Is he still in custody?'

'He was in such a drunken state last night that he wasn't deemed fit for interview. He's still downstairs in a cell, sleeping off the beer.'

'Exactly what has he been arrested for?'

'Assault occasioning actual bodily harm on his wife, Tricia Stevens.'

'Has she made a statement?'

'Yes. All the paperwork's on my desk. I'll fetch it.'

Tina returned a few seconds later clutching the arrest file.

Danny asked, 'What else did the police surgeon say, other than it could be a knife wound?'

'He thought the wound was probably two to three days old and had been stitched by a medical professional. But that it had been subsequently neglected and was now badly infected.'

'Has the hospital been checked to see if there's any record of Craig Stevens attending?'

'Not yet. There was nobody able to check records last night when the arresting officer made the enquiry.'

'Who's the arresting officer?'

'PC Jamie Collins; he works that area regularly.'

'Stevens' attendance at the hospital needs to be established as a top priority. At least then we'll know when this happened and whether Stevens is a viable suspect for the Randall Clements investigation.'

'It's not in the wife's witness statement, but she told PC Collins that Stevens had been on a drinking binge in Nottingham all day on the ninth and had returned home in the early hours of the morning on the tenth with the badly injured hand.'

After a few moments of deep thought, Danny said, 'We need to establish if Craig Stevens is a suspect or not – before he's released from custody. I want detectives to visit the hospital as soon as possible and get a detailed account of when Stevens attended. I want to know exactly what treatment he had and whether he gave any account for how the injury had been sustained.'

He paused and then said, 'I know he hasn't been formally interviewed, but has Stevens given any explanation as to how he got the injury?'

'He told the custody sergeant that he cut his hand while trying to climb over some locked metal gates at his home address.'

'Has Tricia Stevens confirmed that account?'

'No.'

'Right, I want detectives to go to the home address and speak to her again. I want to know exactly what happened when Stevens got home on the night of the tenth.'

20

8.40 a.m., 13 January 1991
20 Western Avenue, Mansfield, Nottinghamshire

Tricia Stevens was feeling weary and sore. Her back ached and her face still bore the swelling and bruising from the previous night's assault.

She watched from behind the net curtains of the living room, as the car slowed to a stop directly outside the semi-detached property.

She could see one of the two men in the car peering down the driveway, towards the house.

After a couple of minutes, the two men in suits left the car and walked down the driveway. She waited for the inevitable knock before opening the front door.

The older of the two men took out his identification card and said, 'I'm DS Wills and this is DC Singh. We're from the Major Crime Investigation Unit and need to ask you a few questions about your husband, Craig. Can we come in and talk?'

Without saying a word, she opened the door wide and walked back into the house, followed by the two detectives.

Once in the living room, she said timidly, 'Is Craig coming home soon?'

Andy Wills replied, 'Not for a while, he's still in custody. We are here because I need to ask you about the night he came home with the injured hand.'

After what PC Collins had told her about the incident in Nottingham the same night that Craig had injured his hand, Tricia had watched the television news and seen the press appeal for the incident in Nottingham where a man had been killed. She knew exactly how her husband had injured his hand, but she now saw a real opportunity to seize some respite from his abusive ways.

She sat down heavily in an armchair and indicated for the two detectives to take a seat on the settee. As they sat, she asked, 'Why do you want to talk about Craig?'

Andy Wills said, 'We're currently investigating an incident in Nottingham where a man died, and we believe another man may have been stabbed. The police doctor who treated your husband last night believes the injury your husband has to his right hand could have been caused by a knife. Did your husband say how he got the injury?'

The lie when it came slipped out easily, 'No, he didn't say anything to me about his hand. Like I told your colleague last night, he often comes home a bit battered when he's been out drinking. My husband likes to drink, and he likes to use his fists, as you can see.'

She pointed to her own face and then continued, 'That

night was no different. He was very drunk when he staggered in.'

Jag Singh asked, 'Did you see the injury, that night?'

'Yes. I told him to go to the hospital. It was a deep cut and I thought he should get it treated properly. It needed stitches.'

'Did he go?'

'He wasn't very happy about it, but he went.'

'To King's Mill Hospital?'

'Yes, it's not far from here, so he walked.'

Andy Wills said, 'So, if we check the hospital records, they will show your husband attending A&E during the early hours of the tenth of January?'

Tricia Stevens nodded. 'Yes, it would have been the tenth. He went out drinking on the ninth and didn't get back until the early hours.'

'What time was that?'

'Around three in the morning, I think.'

'Did you go with him – to King's Mill?'

'No chance. I had to be up for work. He could sort his own mess out.'

Jag said, 'Your gates are very impressive. Do you close them at night?'

'Usually.'

'Can you remember if they were closed that night?'

Another lie slipped out effortlessly. 'I didn't close them that night because Craig was still out.'

Andy said, 'When you close them are they locked?'

'No. We never lock the gates, just close them.'

'That's all we need to ask for the moment, thank you.' Andy looked directly at her. 'Do you have any questions for me?'

'What's going to happen to Craig now?'

'We'll need to ask him some questions about that night and what happened here last night. How are you feeling now?'

'Worried about what will happen when he gets home.' She twisted her hands in her lap. 'More than worried. Terrified.'

'I understand. I can assure you that will be some time yet. I'll stay in touch and let you know what's happening.'

'Thanks. Could you ask PC Collins to call me when he can? I'd like to find out more about the hostels he mentioned. I really can't be here if Craig is released.'

'I'll make sure you get that information.'

With an odd feeling of dread and elation, Tricia Stevens watched as the two detectives drove away. There were a few things she needed to do, before they returned, if her fledgling plan was going to succeed.

21

10.00 a.m., 13 January 1991
King's Mill Hospital, Mansfield, Nottinghamshire

A ndy Wills and Jag Singh sat patiently outside the office of the Casualty Department's consultant's secretary. Andy had already made the request to try and establish if Craig Stevens had presented with an injured hand during the early hours of the tenth.

It was always a nightmare to obtain information from medical professionals about treatment provided to suspects. But that nightmare had been eased on this occasion, as Craig Stevens had already willingly signed a medical consent form that allowed the detectives to establish exactly what treatment he had received that night.

Still, even with the medical consent form, the delay in obtaining any information from the medical secretary was beginning to grate on Andy Wills.

He knocked on the door, walked in and politely but firmly asked the woman, 'Have you located the paperwork for Craig Stevens yet?'

The secretary grabbed a folder from her desk. 'I was just going to come and find you,' she blustered. 'This is the record of treatment given to Craig Stevens.'

She handed the folder to the detective and as he began to read the documents, she said, 'As you can see, Mr Stevens presented with an open laceration to the palm of his right hand. This wound was thoroughly cleaned and required twenty-two stitches. He was also given both a precautionary tetanus injection and a course of antibiotics to help ward off any potential infection.'

Andy quickly scanned the documentation that confirmed what the secretary was saying. He said, 'I see the attending doctor was the consultant Mr Wilberforce. Is it possible for us to speak with him today?'

'Mr Wilberforce is on duty as the senior consultant on the Casualty Department today. The reason for the delay was because I'd left a message for him to contact me as I thought you would wish to speak with him. He's just called me and is making his way up here to speak to you now. If you take a seat outside the office, he shouldn't be much longer.'

Effectively dismissed from the office, Andy stepped back out and obediently sat down next to Jag Singh again.

Ten minutes later and the detectives saw a grey-haired man in dark corduroy trousers and a blue open-necked shirt with rolled-up sleeves striding down the corridor towards them.

Andy stood up. 'Mr Wilberforce?'

The consultant, who was out of breath, nodded and said, 'Will this take long? It's crazy busy downstairs.'

Andy opened the folder, showing the consultant the contents as he said, 'We just need to know if Craig Stevens said anything to you about how he had managed to cut his hand so badly that night.'

The consultant was thoughtful, as though scrolling back through his memory to remember this one individual patient. After a minute or so, he said, 'I do recall him saying something about cutting his hand at home – something to do with climbing over the locked gates at his house.'

'What did you think at the time?'

'I thought no chance has that injury been caused by gates. It looked like something extremely sharp had caused it; the wound was very deep and required a lot of stitches. His hand was a mess, and I just didn't see how a spike on a gate could have caused such an injury. This is only my opinion, of course, and I haven't seen the gates. If I'm being honest, I thought that wound had been caused by a blade of some sort.'

'Would you make a statement to that effect, Mr Wilberforce?'

The weary consultant sighed. 'I will, but I'll make it in those terms – that I couldn't be certain either way.'

'How soon can you let us have the statement?'

'I'll draft something to my secretary, and she will then contact you when it's ready for collection. Now, I really need to get back downstairs.'

'No problem. Thank you for seeing us and I'll express to your secretary how important it is that she contacts us in timely fashion. This could prove pivotal in an ongoing investigation.'

The consultant was already striding purposefully along the corridor, but he called back, 'I'll make sure I draft something before I go off duty today, so Mrs Kinnear will have it ready for you by tomorrow morning.'

Andy shouted after the disappearing consultant, 'Thank you, sir.'

22

11.00 a.m., 13 January 1991
MCIU Offices, Mansfield, Nottinghamshire

Andy Wills knocked once before walking into Danny's office.

Danny put his pen down and said, 'Have you spoken to Mrs Stevens?'

'We've spoken to her, and we've also seen the doctor who treated Stevens at King's Mill Hospital. Like the police surgeon who treated his infected wound here, Mr Wilberforce, the hospital consultant, believed the injury was probably caused by a blade of some sort rather than an accident on metal gates.'

'And what did Mrs Stevens say about the injury?'

'She repeated what she told PC Collins – that her husband had arrived home at around three in the morning with a badly cut hand and marks to his face. She did say that whenever her husband goes into Nottingham drinking, he often gets so drunk that he starts trouble and ends up having fights. It's not the first time he's come home from a night out with injuries.'

'Did she say anything about her husband's version of how he got the cut?'

'I asked her that very question. She said he didn't offer her any explanation of how he'd received the injury.'

'He didn't tell her about cutting his hand climbing over the gates?'

'Not a word. She also says the gates had been left open that night, as he hadn't returned home.'

Danny was deep in thought, then he said, 'We now have two medical professionals who are of the opinion that this injury was likely caused by a blade of some description. We know that Stevens was in Nottingham at the time of the incident and had been drinking and that he didn't have the injury prior to going out. His wife has cast doubt on the initial explanation he provided to the arresting officer and the custody sergeant. I think it's time we got Craig Stevens on record. I'm told by the custody sergeant that he's refused legal advice at this time and is now fit for interview. Let's go and hear what he has to say about how he received that injury to his hand.'

23

11.30 a.m., 13 January 1991
Mansfield Police Station, Nottinghamshire

Danny and Andy sat directly opposite Craig Stevens in the interview room. As Andy carried out the introductions and repeated the rights Stevens was entitled to while in custody, Danny observed the man with the freshly bandaged hand. He cut a forlorn figure. He rested his head on the desk and with his unbandaged hand tousled his messy black hair.

As soon as Andy had finished opening the interview, Danny said, 'How's your hand?'

Stevens sat up and looked at Danny. 'It's much better now. Your doctor said it was infected and has given me some tablets to take.'

Danny could see the man's eyes were bloodshot and his face florid. He had the look of a heavy drinker.

Maintaining eye contact, Danny said, 'I understand you've already been questioned by PC Collins about the reason for your arrest. Is that correct?'

'Yes, and I've admitted the assault on my wife. I'm sorry for that. It's the beer. I get angry and lash out. I already told the other officer; I won't do it again.'

'I'm not here to ask you about the assault on your wife. I'm currently investigating a serious incident that occurred in Nottingham city centre where a man suffered a fatal head wound following a fight on the tenth of January. We believe the person responsible also received a severe cut at the same time. I am now arresting you on suspicion of the murder of Randall Clements.'

Stevens reeled backwards as if hit by a hammer blow. 'You what?' he almost spat, aghast.

Danny repeated the caution and said, 'We need to talk to you about that incident on the tenth of January. Were you in Nottingham on the night of the ninth?'

Stevens slowly nodded, finally saying, 'Yeah. I was in town that night, but I wasn't involved in any fight.'

'It's a long way to go to have a drink. Why don't you drink here in Mansfield?'

'I prefer the city centre. Too many landlords are funny with me in Mansfield.'

'In what way?'

'People take offence with me easily and start trouble. I've been barred from a few of the Mansfield pubs for fighting, but it's not my fault. I just go out to have a quiet drink and then you get some prick saying stuff like, "What are you looking at?" and it all kicks off. I don't go out looking for trouble, but I won't take shit off anybody either.'

'And that's different in Nottingham, is it?'

'Yeah. People are more chilled in the city. They don't want trouble.'

'I can still see faint bruising on your face, so did you have some trouble in Nottingham on the ninth?'

'No. Those marks were from a couple of days before. I got into a bit of scrap outside the local chippy. A couple of twats were making smart-arse comments.'

'You seem to attract trouble.'

'I never start anything.'

Danny pointed at the bandaged hand and asked, 'How did that happen?'

'I cut it on my gates at home.'

'How did you manage that?'

'When I got home that night, my wife had padlocked the gates, so I couldn't get in. I had to climb the gates.'

'Wouldn't it have been easier to climb the wall?'

'This is going to sound stupid now.' Stevens gave a wry half-smile. 'I didn't climb the wall because there's shards of glass set in the concrete top, and I didn't want to cut myself.'

'I haven't seen these gates; can you describe them to me?'

'Yeah. They're eight feet high, have a curved top with sharp spikes and they're made of metal.'

'So not an easy climb then?'

Stevens grinned. 'Not at all, especially if you've had a bevy.'

'Why did you have to climb them?' Danny asked. 'They're your gates – couldn't you have just opened them?'

'My stupid bitch of a wife had put the padlock on them, that's why.'

Danny glanced at Andy and the two detectives shared a look. 'I see. So, exactly how did you cut your hand?'

'From what I can remember, I got to the top okay and

managed to get my legs over. I was going to drop to the ground, but somehow my hand caught one of the spikes. I don't really know how it happened. I wasn't aware I'd cut myself at first. It was only when I started banging on the front door that I noticed the blood.'

'And you went straight to the hospital?'

'I had a word with my wife about her locking the gates. She told me I should get my hand stitched, so I unlocked the gates and walked to the hospital.'

'And before all this,' Danny said, 'how did you get home from Nottingham?'

'I bummed a lift off some bloke.'

'Who?'

'I don't know. I'd been drinking with him in town, and he offered. I've never seen him before that night. He dropped me off in Mansfield and I walked the rest of the way.'

'What was his name?'

'Geoff something. Can't remember.'

'Didn't he mind your cut hand in his car?'

'What? I hadn't cut my hand then. I told you, I did it when I got home.'

'Is there anybody who can support what you're telling us about how you sustained the injury to your hand?'

'Yes. I told my wife and the doctor at the hospital how I'd done it. My wife will confirm that she had closed and locked the gates. I'm telling you the truth. I wasn't involved in any fight in the city centre.'

'A lot of blood has been found at the scene of the incident we're investigating. Would you consent to a police surgeon taking a sample of your blood to compare against the blood we recovered at the scene? This could help prove your innocence if, as you maintain, you weren't involved.'

Craig Stevens knew exactly where he had cut his hand and it wasn't in bloody Nottingham, so he blurted out, 'Yes. Take my blood. I cut my hand on my gates. I wasn't involved in any incident in Nottingham that night. I'm telling the truth. Get your doctor here, you can have my blood. I just want to get out of here.'

'Okay. I'll get a sample organised. Is there anything else you want to say?'

'Yes. Talk to my wife. She'll tell you how I cut my hand. This is fucked up.'

While Andy escorted Stevens back to the custody sergeant, Danny remained in the interview room for a few moments, reflecting on the interview.

He was surprised at how readily Stevens had agreed to providing a blood sample and how adamant he'd been in his denials. It conflicted massively with the account given by his wife and the doctors. The question Danny had to answer was: who was telling the truth?

The blood sample and subsequent DNA test would go a long way to answering that but, in the meantime, there was something else he needed to do.

He found Andy at the custody sergeant's desk and said, 'Organise the police surgeon to come out and obtain the blood sample for DNA profiling. I need to get a forensic team organised. I want those gates at Stevens' home address testing for any trace of his blood. Something doesn't feel right about this. In that interview he spoke like a man who knew he wasn't involved in what happened to Randall Clements.'

24

It had taken her the best part of two hours to completely wash the gates. She had used a weak bleach solution and needed step ladders to reach the top spikes.

She hadn't seen any splashes of blood on them, and after all the heavy rain they had experienced in the last couple of days she wasn't too surprised. She didn't want to risk the police finding blood on them, after she had lied so blatantly. She knew she would be in serious trouble if the truth ever came out.

Her desperation to escape her abusive husband's constant assaults and bullying had forced her into the lie, but she had watched enough television police dramas to know they would double-check her husband's story about climbing those gates by examining them.

The padlock and keys she'd used to secure the gates had been thrust deep into the dustbin containing the food waste.

She walked back into the kitchen and put the kettle on. As she made herself a cup of tea the phone began to ring.

She picked up and said timidly, 'Hello.'

'Hello, Mrs Stevens. It's PC Collins. I've had a message to contact you?'

'Thank you. Yes. I was wondering if you could come and see me with the details of those hostels you mentioned. I don't want to stay in this house a moment longer. I've had enough of being constantly frightened.'

'No problem. I'm going on patrol shortly; I'll grab some information leaflets and call round.'

'Is there any news on my husband? Will he be getting out soon?'

'I know the detectives are very interested in talking to him about that incident in Nottingham I mentioned to you.'

'Detectives came to see me this morning. They didn't seem that interested then.'

'Things must have changed a bit since then. I don't know all the ins and outs of that job, just that it's very serious. Have our scenes of crime been to see you yet?'

'No. Who are they?'

'The people who look for fingerprints and stuff like that. I heard one of the detectives saying that was being organised for your house.'

'Well, they haven't been yet. I don't know what they think they'll find here.'

'Me neither. I'll try and confirm they're coming out to your house before I leave the station. I'll only be ten to fifteen minutes. You might want to pack a bag with some belongings. We may be able to get you fixed up with a place in a hostel today.'

'That would be great. I'm terrified that Craig is going to be released. I know he's going to blame me and when that happens it always ends badly for me.'

PC Collins was quietly seething on the phone and through gritted teeth he said, 'Don't worry, Tricia. I won't let anything bad happen to you. I'll be over to see you in the next ten minutes. I'm sure we'll be able to get something organised at a hostel today.'

'Thank you.'

As she replaced the telephone, she allowed a smile of satisfaction to creep over her face. She felt pleased that she had foreseen the scenes of crime people coming and knew that when they couldn't find any corroboration for the story Craig was telling the police, it would look even worse for him.

She felt no guilt about trying to set him up.

In her eyes, this was a justifiable payback for all the beatings and intimidation she had suffered at the hands of her drunken husband over the years.

As Tricia Stevens sipped her hot tea, she muttered, 'Karma's a bitch.'

25

Danny sat in his office, deep in thought. At the same time as going over his own thoughts on the interview he'd just had with the suspect Craig Stevens, he was listening to the conversation between Tina Cartwright, Andy Wills and Jag Singh.

His own thoughts were interrupted when Tina asked, 'What do you think, boss? Do we have enough to charge and remand in custody?'

Danny's reply was measured. 'Stevens has admitted being on a drinking binge in Nottingham at the time of Clements' murder. He denies being involved in any kind of violent confrontation while in the city, although he has some facial injuries and a significant cut to the hand.' He paused before adding, 'He also denies being in the part of the city where the body of Randall Clements was found.'

Andy Wills said, 'But we seem to have caught him out in a significant lie about how he received that hand injury. According to his wife, there's no way he could have sustained the injury climbing those gates as they were unlocked and open when he returned from the city.'

Danny asked, 'Andy, did the wife say how the gates were shut?'

'She told us that they were never locked, just closed.'

Andy waited before adding, 'And we have the two medical professionals who both say they think his wound has been caused by a sharp instrument. The consultant even went as far as saying a blade of some kind. I've seen the spikes on those gates, and while they do look like they'd be a genuine deterrent to anybody thinking of scaling them, I wouldn't describe them as a sharp blade.'

Danny nodded. 'All good points, Andy. Are scenes of crime travelling to the Stevens address yet?'

'Yes. They should be there in the next ten minutes.'

Danny turned to Jag Singh. 'What have you found out, intelligence-wise, on Craig Stevens?'

Jag flicked open his notebook. 'I've checked with our local intelligence officer here at Mansfield. Craig Stevens is very well known to all the town centre officers. He has a reputation as a regular troublemaker in licensed premises and has numerous arrests for drunk and disorderly, and for assaults.'

'Has he served any custodial sentences?'

'According to the criminal records office he has served two jail terms, both issued by local magistrates for offences of actual bodily harm. Three months custody on each occasion. That really is the tip of the iceberg, though. He has numerous arrests that have gone either unpunished, or been dealt with by way of cautions, fines or suspended sentences.'

'So, it's fair to say that Stevens is a violent individual not averse to using his fists.'

'Not just in licensed premises either. There are numerous intelligence reports of domestic violence calls to his home address. His wife is a long-suffering victim of violent domestic abuse.'

'What do we know about his background – career and suchlike?'

Again, Jag flicked over the page in his notebook. 'Stevens is ex-military. He served two years in the Royal Green Jackets, but was dismissed and issued with a dishonourable discharge. I haven't been able to find out all the details behind that discharge yet, but apparently it stemmed from an incident that occurred while his regiment was stationed in Germany. The only detail I could find was that it involved a violent dispute with some locals.'

'Violence again. Is he currently working?'

'Long-term unemployed and claiming benefits. From what I've found so far, he hasn't held down a job since leaving the army.'

'Thanks, Jag. I'd like to know all the detail of the dishonourable discharge. See what you can find out from the army.'

'Will do, boss.'

Danny addressed everyone in the room. 'There's a lot of circumstantial evidence that makes Craig Stevens a good suspect, but he was adamant throughout the interview that he wasn't involved in the death of Randall Clements and was very quick to provide a blood sample for a DNA comparison with the blood found at the scene. He seems very confident that will clear him and prove he wasn't involved. Does that seem like the actions of a guilty man to you?'

Tina replied, 'I still think we need more than what we've already got.'

'I agree. Let's use what time we have available, even if that means an application to the magistrates for an extension in custody, and let's wait for the science. Scenes of crime will be able to tell us soon enough about the tests being done on the gates and hopefully we'll get a definitive result from the DNA profiling of the blood samples. Tina, I want you to chase the Forensic Science Service for that result.'

'That result will be some time in coming,' Tina pointed out. 'It will definitely go beyond any detention time we have left.'

Danny weighed up his options before saying, 'I don't want to risk bailing Stevens, as I see him as a genuine flight risk. I think we should charge him with the assault on his wife, that he was initially arrested for, and apply at the magistrates' court to remand him in custody pending his court date.'

Tina said, 'With all the previous calls of domestic violence at that address I'm sure the magistrates would look sympathetically on a remand application. Specifically, on the grounds that he is likely to commit further offences and could interfere with the witness for his current charge.'

'Start preparing the paperwork for that remand application. That would be the best-case scenario and means we will receive the DNA results while he's still on remand.'

'I'll get straight on it, boss.'

'Andy, I want you to follow scenes of crime to Craig Stevens' address. I want to know as soon as possible what the results of their examinations are.'

As the three detectives left Danny's office, he was still feeling troubled about the certainty shown by Stevens of his innocence. In particular, the speed to which he had agreed to provide a blood sample. He'd spoken in such a way that there clearly wasn't a shred of doubt in his mind that he wasn't involved in the death of Randall Clements.

Craig Stevens knew he was innocent.

26

10.00 a.m., 17 January 1991
MCIU Offices, Mansfield, Nottinghamshire

A week had passed since the murders of Lionel Wickes and Randall Clements. Although some progress had been made on the Clements investigation, Danny was concerned about the lack of any genuine progress on the other investigation.

He had asked Rob Buxton to give him an update on the current state of their enquiries.

Rob looked exhausted and it was obvious to Danny that he had spent long hours at work. When the detective inspector spoke his voice was hoarse. 'I don't know what to say, boss. We're getting absolutely nothing from the house-to-house enquiries. The SOU lads have been putting the hours in and have made real progress on the numbers of people they've spoken to in what can be an extremely challenging environment. The police aren't exactly welcomed with open arms in the Meadows area.'

'I get that, Rob. I know how hard it is to get people to talk to you on that estate. Haven't we managed to find any witnesses?'

'Nobody with anything useful to say. There's been a lot of second-hand information about who may be stealing cars in the area, but nothing concrete towards solving this case.'

'Have we found any associates of Lionel Wickes, who could help us with some more background on him?'

'A statement was taken by one of the SOU teams two days ago. A man by the name of Franklin Pennant stated he knew Lionel Wickes as a young man, but that he hasn't seen him in over twenty years.'

'Then why take a statement?'

'Franklin Pennant used to box for the same amateur boxing club as Lionel Wickes. That club has long since closed but apparently in his day Lionel was a champion boxer. He represented Jamaica in international matches, but never quite made the Olympics, and after his amateur days had a successful career as a professional boxer.'

'That's interesting. Quite the life story. Make some enquiries with any amateur boxing clubs in the city and see if we can find anybody else who knew Lionel from that part of his life.'

Rob made a note in his book and said, 'I'll get Jane and one of the new lads to look into that.'

'How are the new guys settling in?'

'It's early days but they're both good lads and keen to learn.'

'Helpful having them here then?'

'Definitely. Although I've said there's nothing of any

consequence from the house to house, there's still a ton of rubbish that needs to be bottomed out and checked properly. You know how it is, boss. Those two have both worked extremely hard no matter how mundane the task they've been given.'

'Good to know, thanks. What about local car thieves?'

'We've carried out several dawn raids on likely suspects but have drawn a blank as far as the Wickes inquiry goes. We found evidence of car crime at several of the addresses we raided, and charges will follow, but we've got nothing that assists our investigation.'

'Any fallout from those raids? Any unofficial information or gossip coming in from the streets?'

'Nothing at all. Nobody's talking to us.'

Danny could see the investigation stalling before his eyes. This new lead on the victim's boxing career might yield something, but it really felt like he was running out of options.

'All we can do is keep pushing, Rob. I'll widen the area of house-to-house enquiries and arrange another press appeal. We need to generate a witness from somewhere.' He looked hard at his friend and colleague. 'When was the last time you had a day off?'

'Twelve days ago.'

'Has Rachel got things in hand?'

'Of course. She's on the ball, as always.'

'Right. Take the next two days off, that's an order. You look shattered and need to rest.'

'I'm fine, boss.'

'No, you're not fine. Two days and make sure you get some sleep.'

27

11.30 a.m., 17 January 1991
Police Headquarters, Nottinghamshire

Danny finished briefing Mark Slater on the progress, or rather lack of it, on the Lionel Wickes murder before turning to the more positive news about the Randall Clements investigation.

'We were successful in getting Craig Stevens remanded into custody for the horrific assault on his wife. He's currently in Lincoln prison pending a Crown Court trial date. He was charged with grievous bodily harm in the end, after we discovered that his wife had suffered a fractured vertebrae during the assault. The fracture is believed to have been caused by Stevens kicking her.'

Mark Slater frowned and said, 'Sounds like an arsehole who's in the right place. Any news on the blood sample results?'

'DI Cartwright is in constant liaison with the FSS. They are fully aware of the importance of the profiling and I'm hopeful that we'll have a definitive result in the next week or so. In any case it will be well before any trial date for the assault has been set.'

'Did Stevens' solicitor make any application for bail?'

'He didn't at the original remand hearing and I've no reason to think he will at any subsequent hearings. I think he's of the opinion that it would be unsuccessful because of his client's antecedent history.'

'That's some good news, at least. If the blood samples do come back as a positive match, are you then able to charge Stevens with Randall Clements' murder?'

'Stevens would need to be re-interviewed considering the new evidence, but DNA doesn't lie. If it's a positive match he's going to have some serious questions to answer.'

'Indeed. Keep me informed please, Danny.'

'Will do,' Danny said as he started to stand.

As he reached the door of Slater's office, the chief super-intendent asked, 'How are the extra detectives settling in?'

Danny turned and said, 'They're doing great. All four have settled in well to the new way of working. They all work hard and are keen to learn. It's been a real bonus having them on board and has massively helped with the workload of enquiries generated by the house-to-house teams.'

'Are they being trusted to generate their own lines of questioning yet?'

'I've still got them teamed up with experienced detectives who are well used to the lengths we go to when following through an inquiry. They need to get used to the mindset that every question needs a substantive answer before moving on to the next one.'

'Sounds like it's a success.'

Danny could see that Slater was seeking an acknowledgement that the extra staff was his idea and so he said, 'It's a great success, Mark. And from my point of view, it's refreshing to have the level of support you've shown the MCIU.'

Slater sat back in his chair and said, 'I'm here to support you and your team, Danny. We want the same thing. People need to see that the headline-grabbing offences are being dealt with swiftly, and that the offenders are being brought to justice. It helps to build the public's confidence in the police. Let's hope that blood comes back as a positive match, and you can charge Stevens with Randall Clements' murder.'

Danny nodded and said, 'I'll keep you informed.'

But as he walked out of Slater's office Danny felt troubled.

He wasn't at all confident that the blood tests would come back as a positive match.

28

9.00 a.m., 19 January 1991
MCIU Offices, Mansfield, Nottinghamshire

As Danny walked into the MCIU offices, he saw Andy Wills at his desk.

'Andy, give me five minutes then come and see me in the office. I'm going to chase Tim Donnelly for those test results on the gates at Stevens' home address. I don't see what the delay is in getting a few swabs tested.'

'Will do, boss,' Andy said. 'Do you want a coffee bringing in?'

'Now you're talking. See you shortly.'

Five minutes later Andy walked into Danny's office, placing the two mugs of coffee on the desk.

Danny was already on the phone to Tim Donnelly. 'So, the results are finally in?'

'Yes, sir. They were sent over late last night. There's no

trace of any blood on any of the swabs we took from the gates at Craig Stevens' home address.'

Danny punched the air and said, 'Yes!'

He put his hand over the receiver and said to Andy, 'No blood on the gates.'

Speaking into the telephone again he said, 'Did you find any traces of blood on the floor near the gates?'

'Nothing, but we have had some heavy rainfall between the dates in question. Any blood droplets would have been washed away.'

'Anything else I need to know from your examination?'

'I've only one word of caution. When I examined the gates, I found evidence of wear and tear on the metalwork around the latch. In my opinion that wear could have been caused by the constant use of a padlock on the latch to secure the gates.'

'Okay. That's great. Thanks, Tim.'

Danny replaced the phone and said to Andy, 'No blood anywhere but Tim's concerned that a padlock may have been used on the gates.'

Andy took a sip of his hot coffee before saying, 'Which would support what Stevens said in the interview.'

'Exactly. When you've finished your coffee, take Jag and revisit Tricia Stevens. Let's see what she has to say about this padlock business. If needs be, get a further statement from her.'

'Will do, boss.'

29

10.30 a.m., 19 January 1991
20 Western Avenue, Mansfield, Nottinghamshire

Tricia Stevens was worried when she saw the two detectives pull up in their car outside her house. When Craig had been remanded in custody, she had declined a place in a women's refuge, but now spent her days living in fear that the police would contact her to inform her that her husband was about to be released from prison.

She opened the front door before the officers knocked. The taller of the two men said, 'Hello again, Tricia. I don't know if you remember us. I'm DS Wills and this is DC Singh. Can we come in and have a quick chat?'

With a nervous tremor in her voice, Tricia stammered, 'Are you letting him go?'

Andy Wills said, 'Craig isn't going anywhere. He's still in

Lincoln prison and will be staying there until he goes to court. How are you coping? Are you in much pain with your back?'

As the relief washed over her, she beckoned the two detectives inside the house. 'I'm doing okay,' she said, her voice on an even keel now. 'I just worry that he's suddenly going to turn up on my doorstep again. I was so relieved when I didn't have to go to that hostel; it looked like such a scruffy place.'

She gestured for the detectives to take a seat and said, 'Can I get you a cup of tea or coffee?'

Andy glanced at Jag before saying, 'No thanks, we're fine. I don't want to keep you too long. You never said how the pain was?'

'Most of the time it's fine. According to the doctors, the fracture is miniscule and will heal completely with rest. It's only sore if I'm on my feet for too long, or if try to lift anything heavy. I've only done that once and it proper winded me.'

As Tricia carefully sat down opposite the detectives, Andy said, 'I need to ask you a couple of questions about the gates.'

'Okay. I thought that was all done with after your scientific blokes examined them?'

'The good news is they didn't find anything on the gates that would support Craig's version of events. However, they did find some wear and tear around the latch that looked as though it may have been caused by a padlock. Have you ever had a padlock for those gates?'

The lie came easily to Tricia. 'No. We've never had any kind of lock. I sometimes close the gates but just slip the latch on. We've never used a padlock.'

'How do you explain the wear around the latch?'

'The gates were already in place when we bought the house. I don't know if the previous owners used a padlock on them or not. They never gave us any padlock or keys for the gates.'

'Do you have any contact details for the previous owners? Do you know where they moved to?'

'I've no idea. We've lived here for a few years now.'

'I see. Are you okay to make a quick written statement about this?'

'I've already made a couple of statements; do I really need to make another one?'

'It will help us to refute what Craig may say at his trial. He's adamant that you had locked the gates that night and that's why he had to climb them, subsequently causing the cut on his hand. If there was no lock in existence, how could you have locked the gates?'

'No problem, I'll make a statement. It's the truth anyway. Are you sure I can't get you a drink?'

Jag shook his head as he opened his folder to retrieve sheets of statement paper. 'No thanks, Mrs Stevens, we're fine, honestly.'

Twenty minutes later, Tricia Stevens watched through her net curtains, as the two detectives walked down the driveway. She allowed a smile to form on her lips, then said a silent prayer that what she had told them in that statement would be enough to keep that monster locked up for a long, long time.

30

9.15 a.m., 24 January 1991
Oadby, Leicestershire

Mark Bradbury yawned as he made his way down the stairs of his detached house. It had been well past midnight when he finally arrived home the night before. The drive back to Oadby from Birmingham airport had been horrendous. Torrential rain had greeted him as he walked out of the airport terminal building and by the time he reached the nearby car park he was drenched.

He had been grateful that he'd recently decided to invest in a new car. His brand-new, top-of-the-range BMW 5 series had started first time, its powerful engine purring.

His suitcase was still where he had dumped it the previous night.

He made his way past the suitcase and into the kitchen, where he flicked the electric kettle on to make a coffee.

Taking his first sip of the hot drink, he started thinking about what he would need to do today. This latest trip to the Guangdong province of China had generated a lot of interest in the company he worked for. He knew that with the right follow-up calls he would be able to convert most of that expressed interest into concrete trade links.

Before he started to make those calls, he would allow himself a couple of days off. Travelling the globe, visiting China, was great fun and exhilarating, but it was also exhausting. He would need those couple of days to recover from the long journey before he started chasing those leads.

The noise of the postman delivering mail through his letterbox dragged him from his thoughts. He walked back into the hallway and retrieved the pile of letters and junk mail that had been shoved through the door.

A large manila-coloured envelope caught his eye, and he wondered if this was the package he'd been waiting for.

He had completed the latest phase of the positive vetting process the security service insisted on, but it had been held up because he didn't have a copy of his full birth certificate. He had contacted his parents to send him a copy. He heard nothing from them for days, then they called and said they were sorry, but they were unable to lay their hands on it. He had been due to fly to China in two days' time, so there had been no time to travel to Dorset to search his parents' house to look for the document. He had been left with no option but to apply and pay for a duplicate copy from Somerset House.

He tore open the envelope and started to quickly read the certificate.

He sat down on one of the breakfast stools as he read. This couldn't be right. The name shown on this document wasn't the same as the woman's name he had called mother all his life.

The space allocated for the father's details was completely blank.

The date and place of his birth was as he thought they should be, but he could not answer the question why his mother's and father's names were not on this official document.

His head was spinning, his mind a torrent of questions.

Was this some sort of administrative error?

Who was the woman named in the document?

Why was his father not named at all?

Had he been adopted?

How could he ask his parents what was going on?

Any thoughts of relaxing before developing Chinese business contacts had now completely disappeared. He knew this was a situation that wasn't going to be cleared up with a quick telephone call.

It would be a long drive to Sherborne in Dorset, but he knew the only way to get the answers he needed was to talk to his parents, or the two people he had always thought of as his parents, face to face as soon as possible.

31

A very excited Tim Appleby walked into Danny's office. Already waiting in the office with Danny was Tina Cartwright.

Danny said, 'I take it you've had the results we've been waiting for?'

Breaking into a broad smile, the scenes of crime supervisor said, 'The bloods are a DNA match.'

'Details?'

'The DNA profile obtained from the blood sample taken from Craig Stevens by the police surgeon is a match to the DNA profile the Forensic Science Service have obtained from the samples of blood found at the scene of the Randall Clements murder.'

A look of concern spread over Danny's face and Tim said, 'You don't look too pleased, boss.'

'I'm a little shocked, that's all. Stevens seemed so confident that by giving us that blood sample he would clear his name.'

'Maybe he was stalling for time,' Tina said. 'By agreeing to the blood sample, he might have thought a court would look kinder on a bail application. Whatever his reasoning, DNA doesn't lie.'

Danny was deep in thought. 'Where are we in respect of the investigation? Do we have all the witness statements in place now?'

Tina nodded. 'Everything's in place. All we'll need is another interview with Stevens, so we can put this new evidence to him.'

'Okay. Arrange for him to be transported to Mansfield from HMP Lincoln, as soon as possible. Let's get him to the station and see what he has to say when he's confronted with this DNA evidence.'

'I wouldn't be surprised if his solicitor tells him to say nothing. He'll have nothing to gain by talking to us. His solicitor will know that with the DNA evidence, we will end up charging his client whatever he says.'

'That's true to a certain extent. I know he's already put himself in the city on the night of the murder, but ideally, I'd like him to admit being at, or near the actual scene of the murder. Even with a DNA match we need to put him in the same vicinity as the offence.'

Tina stood to leave and said, 'I'll get onto the prison and arrange for the first available production date. Do you intend on interviewing him again yourself?'

Danny nodded. 'It makes sense to have the same people in the interview room, so I'll carry out the interview.'

'Are there any dates you won't be available?'

'No. Let's get him out as soon as possible. It would be great to clear one of these murders up quickly, so we can devote all our time to the other case.'

As Tina left the office, Danny turned to Tim and said, 'Good work. Please pass on my thanks to all your staff. It looks like forensic science has solved this murder for us.'

'Will do, boss. As Tina said, DNA doesn't lie.'

32

7.45 p.m., 24 January 1991
Lenthay Road, Sherborne, Dorset

After what felt like an interminable drive from Leicester to Sherborne, Mark Bradbury was tired. There was a reason he always had a couple of days off work after trips to China; the jet lag was a killer.

He had been forced to stop and take refreshments several times as he negotiated the busy motorways heading south. At one point he could feel himself falling asleep at the wheel, so he'd stopped at services just outside Oxford and had a sleep in his car, waking up an hour later.

By the time he reached the picturesque town of Sherborne it was dark and the streetlights were on.

He parked his car directly outside his parents' bungalow and switched the engine off. As he started towards the pretty stone bungalow, he could hear the powerful engine of the car ticking as it cooled.

His thoughts were in turmoil. The information on that birth certificate had turned his ordered life upside down. He desperately wanted to walk down the driveway and confront the people who lived there. He wanted to immediately demand some answers.

But when he reached the front door, he hesitated glancing at his watch. It was gone eight o'clock and he knew his elderly parents would already be thinking about getting ready for bed.

He started the BMW's engine once more. He needed to find a bed for the night in one of the town centre pubs. This mess would keep until the morning. It had been kept secret from him for this long, one more night wasn't going to change anything. It would be better, too, if he showed up in the morning when his parents were rested.

His head was spinning as he glanced back at the picturesque bungalow. He wondered how long it would be before he stopped thinking of the people who lived there as his parents.

33

9.00 a.m., 25 January 1991
Lenthay Road, Sherborne, Dorset

It had been no problem for Mark Bradbury to find a room for the night. It was quiet at this time of year in the sleepy town of Sherborne. He had found bed and breakfast accommodation at the White Hart in the town centre.

The bed had been comfortable and the glass of whisky prior to going up to his room had helped his overactive brain to settle, allowing him to get some much-needed sleep.

After a hot shower and a full English breakfast in the pub he now felt ready to confront Bill and Amy Bradbury, the people who until yesterday morning he had considered to be his mother and father.

As he sat in his car outside the neat and tidy bungalow, he felt conflicted. He loved his parents unconditionally; they had given him the best possible upbringing and he knew he was loved by them. They had paid for private education that had set him up for an adult life that now offered countless opportunities.

At the same time, he was finding it difficult to come to terms with the fact they had never confided in him. Never trusted him enough to tell him the truth of his origins.

He got out of the car, took a deep breath, walked slowly down the drive and rang the doorbell.

The door was opened by Amy Bradbury who exclaimed, 'Mark! What a lovely surprise. We weren't expecting to see you today, what brings you down here, sweetheart?'

'Is Dad at home too?'

Noting the serious tone in his voice, Amy's expression instantly changed. 'Is everything all right?'

Seeing the worry etched on her face, Mark stepped forward and hugged his mother. 'Everything's fine. I just need to talk to you both about something.'

'Dad's in the lounge reading the paper, come through.'

As they walked through the bungalow, Mark heard his father's voice call out, 'Who is it, love?'

'It's Mark. He's come for a surprise visit.'

Without saying anything or allowing his face to betray his feelings, Mark thought to himself, *this is going to be a surprise all right.*

He walked into the lounge and Bill said, 'Hello, boy. It's good to see you.'

With his broad Dorset accent, Bill's traditional greeting of 'hello, boy' had always sounded warm and friendly. Today, it felt like a kick in the teeth to Mark.

As Amy fussed around asking about a hot drink, Mark

said, 'Please. I need you both to sit down. I need to ask you something very important, and I need the truth.'

He could see the worried expressions on his parents' faces but he saw something else too. It was a look of resignation. They already knew exactly what he was going to ask.

Bill took the initiative. 'You know, don't you?'

When he saw the look in Mark's eyes, the old man paused before continuing. 'I bloody knew it. As soon as you started asking about the birth certificate, I knew all this was going to come back and bite us.'

Now he turned to his wife and said, an edge of accusation tainting his voice, 'I told you we should have told the boy years ago. He shouldn't have had to find out like this.'

Mark held up both hands and said, 'Stop, please. I don't want you two to argue. All I want is for you to tell me the truth now. I promise you it won't change the way I feel about you both. As far as I'm concerned you are my mother and father, and I love you. Nothing you can say will ever change that.'

Amy gulped down a sob and murmured, 'Excuse me a second, I need to grab a tissue.'

She returned seconds later, dabbing her eyes and clutching a handful of tissues.

It was left to her husband to do the talking. 'There's no great mystery, boy. We adopted you as a baby and have raised you as though you were our own flesh and blood.'

It was the obvious question and Mark asked it: 'Who are my real parents, my biological parents?'

'I can't answer that. It's something we were never told by the church. It's one of the reasons we decided not to tell you. We knew there would be questions, which we wouldn't be able to answer.'

'What have the church got to do with this?'

'Your adoption was arranged by the Catholic church.' The old man sighed deeply. 'More precisely by an organisation calling themselves the Divine Shepherd.'

Mark couldn't help the shiver of distaste that must have showed in his face. 'Was my adoption even legal?' he demanded.

'Of course, it was. Everything was above board. We signed papers drawn up by a solicitor that ensured it was legal. But it's true that times were different back then. Social services weren't all-powerful like they are now. The church was involved in lots of private adoptions.'

Mark knew this was true, so he shrugged and asked, 'Where was I born?'

'You were born in Nottingham, as we've always told you.'

'You told me that you were working in Nottingham at the time, but that wasn't the truth, was it?'

Bill looked at the floor and shook his head. 'We were living here in Sherborne. Everything was arranged through our church in the town. One of the priests there put us in touch with this Divine Shepherd organisation and everything was arranged through them.'

Mark couldn't quite believe what he was hearing. 'Did money change hands?' He shuddered. 'Did you buy me?'

'It wasn't like that. We were desperate to have a child of our own, but for some reason Amy couldn't conceive. When you arrived, you made our family complete.'

'You never answered my question. Was money involved?'

'We were asked to contribute financially to the church. We were told that the church would use the money we gave to fund charitable activities in less privileged countries.'

Mark shook his head and muttered, 'This is unreal.'

A heavy silence filled the room, its weight growing ever more oppressive until it was eventually broken by Amy who asked, 'Why did you feel the need to get a copy of your birth certificate after all these years?'

'As I explained to Dad on the phone, I'm applying for a new job and part of the application process is to provide my prospective employers with a full family history and background check, so I needed a copy of my full birth certificate.'

'Oh, son.' Amy wiped away a fresh flood of tears. 'Will this stop you getting the new job?'

'I'm not bothered about the job, right now. Why didn't you tell me?'

'It's like your dad said, we knew we wouldn't have the answers to your questions.'

'I can answer one of those questions myself now, after seeing the birth certificate. My mother's name was Millicent Lowe. Did you ever meet her?'

Amy shook her head. 'No. We only ever saw the priest who arranged everything. We went to a building in Nottingham where he handed you to us. I can't remember exactly where that was, but I do remember seeing nuns there.'

Struggling to come to terms with everything he was hearing, Mark suppressed his anger once more as he said, 'So, you turn up at this building in Nottingham, pay your money to the priest, who in return gives you a newborn baby. Is that right?'

'Stop!' Bill snapped. 'You're making it sound sleazy. Everything we did then, everything we've done since, was done out of love.'

'I don't dispute that, and I genuinely appreciate all you've done for me, I really do.' He looked at them both, his body awash with conflicting emotions, before continuing, 'You are my mum and dad, and I'll always love you, but what about the poor woman who gave birth to me, and then had to hand her newborn infant to some priest, knowing in her heart she would never see her child again?'

Once more Amy's tears started to flow. In between sobs she said, 'I've thought about her a lot. The priest told us it was her choice, and that what we were doing was a great service for that poor woman. He didn't go into details, but he left us in no doubt that what we were doing, it was a good thing.'

Mark stood up. 'I need to get back to Leicester. I need time to think all this through. Thank you for being honest with me.'

Bill stood and said, 'Are we all right, boy?'

Mark stepped forward, embraced his father and kissed him on the cheek. 'Of course we are, Dad. It's all been a bit of a shock, that's all. I'm still your boy and that's never going to change.'

He stepped over to Amy, put his arms around her, aware that her body was still convulsing with sobs and whispered, 'Love you, Mum.'

Bill followed him to the front door and said, 'I'm sorry we didn't tell you everything, Mark. It just never felt the right time.'

'Don't worry, I'll get my head around it. I do have one more question. Who was the priest in Nottingham?'

Bill's answer was immediate. 'His name was Father Hennessey. His is a name I'll always remember; he changed our lives, for the better, when he handed you to us.'

'What was the name of his church?'

'I can't remember that, but I do recall it was in an area of Nottingham called Carlton.'

As Mark walked up the driveway towards his car, Bill called after him, 'Don't forget, the organisation that arranged everything to do with your adoption was called the Divine Shepherd.' Then his voice broke a little. 'What are you going to do, Mark?'

Mark stopped and turned to face his father. 'I don't know yet. If I want to continue going for this career change, I may need to find my biological mother. I need time to think before I do anything.'

'I know you'll do what's best, boy. I just want you to understand that me and your mother have done nothing wrong. Hopefully we gave you a good start in life.'

Mark walked the few steps back to his father, embraced him, took his hands in his and said, 'You both gave me the best start, Dad. The very best. Don't worry, everything will be fine.'

34

11.30 a.m., 27 January 1991
Mansfield Police Station, Nottinghamshire

As Danny and Andy walked into the interview room, Danny clocked the worried expression on Craig Stevens' face.

His solicitor, Martin Anderson, had just spent the last thirty minutes explaining to Stevens the reason for this interview. He would now know all about the positive DNA evidence, that conflicted totally with the answers he had given at his previous interview.

Knowing this, Danny fully expected Stevens to answer all of today's questions with a 'no comment' response.

After Andy completed the introductions of the people present in the interview room, Danny said, 'You previously provided a blood sample, knowing that sample would be used to check your involvement, or not, in recent crimes. Is that correct?'

Danny wasn't expecting the outburst that followed such a simple question.

'You can go and fuck yourself! I'm not going to let you fuckers stitch me up for this. I haven't killed anybody!'

Danny allowed a pause before speaking again to try and defuse what was an extremely volatile situation.

When he did speak, he chose his words carefully. 'When I last interviewed you, you told me that you were in Nottingham on the night Randall Clements was killed. Where in Nottingham did you go that night?'

A much calmer Stevens looked at his solicitor before replying. 'That was almost three weeks ago. I can't remember exactly where I went that night. I like to have a drink in lots of different pubs, so I walk around the town quite a bit. It was dry that night, so there would be no reason to stay in one pub. How am I supposed to remember everywhere I went.'

'I think you would remember, if you ended up having a violent confrontation with somebody that night as you walked between pubs.'

'That's just it. I didn't have any kind of violent confrontation. I had a few beers, a lot of beers, and came home. I didn't get in any fights.'

'How do you explain your blood being found near to the scene where Randall Clements was killed?'

Stevens cradled his head in his hands. 'I can't explain it. It can't be my blood you've found.'

'The scientific tests we've carried out have identified it as your blood. It's a match for the blood sample the police surgeon took from you right here at this police station.'

'Something's wrong,' Stevens protested. 'I didn't have an injury that would cause my blood to be on the street in Nottingham.'

'But you did have an injury,' Danny countered calmly. 'A serious hand injury that required medical attention when you arrived home from your trip into Nottingham that night.'

'I told you the last time we spoke. I didn't cut my fucking hand, until I got home.'

Danny could see the rage bubbling below the surface and tried to calm things down again. 'Tell me again how you cut your hand?'

Stevens sighed heavily. 'When I got home, the gate was locked. I had to climb the gate to get in. I slipped and sliced open my hand. I told my wife what I'd done that night. She locked the fucking gate – why don't you ask her?'

'We have asked her. Your wife has made a statement saying that she never locked the gate, that those gates are never locked.'

'What! They're always locked! We use a fucking great big padlock to lock them!'

'Your wife has stated that in all the time you've lived at that address those gates have never been locked. Closed yes, but never locked.'

'Why the fuck is that bitch lying? She had locked the bloody gates that night.'

'There's no reason for your wife to lie to the police, whereas you have a very good reason to lie. If you could blame your hand injury on something else, you might think it would remove suspicion from you cutting your hand during a street fight in Nottingham, a fight that culminated in a man's death.'

'I'm not lying. I told the doctor the exact same story when he stitched my hand up.'

'That doctor has also made a statement to the police. In it he states that, in his opinion, the cut he treated that night was most likely caused by a sharp, bladed instrument, not by a spike on the top of metal gates.'

Stevens turned to his solicitor. 'Why the fuck is this happening? This is bullshit. Can't you do something?'

Martin Anderson, the solicitor, said, 'I've given you my advice already, Craig. You don't have to answer any of these questions.'

Stevens stared hard at Danny. 'Listen to me. I wasn't in a fight that night. I don't understand any of this.'

'Craig Stevens, I believe the reason your blood was found at the scene of the incident where Randall Clements died is because you were involved in a violent confrontation with Clements. During that fight, your hand was cut by a knife, probably used by Clements, and Clements was punched to the face causing him to fall backwards, striking his head on a kerb edge. That injury to his head subsequently caused his death. I believe you are the person who threw that punch, and you are responsible for the man's death. Is it the case that you were attacked by Clements and were simply defending yourself?'

'I don't know Randall Clements; I've never met Randall Clements and I've certainly never had a fight with him. I'm telling you the truth. This is a mistake. That blood you've found isn't mine.'

'Has your solicitor explained to you the significance of a DNA match?'

Stevens nodded slowly before saying quietly, 'All I know is this, it wasn't me. Have you checked the gates at my house for blood? There will be blood on them for sure.'

'A forensic examination of your gates has already been done and there was no trace of any blood on them.'

'I don't know what else to say. I don't understand. Why are my wife and that doctor lying to you?'

'If you were defending yourself that night, you really need to tell me now.'

'I wasn't defending myself. I wasn't in any bother that night.'

'Is there anything else you want to say?'

Stevens was quiet for a long time then said simply, 'I didn't do it.'

35

3.00 p.m., 27 January 1991
Mansfield Police Station, Nottinghamshire

Danny carefully scrutinised Craig Stevens' face, as Andy Wills prepared to charge him.

There was a blank expression on the man's face. It looked like he had detached himself from the whole process. His solicitor was trying to offer words of encouragement, but Stevens didn't even acknowledge his presence.

Andy Wills held the charge sheet and read it aloud. 'Craig Stevens. You are charged that sometime during the ninth and tenth of January 1991 in the city of Nottingham, you did murder Randall Clements. Contrary to Common Law.'

Andy paused briefly before cautioning Stevens. At the end of the caution, Andy repeated, 'Have you anything to say?'

In a flat emotionless voice, Stevens repeated, 'I didn't do it.'

Andy made a note of the reply and then escorted Stevens back to his cell.

Martin Anderson approached Danny and said, 'I'm puzzled, chief inspector. It could be that I didn't explain myself well enough to my client. Craig seems to have no grasp of the significance of a DNA match. Not once has he ever wavered from his story. I think he'll be the same when he gets to court. It's as though he's convinced himself that he hasn't done this thing even though all the evidence is stacked against him.'

Danny said, 'You expect him to plead not guilty then?'

'I don't see him changing his mind. As far as he's concerned, he's an innocent man. And I know you're going to tell me that Lincoln prison is full of innocent men, but I've never known somebody as convinced of that as he is.'

'I wasn't going to say that at all. I was as surprised as you were at just how vehemently he denied any involvement when all the evidence says the opposite. The evidence from his own wife was the clincher for me.'

The solicitor nodded. 'No doubt I'll have my client's instructions in the very near future, but I fully expect this to go to trial.'

10.00 a.m., 28 January 1991
Police Headquarters, Nottinghamshire

Danny should have been feeling elated having charged Craig Stevens with the murder of Randall Clements the day before, but as he walked along the corridor towards Mark Slater's office he was consumed by doubts.

He knocked once on the chief superintendent's door and waited for the instruction to enter.

As Danny walked in and sat down, Mark Slater was beaming. 'Fantastic work, Danny. I can't believe you and your team have got a result in less than three weeks. Is the evidence strong?'

'Some of the evidence is circumstantial and we have no confession, but we do have DNA evidence that puts Craig Stevens at the scene of the murder.'

'That's excellent.'

Danny was thoughtful before saying, 'I do have my doubts over some of the circumstantial supporting evidence, though.'

'Go on.'

'We are reliant on Stevens' wife, Tricia, to refute his version of how he sustained the injury to his hand. The blood found at the scene that's a DNA match suggests he was cut during the confrontation with Clements. His version is that it can't be his blood, because he didn't cut his hand until he was back home in Mansfield.'

'But you've forensically examined the gates, and that examination also supports the wife's testimony. No traces of blood were found on those gates.'

'That's true. I've just never known anybody be so adamant in their denials.'

'Have you any doubts about the wife's evidence?'

'It's more a concern than a doubt. There's a long history of domestic violence at that address. Craig Stevens has convictions for previously assaulting his wife and I wonder if she's seen this as a golden opportunity to remove him from her life.'

'That's a bit of a stretch, Danny. Are you saying she's blatantly lied to the police? I take it she's of previous good character and there's no reason to doubt her word.'

Danny shrugged. 'You asked me my concerns, so I've told you my thoughts. I know it's a stretch to imagine his wife would think along those lines, but it has crossed my mind more than once. I sat in the interview room and saw Stevens be so confident that by giving us a sample of his blood he would clear himself. Surely, if he had been involved in the death of Clements, he would have just refused to give us that blood sample.'

'Maybe he was trying to buy some time,' Slater suggested. 'Thinking he would be granted bail by the court and could then abscond and not face justice. There's not much tying him to this area is there?'

Danny didn't respond and after a brief pause Slater continued. 'I think the science is telling you all you need to know. The only credible explanation for his blood, his DNA, to be at the scene is because he's responsible for the murder of Randall Clements. You've only got to look at the man's previous convictions. He is a violent individual with a string of assault charges against his name.'

Danny nodded. 'I hear what you're saying, and I know my doubts may seem irrational, but ...'

Slater held his hand up and interrupted, 'There is no but here, Danny. You can prepare your case for the Crown Court. DNA evidence doesn't lie. You have your killer and it's Craig Stevens.'

Slater paused again before saying, 'What I need from you now is to concentrate all your resources and efforts into finding the killer, or killers, of Lionel Wickes. I have to say, Danny, that while I'm full of admiration at the speed in which your team located and charged Craig Stevens, I'm equally as disappointed in the lack of progress being made in the Wickes case.'

Danny stood and said, 'Everyone at the MCIU is working flat out to make progress in that investigation, but the amount of information coming in from the public is virtually zero. The media are pushing us to get results, quoting the public's demand for justice, but that's the same public who are refusing to talk to or cooperate with my officers. They can't have it both ways, boss.'

'That's just it, Danny, they can.' Slater shrugged, but his gaze was steely. 'And we must deliver every time. Promise me you won't waste any more time on these so-called doubts about Craig Stevens. He's your man. Now find me the killer of Lionel Wickes.'

37

Craig Stevens lay awake on the top bunk in the cramped cell he shared with one other prisoner. He could hear the other man's rhythmic heavy breathing, interspersed with loud snoring, emanating from the bunk below.

It wasn't his cellmate's breathing, or his snoring, that was keeping him awake. He lay in the dark, eyes wide open, wondering how the hell he had ended up in prison, awaiting trial for something he had nothing to do with.

He repeatedly played out in his head the times when he had been questioned by that detective, wondering if there was anything else he could have said that would have cleared his name.

Every meeting he had with his own solicitor recently had

been spent trying to impress on the man supposed to be helping him that he was innocent. Even his own solicitor was now advising him to enter a guilty plea and accept the mercy of the court. The legal team was insisting that it was the only course of action left open to him and that such a plea might significantly reduce the length of any custodial sentence.

So far, he had been resolute in his refusal to go down that line. He knew he hadn't killed that man. He knew where he had cut his hand, and it wasn't in fucking Nottingham.

He reflected on what the detective had told him about the statement made by his wife, where she had in effect stitched him up. She had deliberately lied to the cops, and as he lay in the darkness with just his own thoughts for company, he began to understand the reason why.

He could feel the tears of frustration sting as they welled up in his eyes as he recalled every occasion he had viciously beaten his wife with his fists or boots.

Finally, his mind clear from the self-justifications usually offered by his huge alcohol consumption, he understood exactly why she had lied. It was her way of taking revenge on him for the countless times he had turned his own anger and rage against her and physically beaten her, intimidating and humiliating her in her own home.

At the stark realisation that his current predicament was all his own making, his eyes began to sting harder, and he felt those tears start to roll slowly down his cheeks. He swallowed hard and as he wiped the tears from his face he made a mental note to send his wife a visiting order tomorrow. It was a desperate tactic and one that in his heart he already knew was doomed to fail. If he could see her just once, he might be able to persuade her to retract her statement, tell the cops the truth and get him out of jail.

He knew it was his only hope.

But those tears of frustration quickly turned into ones of despair, as he came to the even harsher realisation that it would be a cold day in hell before his wife, the woman he had abused all their married life, would do anything to free him from this bleak prison cell.

38

D anny had called a meeting of all his supervisors to inject some much-needed impetus into the Lionel Wickes murder investigation.

Rob Buxton spoke first. 'I hear what you're saying, boss, but it doesn't seem to matter what we try on the Meadows estate, the people there just refuse to engage with the police.'

Danny shook his head. 'I'm not accepting that, Rob. I know it's a difficult place to work and I understand the local problems, but this is different. This is a member of their own community who has been brutally murdered trying to protect his own property. We need to impress on the community that we're working on their behalf to try and find someone who has no qualms about murdering a defenceless old man simply in order to steal his car.'

He looked around the room, wanting to impress the urgency of the situation upon his team. 'It's down to us to get that message across and, if we can do that successfully, I'm sure we'll start to see some cooperation. I want you to arrange with the divisional inspectors for the Meadows area to hold a series of public meetings where the residents can air their grievances with the local cops, while giving us a platform to seek greater cooperation from them.'

Rob let out a sigh of resignation and said, 'I'll get the meetings arranged.'

'Come on, Rob. We need some positivity here.'

'Just then,' Rachel interrupted, 'you described Lionel Wickes as being a defenceless old man. I think we can show that wasn't necessarily the case.'

'Go on.'

'Jane Pope and Steve White have been making enquiries at the boxing clubs in and around the city, and they've come up with something interesting.'

She paused and Danny nodded at her to continue.

'Yesterday they visited the Phoenix amateur boxing club in Hucknall. All the club members and trainers there knew Lionel Wickes very well. Even though he's now in his seventies, he still visited the gym to train three times a week. One of the trainers described him as an inspiration to the younger lads on their books. They had his photo on the wall, and a candle lit below it. The lads in the gym seemed genuinely devastated by his death.'

An incredulous Danny said, 'And he was still boxing?'

'Not boxing as such, but training. He had a strict routine, where he would work on the speed ball and the different punch bags. Talking to the trainers, it was obvious they had the utmost respect for Lionel; they all mentioned how he still had very fast hands. Although a little reluctant to talk to the police at first, all the lads there were gutted that he's been killed in such a way. They have promised to encourage some more public cooperation via the city's other boxing clubs.'

'That's great. You see, that's what we need. All it takes is a single act of support and it will grow. Very soon the public will come to realise that we're on the estate to help them remove a dangerous individual from their streets. Good work.'

Rob was thoughtful for a moment and then said, 'That does raise some questions, boss.'

Danny indicated for him to continue.

'Do you remember the mysterious bruising on Wickes' hands and knuckles, which Seamus Carter couldn't really account for? What if our victim had managed to land a few punches on the killer before he was struck with the scaffold pole?'

'It's possible, I suppose, especially if he was still regularly taking part in boxing training, but where does that take us? We certainly haven't found any blood that's unaccounted for at the scene.'

'Maybe we haven't been looking hard enough. I recently read about a case in London where minute droplets of blood had been found on a coat after the offender had exhaled over the garment after cutting his mouth during a fight.'

'And you're thinking if Lionel Wickes had managed to punch his assailant in the mouth, causing a significant injury, prior to being felled by the scaffold pole, the killer could have exhaled blood in a similar way – leaving traces that we haven't yet found?'

'It's just a thought, and I know it's a lot of what-ifs.'

'I want you to follow this idea through, Rob. Talk to Tim

Donnelly and get his opinion about where any such traces of blood could have landed and let's see if we can find something.' Danny looked at his colleague, impressed by his thoughtfulness. 'I'm feeling more optimistic already,' he said warmly. 'Good thinking, Rob.'

Next he turned to Andy Wills. 'Andy, I want you to set up the public meetings, so Rob can follow this line of enquiry, okay?'

'No problem, boss.'

'Rachel, pass on my thanks to Jane and Steve for all their hard work visiting the boxing clubs. I'm aware just how time-consuming that line of enquiry has been – but it seems that it's starting to bear fruit.'

'Will do.'

Danny then spoke to Tina Cartwright. 'Tina. Now that we've charged Stevens are there any of your staff you can release over to the Lionel Wickes murder case?'

Tina was thoughtful. 'Glen has been working with Ray Holden researching previous robberies in the city, but all the information they've gathered will now probably end up as unused material, so they could switch without causing too much of an issue.'

'Good.' Danny clasped his hands together. 'Ask them both to come and see me after this briefing. I've thought of a new angle I want them to concentrate on.'

'Will do.'

'Okay. That's it for this morning. Keep your staff motivated. The answer is out there somewhere, we just need to find it.'

As everyone started to leave, Rachel hung back a little and said, 'Have you got five minutes, boss?'

'Of course, close the door and grab a seat.'

Danny waited for Rachel to get comfortable before saying, 'Is everything okay?'

Rachel remained silent for a while before blurting out, 'I'm pregnant.'

A little shocked both by her news and by the way she had suddenly delivered it, Danny took a couple of moments to recover. 'Okay. And how do you feel about that?'

'That's just it, I don't know. I think I'm going to need some time off to talk everything through with Jack.'

Danny had met Rachel's fiancé, Jack, on several occasions and had always found him to be an approachable, pleasant man.

'What does Jack think?'

'As you know we were planning to get married later this year anyway, but neither of us had factored in having a child this early.'

She paused and Danny remained silent, allowing her the time to say what she needed to say. 'Again, as you know, Jack's a primary school teacher and adores the kids in his class, so he's excited and can't wait to be a father himself.'

'And you?'

'I love my work and don't know if I'm ready to give that up yet.'

Danny nodded in sympathy at her situation. 'I'll authorise any amount of time off you need, Rachel, that's not a problem. This is a massive decision and one you and Jack both need to consider. If you think it would help, why don't you talk to Sue? She's working full time in a stressful job, and is still a brilliant mum to our daughter, Hayley. There were some initial problems for both of us balancing parenthood and work. I'm sure she could talk you through some of those problems – who knows, maybe you might avoid them altogether.'

Rachel nodded before saying, 'I'll use the time off to talk everything through properly with Jack before coming to any decision.'

'Let me have an annual leave pass today, and I'll get your time off authorised. Take what time you need and make sure you reach the right decision for you both. Am I okay to talk to Sue about your pregnancy? I think she could offer you some valuable insight about the pressures involved in juggling a career with motherhood. When our daughter came along everything was a massive upheaval at first, but then you soon work out a routine that suits both of you.'

'Thanks, boss. And yes, please do talk to Sue, I'd love to talk to her, if that's possible. As you know, I don't have anyone else I can talk to about this stuff. I haven't mentioned anything to anybody else yet. I want to wait until I've decided what I'm going to do.'

'I understand. I'll talk to Sue and ask her to contact you at home.'

39

Danny was still considering the news Rachel had shared with him after the briefing when there was a knock on his door.

Glen Lorimar and Ray Holden walked in. Glen said, 'You wanted to see us, boss.'

Danny said, 'Grab a seat. I'm taking you both off the Randall Clements investigation. Any intelligence or reports you've gathered on previous city centre robbery offences, pass them on to DI Cartwright.'

Glen looked shocked. 'We've both put a lot of hours into that line of investigation, boss. Do you mind me asking if there's any particular reason why you're taking us off?'

'Unfortunately, I think all your hard work isn't going to amount to anything evidentially this time. It will probably end up as unused material in the court file DI Cartwright's preparing against Craig Stevens.'

Danny could see the crestfallen look on the faces of both detectives and said, 'However, I've asked you in here because I want you to start working on a fresh line of enquiry in the Lionel Wickes murder.'

Both men now sat up, paying attention.

Glen parroted, 'A fresh line of enquiry?'

'Yes,' Danny said. 'It occurred to me that Wickes was killed trying to prevent the theft of his car. What if the killer was stealing the car for a reason other than joyriding and needed a car urgently that night.'

Glen said, 'Well, there's any number of reasons why somebody could need a car urgently.'

'Maybe wheels for a planned robbery?' Ray added. 'Or simply needed to get somewhere sharpish?'

'Exactly. With that in mind, I want you two to research any cars that were stolen on the night of the murder, in that area of the city.'

Glen nodded. 'How wide an area should we research, boss?'

'Start with any vehicles stolen within a two-mile radius of the murder scene and see how many that turns up.'

'Okay, and then what?'

'Come on, Glen. Use your imagination. I want to know exactly where they were stolen from. And where they were recovered. If they've already been recovered, what forensic evidence was found? Have any suspects been arrested and interviewed in connection with those car thefts? You know what I'm looking for.'

Ray said, 'If we find there are still vehicles stolen that night that haven't been recovered yet, are you going to authorise an information marker on the PNC? That would flag it up for the locating officers to contact us immediately?'

'Good idea, Ray. When you've got a definitive list of any vehicles that are still outstanding, come and see me. I'll authorise the entry on the PNC and flag it so that any vehicles subsequently located are recovered by means of a full lift and preserved for full forensic examination.' He looked both men in the eye. 'This could be another painstaking enquiry for not a lot of reward, but it's got to be worth a try.'

Glen said, 'We're on it, boss.'

As the two detectives were leaving the office, Danny said, 'Don't forget to hand all the robbery intelligence to DI Cartwright and keep me informed of any progress.'

40

11.30 a.m., 2 February 1991
Our Lady and St Edward Roman Catholic Church,
Nottingham

I t had taken Mark Bradbury a week to locate Father Francis Hennessey.

He had tried to locate the Divine Shepherd adoption agency first, but with no success. There were archive records in the main library that gave details of the premises the agency once occupied on Marlborough Road, Nottingham.

Following that lead, he had discovered that the building was now a house of multi-occupancy and had been for over ten years.

Speaking to some of the tenants, who were predominantly students there for the cheap accommodation, he learned that the building now had no connection with either the Divine Shepherd agency or the Roman Catholic church; rather, it was owned by a private letting company.

One of the tenants, an older woman, did inform him that she thought the nuns who had once occupied the building had relocated to premises somewhere in Gloucestershire.

Realising he was going to get no information from the adoption agency, Mark had changed direction and turned all his attention to the Roman Catholic church – in particular, the location of Father Francis Hennessey.

A call to the main offices of the Diocese of Nottingham had finally borne fruit. He had given the woman on the telephone a convincing reason for trying to contact the elderly priest, saying that his terminally ill mother was nearing the end of her life, and she had dearly wanted her son to pass on her regards to Father Hennessey before it was too late.

The woman had been sympathetic to his cause and had readily informed him that Father Francis Hennessey was one of two priests responsible for the congregation of Our Lady and St Edward in the Carlton district of Nottingham.

Now, as Mark sat in his car staring at the brick façade of the church, that was typical of the architecture of the fifties, he wondered exactly how to approach the priest. He was desperate to speak to his biological mother, but at the same time knew if he handled his approach in the wrong way, the priest could easily close the conversation without revealing any of the detail he needed.

He was still holding down a high level of anger and resentment, fuelled by the fact that the church and this priest had taken it upon themselves to take a newborn child from its mother – for monetary gain. He knew that before he spoke to Father Hennessey, he would need to control that emotion and take a conciliatory tone with the clergyman.

He found the elderly priest standing near the altar at the front of the church. He was busily unpacking boxes of tealight candles ready for upcoming services. He heard Mark's footsteps echoing around the spacious church as he approached and turned to face him.

Mark gave a warm smile and asked, 'Father Hennessey?'

'Can I help you, son?'

'My name's Mark Bradbury,' Mark said calmly. 'I am Millicent Lowe's child. I have recently discovered that I was adopted at birth and would dearly love to speak to my birth mother. My adoptive father told me that you arranged the adoption and I wanted to thank you for that. I've had the most wonderful upbringing with two loving parents, but I would dearly love to make the connection with my birth mother.'

Father Hennessey took a moment to process what the smart, well-spoken young man standing before him had just said.

He smiled kindly, peered over the spectacles perched on the tip of his nose and gestured for Mark to sit on one of the pews at the front of the church.

After a brief pause, the white-haired priest also sat down. 'I remember your mother, Millicent,' he said, 'and the predicament she was in at the time.'

'Predicament?'

'Your mother had been married for less than a year, and at that time her husband worked away for long periods of time. She was led into temptation on a night out with her work colleagues and ended up in the family way. It was obvious to both Millicent and her husband that he was not the father.'

Mark nodded and said sympathetically, 'I can see why that would be a huge problem for her.'

'This was the early sixties and society took a harsh view on such matters back then.'

'How did you become involved, Father?'

'Your mother's husband approached me after Mass one Sunday and spoke to me of his family's difficult situation. I offered him a possible solution to the problem.'

'That problem being me?'

The priest shook his head in a kindly fashion and said, 'Millicent was a good Catholic and wouldn't countenance any talk of abortion, and her husband wasn't prepared to raise her illegitimate offspring as his own. That was the problem, not you, my child.'

Mark was taken aback at the seeming kindness of the old priest's words. He'd been expecting much worse. For some reason he couldn't quite fathom, he was pleased the old priest hadn't used the word bastard during their conversation.

'What was the solution you offered them, Father?'

'Back then it was legal for the church to assist in adoptions. I worked with an adoption agency called the Divine Shepherd. We would place unwanted or abandoned children with loving parents, who would then raise them as their own. I offered this as an alternative to your mother and her husband. Millicent could see this was the only way out of her situation. She dearly wanted to give birth to her child but desperately wanted to remain married.'

'So, she accepted your offer?'

The old priest nodded. 'She accepted it with open arms.'

'And how did you find my adoptive parents?'

'I'm afraid most of that part of your story is lost to me. I can't recall those details. My memory isn't what it was, I'm afraid. I do recall that they collected you from the Divine Shepherd maternity home, the day after you were born.'

'And what became of my birth mother, Millicent Lowe? Is she still alive?'

'Millicent is still very much alive. She's a widow now though; her husband passed some years ago.'

'Do you still see her?'

'I haven't seen her for quite a while. Ever since she moved into the nursing home at West Bridgford.'

'A nursing home. Isn't she well?'

'After her husband died, unfortunately Millicent went into a sharp decline and now suffers with dementia. The nursing home is a specialist centre for the care of the elderly with dementia.'

'Would I be able to see her?'

'I don't see why not. Would you like me to come with you?'

Mark was thoughtful for a minute. He had no idea what his mother thought of this priest. It could be that she despised him for taking her child away from her.

He smiled and said, 'No thanks, Father. I'll talk to the staff at the home and be guided by them. The last thing I want to do is to upset her or cause her condition to get worse.'

'I think that's a very wise move, young man.'

'Do you have the address for the home, please?'

'It's in the office, I won't be a minute.'

As he sat waiting for the priest, Mark gazed around the spacious interior of the church and wondered what checks, if any, were done by this priest into his adoptive parents before he handed over a newborn infant to them.

After five minutes, a slightly out of breath Father Hennessey shuffled back into the church clutching a piece of paper that had been torn from a notepad.

'I've written all the details down for you. There's a telephone number as well, in case you wanted to contact the staff before you visit.'

'Thank you, Father.'

The old priest extended his hand and said, 'I'm so very pleased that you had a wonderful childhood, my son.'

Mark shook the priest's hand and found that he was smiling through gritted teeth.

As he walked out of the church back into the bright sunlight, he muttered under his breath, 'More by luck than judgement, mate.'

41

2.00 p.m., 2 February 1991
Briar Lodge Nursing Home, West Bridgford, Nottingham

The matron in charge at Briar Lodge met Mark in the reception area before taking him into her office.

She offered Mark a seat and said in a lively Jamaican accent, 'You're the first visitor Millicent Lowe's had in over six months. Can I ask what your connection to her is, and the purpose of your visit?'

Thinking it best to be honest, Mark replied, 'I recently found out I was adopted at birth. I've since discovered that my birth mother is Millicent Lowe – and I wanted to meet her.'

Seeing the frown pass across the matron's face, he said quickly, 'I realise this could be upsetting for her and I want to assure you that isn't my intention. I'll be entirely guided by you on whether you think this is a good idea or not.'

The matron was thoughtful before saying, 'Millicent is in the early stages of dementia and some days she isn't aware of her surroundings, but most days she is lucid and understands everything and everyone around her. I haven't spoken to her today, so let me talk to her first. That way I'll be able to assess how she's feeling, and if it's worthwhile you talking to her. Make yourself comfortable in here,' she added as she stood up. 'I won't be too long.'

As Mark waited alone in the office his mind was in turmoil.

He had no idea how he would feel towards the woman who had readily abandoned him to strangers, just so she could save her marriage. Part of him felt a massive sense of betrayal and another part huge relief that he had been adopted by two people who loved him unconditionally and cared for him so deeply.

He didn't know what he was going to say to Millicent. The question he needed answering was twofold. Had she wanted to abandon him? Or was it someone else's decision that she had no choice but to go along with? If the latter was the case, he knew it would go a long way towards dispelling the overwhelming feeling of abandonment he had been experiencing ever since he learned the truth about his adoption.

The matron returning to the office dragged him from his troubled thoughts. She smiled and said, 'Millicent's having a good day and is feeling fine. She's quite excited about having a visitor.'

A worried Mark asked, 'Have you told her who I am?'

Shaking her head, she replied, 'No. I think that's best

coming from you. Just take your time and break the news gently. If you do that, I think you'll find Millicent will respond to your news just fine.'

The matron walked with Mark through the nursing home until she paused outside a door saying, 'This is Millicent's room. I'll come in with you to introduce you, then I'll leave you to talk.'

She pointed towards a chair in the corridor and said, 'Don't worry, I'll be waiting outside. When you've finished talking, just open the door and let me know. Okay?'

Mark could feel his hands shaking with nerves, but he nodded and said, 'Okay.'

Walking into the room, the matron said, 'Hello again, sweetheart. This is your visitor. His name is Mark, and he has some news for you.'

She looked at Mark indicating he should sit on the chair opposite the old woman. As soon as he sat down, she said, 'I'll leave you two to chat. I'll be just outside.' With that she left the room.

Mark found himself facing a woman with short grey hair and bright blue eyes.

In a soft voice that was barely more than a whisper, Millicent asked, 'Do I know you? You do look familiar.'

Having wondered what he was going to feel when he met this woman, Mark now realised the only emotion he felt was one of immense sorrow. There was an all-pervading sense of sadness emanating from her, which her sparkling eyes failed to mask. She looked frail and vulnerable.

He tried to imagine her as a young woman stuck in that awful situation, between having her child, or saving her marriage.

Suddenly, realising that he still hadn't said a word, he

spluttered, 'My name is Mark Bradbury.' Composing himself a little, he continued, 'I was raised in Dorset, by two wonderful people, Bill and Amy Bradbury. I always thought I was blessed to have been born and raised by two such loving parents.'

He paused, trying to gauge her reaction to what he was saying, and he detected a hint of a smile on her face.

She said softly, 'That's lovely for you.'

'I recently found out that Bill and Amy actually adopted me when I was still a baby.'

That hint of a smile now turned into a full-blown one that animated her eyes more and showed neat, even teeth. 'You're my baby, aren't you?' Millicent said.

Mark could feel tears stinging his eyes as he nodded. 'Yes. Father Hennessey handed me to the Bradburys – my parents – the day after you gave birth to me.' He paused, wiping his eyes. 'I wanted to meet you and let you know that I had a wonderful childhood, and that my mum and dad were always kind and loving towards me.'

Millicent reached out and took Mark's hand in hers and said, 'I've thought about you every day. Wondering what you looked like? What you were doing? Whether you had a wife and children of your own now?'

'I need to ask,' he started, then swallowed hard. 'I need to ask: why did you give me up for adoption?'

Millicent's eyes held his. 'That was a decision I have regretted all my life. I felt at the time that I had no choice. I was a young Catholic girl pregnant outside of my marriage. I wouldn't hear any talk of abortion and my husband was going to walk out on me.' Then her face changed. 'Father Hennessey' – she almost spat out the name – 'suggested an adoption. My husband wanted it so badly that I felt pressured into going through with it. We should never have been bullied by that priest. I'm sure we could have worked things out given time.'

Now tears were streaming down the old woman's face and Mark only wanted to ease her obvious anguish.

'It must have been such a hard decision for you. I bear you no ill feelings, please understand that.' He reached out, instinctively, and took her delicate, warm hand in his. 'I totally understand why you felt you had to do it.'

He could feel her grip tighten on his hand. 'Bless you, Mark,' she murmured. 'I hope your brother feels the same way.'

'I have a brother?' Mark felt sure that if he wasn't holding her hand so tight he would have – literally – fallen off his chair in shock.

'Yes, you have a brother. I gave birth to twins that day. I had received no antenatal care during my pregnancy, so when I gave birth to twins, it came as a shock to everyone.'

His mind still reeling at what he'd just been told, it took Mark a good minute to find his voice. 'What happened to my brother?'

Millicent shrugged, a faraway, sorrowful look on her face. 'I don't know,' she said in a resigned voice. 'Father Hennessey took both of you away from me. He never told me where either of you went, or who adopted you. That was the way things were done.'

'Has my brother ever contacted you?'

'No.' The old lady frowned deeply, squeezed Mark's hand tighter and made full eye contact. 'Do you forgive me?'

He squeezed her hand back and said softly, 'Of course I do. You did nothing wrong.'

'Thank you. Will you come and see me again?'

Mark nodded, his heart full of emotion. 'I will, and if I can find my brother, I'll bring him too.'

A smile replaced her frown and she said, 'That would be wonderful. I want to know everything about your lives.'

'I've got to go now, but I'll come back soon and we can speak again.'

Mark walked out of the room and found the waiting matron, who with genuine concern in her voice asked, 'How did it go?'

'It was fine, thanks for all your help. Will it be okay if I visit her again?'

'Of course it will.' The matron gave a huge grin. 'She's your mother.'

As he walked back out into the car park, Mark felt conflicted.

He was overjoyed at finally meeting his birth mother, but equally seething over the fact that Father Hennessey hadn't said a word about a twin brother. The visit to the nursing home had been a success, but had left him needing answers to even more questions.

42

7.00 p.m., 2 February 1991
Our Lady and St Edward Roman Catholic Church,
Nottingham

Mark sat in his car, parked opposite the main doors of the church. The last of the parishioners who had attended that evening's vigil Mass were now slowly leaving, shaking the hand of the white-haired priest standing in the doorway as they left.

He slipped out of the vehicle, crossed the road and stood in the shadows to one side of the door. From this position, he could clearly hear an elderly woman, who was the last parishioner to leave, say, 'Thank you again for a wonderful service, Father Hennessey.'

'It was a pleasure, Mrs Finch. And will I see you again this Sunday?'

'Of course, Father. See you Sunday.'

Mark waited for the woman to shuffle out of sight before stepping forward out of the shadows, bundling the priest back inside his church and closing the door behind him in one swift, precise movement.

Father Hennessey started to protest, but fell silent when Mark growled, 'Be quiet. All I want are some answers.'

He saw the look of recognition on the elderly priest's face. 'You again,' Father Hennessey spluttered. 'What do you want?'

'Why didn't you tell me about my brother?' Mark hissed, real venom in his voice.

'I didn't mind giving you details about your mother, I felt you had a right to know about her, young man. But your brother has a right to his own privacy as well. What if he's living a perfectly happy life, ignorant of the fact he was adopted? I needed to take that into consideration.'

After sitting in his car for three hours waiting impatiently to speak to this man, feeling his anger gradually increase, Mark was not going to be fobbed off.

He grabbed the priest by the front of his robes and pulled him in close. 'I'm in no mood to hear any more of your nonsense. You've interfered in my life way too much already. If you don't tell me everything you know about my brother, I won't be responsible for what happens next. That will be on you.'

Mark could see that the priest was terrified by his presence and the threat of violence. He had no intention of harming the old man, but he needed answers, and he hoped his bluff would be enough to get them.

To reinforce the threat, he shouted, 'Talk to me!' and his raised voice echoed around the empty church.

Cowering under Mark's grasp, Father Hennessey panted,

'All right, all right. There's no need for any of this. I'll tell you what I know.'

Mark eased his grip a little but left his face inches from the old man's and snarled, 'Start talking.'

'We need to go into the office. Any details I have will be in there.'

'Okay. Let's go.'

Mark held on to the old man's arm as they walked through the church. Taking a key from beneath his robes, the priest unlocked a plain wooden door, saying, 'It's through here.'

He followed the clergyman into the small room that contained a desk, two chairs and a wardrobe.

Sitting down heavily in the chair behind the desk, Father Hennessey unlocked the top drawer and removed a large hardback notebook.

He flicked through the pages until he found what he was looking for. 'Here it is, Millicent Lowe, seventh March 1964.'

'What does it say?'

'Gave birth to two male infants. First born adopted by William and Amy Bradbury of Lenthay Road, Sherborne, Dorset. Contribution paid in full. Second born to be arranged.'

'To be arranged? What does that mean?'

'Yes. I remember what happened now. Nobody expecting a second child to be born that day, so no prospective adoptive parents had been arranged for your brother. I did enquire with Mr and Mrs Bradbury to see if they would take you both, but they were of the opinion they couldn't afford to raise two children.'

Again, Mark was stunned that his own parents hadn't

thought fit to tell him he had a brother. Still reeling from that revelation he said, 'So, what did you arrange?'

'A few days later, I managed to find a couple who were still waiting to adopt, after being turned down by another agency. I would have made a note in here.' Once again, the priest flicked through the book. 'Here it is. The second male child of Millicent Lowe, adopted by Ray and Martha Stevens of fifty-four Whitfield Street, Newark, Notts. Fifty per cent contribution paid.'

'What does that mean, "fifty per cent contribution paid"?'

'It means I had to find a home for the child in a hurry, so the agency accepted half the contribution.'

'And how much was that?'

'That's none of your business and I'm not going to divulge that. What we did was perfectly legal and above board.'

'And how much of that contribution did you pocket, Father?'

'That's an outrageous accusation. That contribution was only ever used for good causes.'

'How much?' Mark insisted.

'I was paid expenses, that's all.'

Mark turned away in disgust and then said, 'What checks did you do on the people who took these babies?'

'We only ever allowed children to go to good Catholic homes, with well-respected parents.'

'But what checks did you do?'

'We provided those children with safe homes.'

'Did you ever follow up on any of these adoptions, to make sure the kids were safe and being cared for properly?'

The priest now railed against the questioning and spluttered angrily, 'I think it's time you went. If you don't leave this minute, I'm going to call the police. I could already have you arrested for assault.'

'Of course, you could,' Mark said steadily. 'But you won't. I think what you were doing back then, in concert with the Divine Shepherd adoption agency, was morally bankrupt and borderline criminal. This voluntary contribution is another way of saying that you were, in effect, selling children to the highest bidder. It was horrendous.'

'Why are you so angry?' Father Hennessey spat back. 'You told me earlier that you'd had a good childhood.'

'I did, but no thanks to you and your cronies at the agency. I was lucky, that's all. I could have been abused every day of my childhood, and you would have been none the wiser, so call the police if you like. I'm leaving anyway. You disgust me.'

Mark needed some fresh air and a stiff drink. He slammed the heavy door behind him as he stormed out of that godforsaken church.

43

10.30 p.m., 2 February 1991
Mansfield, Nottinghamshire

Danny and Sue stood on their doorstep and waved as Seamus Carter and his fiancé Gemma Coleridge left. It had been a pleasant evening; the two couples had spent it chatting over a home-cooked meal.

As Danny closed and locked the front door, he said, 'What did you think of Gemma?'

'I thought she was lovely. They make a great couple. Obviously, I don't know Seamus as well as you do, but he seems happy.'

'I've known the guy for years and I've never seen him like this. How the pair of them were acting around each other reminded me of us when we first started seeing each other. He looks totally loved up.'

'How we were?' Sue screwed up her face. 'You mean as

opposed to how we are now? Constantly arguing and fighting with each other.'

Danny grabbed her waist, laughed and said, 'Exactly like that, wife.'

Sue turned to face him and smiled playfully. 'You keep digging, husband, and you'll be looking for a new wife.'

As they sat down in the lounge, Danny said, 'Shall we finish what's left of the wine?'

Sue nodded. 'That sounds like a plan.'

As she walked into the kitchen to get the bottle and two glasses, Danny said, 'Leave the dishes, I'll do them in the morning.'

Sue walked back in and poured two generous glasses. 'The dishes are already done. Gemma helped me do them earlier while you and Seamus were rattling on. I thought she was lovely, and I'll be glad to help her settle into this area. I remember what it was like for me when I first moved here and didn't know a soul. I know she has Seamus, and they seem a perfect match, but it's nice for a woman to have some girlfriends to confide in as well.' She giggled. 'Who knows, she might even talk him into getting rid of that awful beard.'

'I doubt that. He was telling me earlier she adores the beard.' Danny took a sip of his wine and said, 'I do have some other news, that is for your ears only and mustn't be repeated.'

'Sounds ominous.'

'It's nothing bad. I had a conversation with Rachel yesterday and she told me she's pregnant.'

'Wow! I didn't see that one coming. I always had Rachel pegged as more focused on her career than starting a family just yet.'

'Exactly. But she's expecting and is torn about what to do.

She's taking some time off work to talk things through with Jack.'

'They're getting married in October, aren't they?'

'That was the plan.' Danny looked at his wife, who was thoughtfully swirling the wine in her glass. 'I asked Rachel if it would be okay to talk to you about the pregnancy. I was hoping the two of you could get together and have a chat. I think she'd really value your thoughts on how to juggle a high-pressure career and being a mum.'

'No problem. I'd be glad to. It was a lot of trial and error for us two, wasn't it, so hopefully I could steer her away from some of the pitfalls. She's already in a good position as Jack's a teacher. I'm sure his hours are far more regular than yours, so splitting the childcare between them won't be so much of an issue, as it was for us at the beginning.'

'I knew you'd be able to help, thank you.'

'When should I call her?'

'I'd give it a few days to let her and Jack thrash things out first.'

Sue snuggled into his side. 'No problem. I've had enough of the vino, let's go up.'

44

Mark Bradbury glanced at the notepaper that Father Hennessey had given him and checked the address on it one more time.

At least he didn't have to worry about work now. After the conversations with Father Hennessey, he had contacted the office and told them he was suffering from a crippling stomach bug, which he must have picked up on his travels, and that he would be back in work as soon as possible.

Now he was sitting in his car outside the home of his brother's adoptive parents, Ray and Martha Stevens.

The scruffy terrace in the centre of Newark couldn't have been more different from the neat, detached bungalow where he had been raised. He wondered how different his brother's upbringing had been from his own privileged beginnings.

He reflected on how Bill Bradbury had worked long hours to be able to afford to send him to a private school. Sherborne Academy had given him an excellent education and was the perfect place to hone his undoubted prowess at learning foreign languages. It had been no surprise when he had been offered a place at Oxford, where he achieved his first-class degree in business studies.

Looking at the house and surrounding neighbourhood, he was almost certain that any such advantages had been thin on the ground for his brother. These were mean streets.

He wondered exactly how much, if anything, the two men would have in common. As he opened the car door, he muttered to himself, 'You've got to find him first, idiot.'

Stepping from his vehicle, he knocked loudly on the front door.

A man's voice shouted from within, 'Just a minute, I'm coming.'

Mark could hear shuffling feet approaching, and eventually the door was opened by an elderly man. The man was wearing stained jeans and a grubby white vest. His hair was uncombed, and he had three or four days of stubble on his face. His eyes were bloodshot, and his face crisscrossed with thread veins, giving him a florid complexion.

He looked like a heavy drinker.

The man was waiting for Mark to speak, so he said, 'Mr Stevens?'

'Who wants to know?'

'I'm sorry to bother you, Mr Stevens. My name's Mark. I recently found out I was adopted. I believe you may have adopted a child at the same time.'

'Do you now?'

'Both the adoptions were arranged by Father Hennessey and the Divine Shepherd agency.'

The man took a packet of cigarettes from his pocket and lit one. Taking a long pull on the cigarette, he said, 'I don't know why you're here, mate. I've got nothing to say to you about all of that.'

'Please. All I'm trying to do is locate the boy you adopted. I think he may be my brother – my twin.'

With an air of resignation, the man leaned on the door frame and said, 'You're not going to go away, are you?'

Mark shook his head and smiled. 'All I need is five minutes of your time.'

'You'd better come in.'

The front door opened directly into the small living room. There were old newspapers strewn everywhere, plates of leftovers from previous meals, and empty cans of strong lager. The room held a blue haze of smoke, and the smell of stale cigarettes was almost overpowering.

'If you can find somewhere to sit, take a seat.'

Mark shifted some old newspapers from an armchair and sat down. 'What did you name your son?'

'His mother named him. The adoption was all her idea. I could quite happily have done without having another bloody mouth to feed but Martha wanted a kid. We couldn't have children of our own, so she tried to adopt through the church. We got a phone call out of the blue from this priest who said he had a male child who needed a home urgently, and that we could have him for a small fee.'

'What did you do?'

'Like I said. I wasn't bothered, but Martha insisted on taking the kid. I spoke to the priest and offered him half the money he'd originally quoted. I couldn't afford any more than that, so it was take it or leave it. Anyway, he accepted that offer, and we drove to Nottingham and brought the kid home.'

'What did Martha call him?'

'Craig. His name's Craig Stevens.'

'Does he still live here with you and Martha?'

'Martha's dead. She passed five years ago. That little shit never even turned up for her funeral. He always was a wrong 'un.'

'When did you last see Craig?'

'Haven't seen him in years. He pissed off when he was sixteen and joined the army. I'll be honest with you, by then both of us were glad to see the back of him. He brought nothing but trouble to my door, always getting into fights. I got sick of the cops coming round here, telling me he was locked up again and did I want to fetch him from the station. He was a proper tearaway, God knows why the army took him.'

'So, you haven't heard anything from him since he left to join the army?'

'The last bit of news I heard was from one of his old school mates. He had heard that Craig had married a lass he met in Northern Ireland when he was still a serving soldier. This school mate told me he'd now left the army and was living in Mansfield somewhere.'

'But you haven't spoken to him yourself?'

'No, and if you do find him, don't go telling him to visit me. I couldn't care less if I never see that piece of shit again. Are we done?'

Mark stood and said, 'Thanks for your help.'

As he walked out the front door, Ray Stevens opened the

tab on a can of lager and said, 'Take my advice and don't bother looking for Craig.' He took a long swig and held Mark in his unsteady gaze. 'You seem like a nice bloke, nothing like him. Trust me, he was trouble then and he'll be bigger trouble now. Go back to wherever it is you came from and forget you ever spoke to that priest.'

45

4.30 p.m., 3 February 1991
20 Western Avenue, Mansfield, Nottinghamshire

Mark slowed his car to a stop outside the property on Western Avenue. This would be the fifth house he had visited since he started his search.

After leaving Newark he had driven straight to Mansfield. His thoughts on that journey had been consumed by the parting words of Ray Stevens, but the urge to track the man down who could be his brother was too strong to resist.

When he arrived in Mansfield, he stopped at the first public telephone box he saw. Even though the handset had been smashed and was hanging by one exposed wire, the phone directory was still on the shelf.

He had quickly scanned the pages until he found the listings under Stevens and Stephens. When he saw how many names were listed just under those two surnames, he cursed himself for not asking Ray the correct spelling of his surname.

He had carefully ripped out the pages for those two surnames and started the laborious process of visiting every address listed. He had started with the entries for C. Stevens, of which there were twelve.

It was starting to get dark and, when he glanced down the driveway leading to the house, he could see there was already a light on.

As he walked towards the front door wondering what he was going to say to this man, who was his brother, his mind was in turmoil.

He knocked on the door and waited patiently.

When there was no answer, he knocked again.

A woman's voice said timidly, 'Who is it?'

'My name's Mark Bradbury, I'm sorry to disturb you. I wanted to talk to Craig Stevens if he's home.'

There was a long pause before the woman said, 'Craig's not here; he's away right now. Why do you need to speak to him?'

'It's a long story,' Mark said carefully. 'Would you mind opening the door?'

'You'll have to come back tomorrow. It's getting dark now and I don't know you from Adam.'

'I understand. What time would be best for you?'

'I don't know. In the morning, around eleven.'

'Okay. I'll come back then. There's nothing to worry about and I promise I won't take up much of your time.'

The woman didn't answer, so it was with a real sense of frustration that he walked slowly back to his car.

As he drove away, he pondered on the woman's words:

he's away right now. He wondered where he might have gone, and why. *Was he still in the army? Had he been posted overseas?*

Feeling a little more positive, he screwed up the pages of the telephone directory and hurled them on the backseat. At least he now knew where Craig Stevens had been living and, hopefully, if he got to speak with the woman properly tomorrow, he would get some answers.

46

11.00 a.m., 3 February 1991
20 Western Avenue, Mansfield, Nottinghamshire

PC Jamie Collins was looking through the net curtains, watching the man as he walked down the drive. He said, 'Is this him?'

Tricia Stevens looked over the police officer's shoulder and said, 'That's him. I reckon he's from the papers or something. He scared me to death last night calling round when it was dark. I don't want to talk to him. Can you talk to him and see what he wants?'

Jamie opened the front door just as the man was about to knock. The officer could see that the stranger was startled, obviously not expecting to see a police officer in uniform.

He used the pause to his advantage and said firmly, 'Can I help you?'

The man said, 'I was hoping to speak with Craig Stevens, or his wife. Has something happened?'

'Who are you? And what do you want?'

'My name's Mark Bradbury. I have some important news for Craig Stevens about his upbringing. I didn't mean to cause any trouble.'

'I'm afraid you've had a wasted journey, Mr Bradbury. Craig Stevens is away, and his wife doesn't want to speak to you. She wants you to leave.'

'No problem.' The man held his hands up. 'I'll leave. Like I said, I don't want to cause any trouble. Can you tell me where Craig is, and when he's likely to be back?'

'He's locked up and hopefully won't be back for a long time.'

'What do you mean locked up?'

'He's in prison, so I doubt that you'll be able to talk to him anytime soon.'

'I don't understand.'

'Look. I've probably said too much already, Mr Bradbury. Mrs Stevens doesn't want you hanging around here bothering her. If I give you the name of Craig's solicitor, you can contact them about whatever it is you need to speak to him about. Does that seem fair?'

'That would be great, thanks.'

Jamie flicked through his notebook until he found the entry for the night he had arrested Craig Stevens, 'Okay. Try Anderson and Phillips. They are based in Mansfield town centre on Leeming Street. Talk to them.'

'Thanks. I didn't mean to alarm Mrs Stevens, and I hope I haven't wasted your time.'

'No problem. It might be an idea if you write to his solicitors and let them know what this information you have is all about. They may be able to organise a visiting order for you to see Craig in prison.'

'I will, thanks.' Mark turned away, relieved. His brother felt a little nearer now. But prison – what was all that about?

47

10.00 a.m., 7 February 1991
HMP Lincoln, Greetwell Road, Lincoln

C raig Stevens had been assaulted the previous night by another inmate and his mouth felt bruised and sore. He was feeling reluctant to talk to his solicitor.

Martin Anderson had been a solicitor many years and understood what a harsh regime it was in prison for prisoners on remand. They had few of the privileges offered to inmates who were already serving their custodial sentences, and their supervision was sketchy to say the least.

He knew sympathy would be wasted on Craig, so he pointed at the bruising and said bluntly, 'Any witnesses?'

Stevens shook his head but didn't speak.

'Have they given you anything for the pain?'

Wincing as he spoke, Craig mumbled, 'One of the screws

arranged for me to be seen by the doctor before you came. He's given me a couple of paracetamol, that's it.'

There was a silence between the two men that was eventually broken by Craig. 'If you haven't got any news on a trial date, why are you here?' he said. 'I just want to go back to my cell, so I can get some sleep.'

'I'm here because I had an interesting telephone conversation with a man named Mark Bradbury. Does that name mean anything to you?'

'No. Should it?'

Anderson didn't feel the need to beat about the bush. 'He claims,' he said, 'that he was adopted a few days before you were and that he thinks you could be brothers.'

'What?'

'He claims to be your brother, your twin brother. Were you adopted as a child?'

An incredulous Craig sat up straight. 'Yes, I was. It's no secret, the local cops all knew it too.'

'Are his claims plausible?'

'I don't know,' Craig said, shaking his head as he tried to process the news. 'All I know is what my adoptive parents told me when I was about fourteen, that I wasn't their real son and that I'd been adopted at birth.'

'Did they tell you anything about the adoption?' the solicitor pressed. 'Where you were adopted? Who your real parents are?'

'That lousy drunk, who was supposed to be my dad, couldn't be arsed to tell me anything. My mum told me that she had collected me from a big house in Nottingham and that there were nuns working there.'

He paused before continuing, 'To be honest, I never really asked them any questions about it. By that time, I wasn't bothered; it made no difference to me. I was never at home anyway.' Craig paused, then ran his hands over his face. 'What's this Bradbury bloke like?'

'I haven't met him, just spoken to him on the phone. He seems genuine to me. I didn't get the impression he was playing games.'

'What does he want?'

'He wants to meet you. He's asked me to ask you if you would send him a visiting order.'

'What do you think?'

'I don't see what harm it can do. I've got his address and details here if you want to send one.'

'Why not.' Craig shrugged, resuming his mask of indifference. 'I didn't think I had any proper relatives anywhere. Knowing my luck, he's probably some nutter who's seen my name in the papers.'

48

1.00 p.m., 7 February 1991
MCIU Offices, Mansfield, Nottinghamshire

Danny was trawling through the pile of witness statements that had been taken during the house-to-house work on the Meadows estate.

Those enquiries were now all but finished, and Danny had no plans to extend the parameters. He was desperately searching for something that may have been overlooked previously. A nugget of information that could provide a new, vital lead.

He knew the entire investigation into the death of Lionel Wickes was floundering, despite the best efforts of him and his team.

He pinched the skin on the bridge of his nose and rubbed his eyes. It felt like he had been reading all day and his eyes were stinging. He stood up, stretched and walked into the main briefing room. He saw Rob Buxton at his desk, head down also reading reports.

He walked over and said, 'Have you found anything?'

'No, boss. And I must have read these reports a dozen times now.'

'I know what you mean. I've been rereading the witness statements from the house to house all day. Nothing.'

'I thought that's what you were doing. That's why I didn't disturb you.'

'Did you want to see me about something?'

'I chased Tim Donnelly this morning about that blood spray idea we spoke about at the last briefing, and he's agreed to carry out a luminol procedure on the external surfaces of the Ford Fiesta – the vehicle owned by Wickes.'

'That's great. He must be hopeful of finding something to agree to it.'

'To be fair it was his idea. A couple of days ago, I explained what we suspected about Wickes landing a few punches on his attacker before he was brought down, and he said he would look at the best option to detect and retrieve any blood particles caused by exhalation. Apparently luminol is that best option, and because the vehicle has been under cover in a dry and stable environment since the morning of the murder, if there are any particles of blood, they should still be there.'

'This is great news. When's the procedure being done?'

'Unless another job breaks overnight, he plans to do it tomorrow morning.'

'I think we should be there. What time?'

Rob glanced at his notepad. 'Provisionally booked in for eleven o'clock, in the forensic bay at HQ.'

'Fingers crossed that nothing comes in overnight. Are you free tomorrow?'

'I am now, boss.'

49

1.30 p.m., 8 February 1991
Police Headquarters, Nottinghamshire

Danny and Rob had waited patiently in Tim Donnelly's office at the Scenes of Crime Department. They were not allowed to observe the luminol procedure for themselves. Only the scenes of crime technicians in full protective equipment, who were carrying out the procedure, were allowed inside the confines of the forensic examination bay. The chemicals used were extremely hazardous, so no unnecessary risks were being taken.

Danny paced up and down in the cramped office. 'Why is it taking so long? Surely, they must be almost done by now?'

Rob shrugged. 'If they're doing the entire vehicle, it's bound to take some time. Do you want another coffee?'

'No thanks, Rob. I'm just desperate for some good news.

You know as well as I do, this investigation is dying on its feet. Unless we get a breakthrough soon, this murder's going to remain unsolved.'

That last comment hung heavy in the air, creating a sombre mood in the room.

Suddenly, the door burst open and a beaming Tim Donnelly strode in. 'We've found something.'

Danny snapped, 'Don't keep us in suspense, man.'

'We've located minute particles of blood on the offside front wing of the vehicle. This is the opposite side to where the body of Lionel Wickes was found, which means it's unlikely to be blood spray caused when the metal bar struck his head.'

'Do you think it could be from an offender?'

'We need to do more tests. We've taken samples of the blood found on the car that will need to be compared to the blood we took from Lionel Wickes. We've also got photographs showing the extent of the spray on the vehicle. These photographs also show clearly that it was aerosol blood.'

'Aerosol?'

'It's what we see when someone's exhaling and there's already blood particles in their mouth.'

'Yes!' Rob exclaimed, exuberantly punching the air. 'Good old Lionel. I knew he'd belted this toerag before he got dropped.'

'We won't know that for sure until we've completed those blood comparisons, but it's looking good.'

Danny sighed. 'And how long will that take?'

'I'll fast track it and hopefully we'll have an answer within a couple of weeks.'

'Good. As quick as you can please, Tim.'

'Can you get a DNA profile from a sample of aerosol blood?' Danny asked, thoughtful now.

'I'm very hopeful that, on this occasion, we should be able to, simply because there's a lot of it. It's all minute particles, but it's spread over a wide area, so we've managed to obtain a lot of samples.'

'That's great. I need to be notified as soon as you get the results of the initial blood tests, Tim.'

'No problem,' Tim said smartly. 'I'll make a start on the paperwork straight away.'

'Brilliant. Good work!'

50

Rachel was pleased to see the main briefing room was empty and there was still a light on in Danny's office.

She tapped lightly on the door before opening it. 'Evening, boss. I'm pleased I caught you.'

'Come in, come in. How's it going with Jack?'

As Rachel sat down, she said, 'I don't think we've ever done so much talking. We took ourselves off to the Peak District for a few days. It was great to totally switch off from everything else, to just concentrate on the two of us and what we both wanted for the next stage of our life together.'

'I bet it was a bit wet and wild on the peaks at this time of year.' Danny smiled at his colleague. 'Did you come to a decision?'

She returned with a wide smile of her own. 'It certainly was and yes, we have. We're going to bring the wedding forward and have the baby.'

'That's fantastic news, congratulations. I know that for me becoming a father was one of the best things to happen in my life. How does Jack feel?'

'Jack adores kids; he's always wanted to be a dad. I was the one having doubts, but they've all gone now. The more I think about it now, the more excited I am about becoming a mum. I still want to be a working mum, though. I love my job and Jack has promised that everything will be a team effort. He reckons we can manage raising a child and both continuing with our careers.'

'He's so right. You'll cope. It'll just take a bit of adjustment from both of you.' Danny paused. 'Can I ask, what about your wedding?'

'It's going to be a quiet registry office ceremony now. We'll organise everything so we can get married early next month.'

'I'm so pleased for you both. You know I'll support you in any way I can, both through the pregnancy and afterwards when you're ready to return to work.'

'Thanks, boss.' Rachel looked down at her hands. 'I do have a massive favour to ask as well.'

'Go on.'

'As you know, my brother Joe's in the military. I'd love him to be able to walk me down the aisle, but he's currently in Iraq because of the war, and may not be able to get leave.'

'I didn't realise Joe was in Iraq. Do you know what he's doing over there?'

'Since he left the Marines and joined this other unit, I never know what he's doing, or where, or when. It's all very secretive. He can't tell me, and I don't ask. I've sent a letter to his base, telling him about the wedding and what I had planned for him, but I don't know if he'll even get the letter, never mind be able to come home. There doesn't look like any end to this bloody war soon.'

'I can see that's going to be a problem,' Danny agreed. 'What can I do?'

'I know this is cheeky, but if Joe can't get home, would you be prepared to be my first reserve and walk me down the aisle?'

'I'd be honoured to, Rachel.'

'Thank you, that means a lot. And I'd still love to talk to Sue, if that's possible?'

'No problem. I did tell her what was happening, and she would love to hear from you. Just give her a call and go out for lunch, or something. She'll be delighted with your news.'

'I'll do that. I'm back at work tomorrow, but I wanted to talk to you alone first and let you know what was happening.'

'It really is such happy news, Rachel. Please pass on my congratulations to Jack.'

Rachel nodded as she stood to leave. 'One last thing, make sure you keep the fifth of March clear. I don't want work to get in the way of my wedding.'

'Don't worry,' Danny promised. 'We'll be there.'

51

10.00 a.m., 15 February 1991
HMP Lincoln, Greetwell Road, Lincoln

M ark Bradbury was feeling apprehensive as he drove his car into the visitors' car park opposite the imposing twin turrets that stood either side of the huge wooden gates. The façade of HMP Lincoln was enough to fill anybody with a sense of foreboding; it did nothing to calm his already nervous mood.

Having worked so hard to locate the man who could be his biological brother, he was now worried about finally meeting him, unsure of what he was going to find and what he was going to say.

When the visiting order had arrived in the post he just sat and stared at it for over an hour. Part of him wanted to throw it in the waste bin and move on with his life, but another part was desperate to discover if he had any blood family. The visit to his biological mother in the nursing home had moved him deeply and he now felt an obligation to speak to his brother for her sake as well as his own.

He got out of the car and stretched his back. It had been a long drive across country to get from Leicester to Lincoln, and he had reached the city at the peak of rush hour which had also delayed him. Even so, the visiting order said arrival time was ten thirty, so he'd still arrived in good time despite the heavy traffic.

He walked to the visitors' entrance where he was met by a prison officer who used a hand-held scanner to search him. He had taken note of the literature that arrived with the visiting order and had brought nothing with him that would need to be placed in a locker or confiscated. He had deliberately left all his valuables, his watch and so on, locked in his car and out of sight.

He produced the visiting order and the officer checked it thoroughly before ticking his name off the list on his clipboard. Then the officer directed him to take a seat in the waiting room and informed him that he would be escorted to the visiting area in fifteen minutes' time.

The small waiting room was already crammed with women; there was a mix of hard faces and homemade tattoos on bare arms, alongside women who looked simply vulnerable, twisting their fingers in their laps or gazing at the scratched lino floor. Some carried their babies, while others grabbed and pulled at boisterous toddlers. All were waiting to see their men, who were incarcerated within these walls. The room was heavy with cigarette smoke, as the visitors took the opportunity to have one last cigarette before going in.

He was one of only three men in the room. One of those

men, the older of the two, had a badly broken nose and heavy scar tissue over both eyebrows. The younger man had flamboyantly dyed green hair and was wearing heavy eye liner and mascara.

Mark felt totally out of place; he kept his head down, keen to avoid eye contact with anybody. The last thing he wanted was to upset or annoy someone by inadvertently doing something wrong.

When the prison officer arrived to escort everyone to the visiting area, Mark's eyes were stinging and sore from the cigarette smoke. As he stood up, he felt a palpable sense of relief, to finally be moving out of the cramped waiting room.

He hung back and joined the end of the queue. He was the last to enter the visiting hall. There was only one prisoner who had no visitors in front of him, so Mark made his way over to the table.

As he walked slowly towards the vacant chair opposite the lone man, he noted that he bore a strong physical resemblance to himself.

He said, 'Craig?'

'That's me,' the man barked. 'Sit down.'

A little taken aback at the abrupt nature of Craig's first words, Mark said nervously, 'Thanks for seeing me.'

Again, the reply was brusque and to the point. 'You're here now. I only sent you the VO because my solicitor thought it was a good idea. What do you want from me?'

'I don't want anything from you. I just want to talk.'

'What about?'

'I recently found out that I had been adopted at birth and made efforts to trace my real mother. When I located her, she told me that when I was born, she also gave birth to another boy. From everything I've learned since, I believe you were that other child. I think you're my twin brother.'

Other than uttering a loud tutting sound, Craig remained silent.

Mark persevered. 'What do you know about your background?'

After a long pause, Craig sighed and said, 'I was adopted. The only thing I know about it was that my parents fetched me from a place in Nottingham, and that nuns worked there.'

'That would have been the Divine Shepherd clinic on Marlborough Road in Nottingham.'

'If you say so.'

'That's where I was born. My parents collected me from there as well. Everything was arranged through the Catholic church – that's why nuns were involved I think.'

'Whoever arranged it didn't do me any fucking favours.'

'What do you mean?'

'I don't know what happened to you after you were adopted, but my life as a kid was a fucking nightmare. My so-called father was a useless drunk and my mother was a weak, downtrodden woman who did everything her husband told her. As a youngster I was often on the wrong end of a beating from that drunken dickhead. That stopped as I got older and started hitting him back.'

'I'm sorry to hear that. Our childhoods were obviously very different. My adoptive parents really cared for and looked after me.'

There was heavy sarcasm in Craig Stevens' voice when he replied, 'Good for you, mate. I suppose you were brought up somewhere posh and went to a private school or something.'

Picking up on the sarcasm and not wanting to antagonise the man in front of him any further, Mark said carefully, 'I was looked after well.'

'Well, I was raised on a rough council estate in Newark and went to a shit school which didn't give a toss about giving me an education. I've had to fight and scrap for everything I've ever had. Nobody ever looked after me.'

There was a long pause and Mark could see Craig shifting uncomfortably in his seat. Not wanting to ruin this one chance of finding out more about his long-lost brother, he decided to change direction. 'What did you do when you left school?'

'I hardly ever went to school for the last couple of years and left home when I was sixteen. I joined the army.'

'What was that like?'

'The army was great. I stayed in for six years and was going to sign on for another three, but my wife didn't want me to. The army was the only time in my life I felt like I belonged. I was in the infantry and did tours of Northern Ireland, Hong Kong and Germany, so I saw a bit of the world. I was pissed off that my wife didn't want me to sign on again and I got in a bit of bother at my last posting in Germany.'

'Bother?'

'I had a few drinks and ended up scrapping with some Krauts in a bar in Dusseldorf. The army got rid of me after that.'

'You spoke about your wife, are you still married?'

Again, there was a long pause. 'I don't really want to talk about that bitch. Yes, we're still married and she's the main reason I'm stuck in here. The snide cow set me up.'

'What do you mean?'

'I don't know what my solicitor told you when you spoke to him, but I'm banged up in here on suspicion of murder. I had nothing to do with this murder and was nowhere near the area where it happened. I'm rotting away in here for something I haven't done, and it's her lies that have helped put me in here.'

'If you're innocent, can't your solicitor get you out?'

'What planet do you live on? All he's interested in, is me copping a guilty plea at the trial, so he can pick his legal aid money up.'

'That can't be right. If you're innocent, he's got to fight your case, surely?'

'I am innocent. In an ideal world he should, but he won't, and I'll end up being stuck in this shithole for the rest of my life.'

'Is there anything I can do to help?'

'I don't know, is there? Are you a Crown Court judge or something?'

Again, the comment was laced with heavy sarcasm.

Mark ignored it and said, 'It's up to you, but if you tell me the details of why you're in here, I can at least do some digging. You never know, I might be able to turn up something your solicitor hasn't found.'

'That wouldn't be hard, because that prick isn't looking.'

'Look, the offer's there. Let me help you. What have you got to lose?'

Mark could see his brother thinking about the offer. After a long pause, Craig started to talk.

Leaning forward and speaking in hushed tones, he quietly related in detail everything that had happened on that fateful night out in Nottingham. He followed that up by what had happened when he arrived home in Mansfield and the circumstances leading to his arrest. He gave a thorough account of all the evidence that was stacked against him.

Mark sat and listened.

He could hardly believe what he was hearing.

52

7.30 p.m., 15 February 1991
Oadby, Leicestershire

As soon as he left Lincoln prison, Mark Bradbury had driven to Nottingham and visited the offices of the *Evening Post*. Under the guise of wanting the information for an essay he was writing for an Open University course, he had managed to obtain copies of all the newspaper articles that covered the murder of Randall Clements in the city centre, and the subsequent arrest and charging of Craig Stevens for that offence.

Clippings of those newspaper reports were now spread out across his dining room table.

Mark stood transfixed, staring at a photograph of the dead man.

As he had listened to Craig Stevens describe the events leading to his arrest – and what he had been accused of – he had thought at the time that the date and location had sounded familiar. Now, as he stared down at the grainy black-and-white image of the victim, Randall Clements, Mark was left in no doubt that this was the man who had tried to rob him at knifepoint. The same man who, in a desperate attempt to protect himself from a knife attack, he had punched and knocked to the floor.

Picking up another of the clippings he read a report of a witness appeal made by the police, in which a man carrying a knife had been seen running from the scene. The description of that man, although very basic, fitted him and he remembered that after he had fled from the would-be mugger, he was still carrying the knife his assailant had dropped. He recalled plunging the knife down a drain after putting some distance between himself and his attacker.

With the realisation dawning on him that the single punch he had delivered to the mugger had killed the man, his mind became overwhelmed with disturbing questions.

If I go to the police, will I spend the rest of my life in prison?

If I admit my involvement, can I forget about a career in the security service?

If I tell the police, will my life as I know it be over?

How will all this affect my elderly parents?

If I do nothing, will an innocent man spend the rest of his life in prison?

Not just any man, my own brother. My own flesh and blood.

Mark stepped away from the table, walked through to the lounge and sat down heavily on the settee. He allowed the darkness in the room to envelop him.

He needed to think, and he'd always found that sitting alone in the dark helped him to process his thoughts.

After an hour of deliberation, he came to the realisation

that he needed to share this dilemma and find someone who could help him.

But who?

After another long period sitting alone with his thoughts, weighing up his options, he finally came to a decision and picked up the telephone. He had decided to call Mike Hermitage, a good friend who he had first met at Oxford. He was aware that Mike, now a qualified solicitor, had set up his own legal practice in Leicester a few years ago.

He had chosen Mike because he was aware of the legal privilege rule that stated anything he shared with his legal representation couldn't be used as evidence against him in any subsequent legal proceedings.

The telephone rang four times before it was answered. 'Mike Hermitage.'

'Mike, it's Mark Bradbury. Are you okay to talk?'

'Hello, mate, long time no hear. Yeah, I can talk. Are you okay? You sound a bit stressed.'

'I'm okay, but I think I have a problem and I could do with your advice.'

'Personal or professional?'

Mark hesitated and then said, 'I need your professional advice about something I'm involved in.'

Now it was Mike's turn to pause. 'Doesn't sound good, but fire away.'

'Not on the phone, mate. Can we meet and have a chat over a beer tomorrow?'

'Let me check what I've got on.'

Mark heard the telephone being put down and waited while his friend checked his diary. Eventually, he heard the telephone being picked up again and Mike said, 'I've a window between two and three tomorrow afternoon, if that's any good.'

'That's great, thanks, mate. Shall we say the Red Lion on Haymarket Street, that never gets too busy in the afternoon, so we should be able to talk.'

'No problem, Mark. I'll be there. Are you sure you're okay?' He paused. 'You sound really worried, mate.'

'I'm fine. I just need to run this by you, that's all.'

'No problem. You can get the beers in.'

53

5.00 a.m., 16 February 1991
Chesterfield Road, Mansfield, Nottinghamshire

It had been Jamie Mullins' turn to drive. Before he could start the engine, he had to shove the driver's seat as far forward as it would go, then raise the seat, so he could see over the dashboard. Even doing all that, his feet only just reached the pedals.

He could hear Reggie and Paul sniggering as he made the adjustments. Both youths were taking the piss, big style. Reggie sneered, 'Are you sure your little legs can reach the pedals, Jamie boy?'

'Fuck off,' he snarled.

Paul now joined in. 'We'll nick you a pedal car next time.'

Both youths laughed loudly, and Jamie yelled, 'Bollocks!'

He made one final adjustment to the rear-view mirror

and then twisted the screwdriver. The car roared into life and clouds of black smoke belched from the twin exhausts.

Jamie said, 'Did you see all that smoke, Reggie. Do you think it's okay to drive?'

'Course it is, you numpty. Get going. Or are you losing your bottle?'

Jamie instantly engaged first gear and took off. Driving the car at speed he headed towards the motorway. He had been driving stolen cars since he was eleven and was a more than competent driver.

He soon had the car topping a hundred miles an hour as he drove north on the M1 towards Leeds.

Glancing down at the petrol gauge, he said, 'I'd better turn round and head back, we're getting low on juice.'

Paul said, 'I'll fetch some from the garage tomorrow. I've got a couple of petrol cans at home.'

The potential shortage of fuel didn't stop Jamie hammering the car back down the motorway. He looked nervously in the rear-view mirror as every time he changed gear, a cloud of black smoke erupted from the twin exhausts.

He was relieved when he finally exited at junction twenty-nine and headed back towards Mansfield. Even driving at much slower speeds, every gear change was now accompanied by clouds of black smoke and he was finding it harder and harder to select a gear.

As the gears crunched yet again, Reggie said, 'For fuck's sake, Jamie, sort yourself out. Your driving's shit.'

'It's not me,' Jamie protested. 'I'm telling you, this car's fucked.'

As he said that he tried to change gear again. This time it didn't matter how hard he tried to get the gearstick to select a gear, it wouldn't go in. The car slowly coasted to a spluttering stop before the engine cut out completely.

'Fuck me, Jamie,' Paul said. 'What have you done?'

'I don't know. It's fucked.'

Reggie shouted, 'Well don't just sit there, you numpty. Get the fucking thing started. We can't sit on a main road like this for long.'

Jamie tried several times to turn the screwdriver and start the ignition. The engine and gear box were well and truly broken; the car wouldn't start.

He looked at the other two and said, 'I reckon the gear box is fucked.'

Reggie sneered, 'And what do you know about cars? You can't even drive properly, you little prick. Where are we anyway?'

Paul said, 'Near Bull Farm. Chesterfield Road, I reckon.'

Reggie laughed and said, 'Is anybody in the RAC?' before opening the car door and saying, 'Well, it was fun while it lasted. Come on, boys, let's get the fuck out of here, before the cops come calling.'

Leaving the car doors wide open, the three youths bolted from the car and ran into the dark streets of the Bull Farm estate.

54

7.30 a.m., 16 February 1991
Chesterfield Road, Mansfield, Nottinghamshire

Glen Lorimar parked in the car park of the Rufford Arms. He and Ray Holden then walked along the busy Chesterfield Road to where the Ford Sierra RS Cosworth had been abandoned.

Chesterfield Road at this location was a dual carriageway, and one lane was now effectively blocked. The police patrol car that had found the stolen vehicle was parked behind it and the officer had placed warning signs and cones out to alert other road users of the danger and to try and ease traffic flow around the obstruction.

Glen took out his warrant card and approached the uniformed officer standing by the side of his car. 'Morning. I'm DC Lorimar and this is DC Holden from the MCIU. What time did you find the vehicle?'

'A Mr Gerald Burgess of 317 Chesterfield Road called it in a couple of hours ago. He told the control room he'd seen three youths running from a car and he had the impression they'd stolen it. He also told the control room operator that he didn't want a uniformed officer to visit him at home, as he was worried about reprisals. I got here just after six o'clock, when I started my shift, and I've been here ever since. I'm hoping the vehicle examiners aren't going to be too long, or the tailback into Mansfield from the motorway will be horrendous.'

Glen nodded. 'I can see it's already getting bad. The control room notified me at seven o'clock when I came on duty. The first thing I did was fire a call into the examiners, to arrange for a full lift recovery. They should be well on their way by now. Have you been inside the car?'

The officer shook his head. 'No. When I first got here, three of the four doors were wide open and sticking out into the road, making the hazard even worse, so I closed them with my boot. Then, when I called in the vehicle check and it came back as being a stolen vehicle, and to preserve for a full forensic analysis, I thought I'd better not.'

'That's good.'

Ray Holden said, 'I take it you didn't see anybody with, or hanging around, the car when you arrived?'

'Nah. Whoever abandoned it had long gone by the time I got here.'

'Do you know which house on Chesterfield Road this Mr Burgess called from?'

'I did have a look when I first got here. It's the one right behind me, the one with the blue door. I've seen the old guy peering out of the upstairs window from time to time.'

'Has he spoken to you?'

'Nope. Hasn't even offered me a cup of tea.'

Glen said, 'We're going to do some door knocking to see if anybody else saw the car being dumped.'

The young cop nodded. 'I'd give you a hand, but I've got to keep an eye on the traffic flow. If I'm not here, drivers will start pushing in and people will get irate. Let's hope the examiners aren't too much longer, I really need to use the toilet.'

Glen grimaced. 'There's nothing worse, mate. We'll watch the traffic flow while you nip to the pub. I'm sure the landlord will let you in to use his toilets.'

The young cop grinned. 'Cheers, gents. I won't be a minute.'

Glen turned to Ray. 'We'll start with Gerald Burgess, then make our way along this side of the road first. Hopefully, as we're not in uniform, he'll talk to us.'

Ten minutes later, and with the young cop now back by the side of the road, the two detectives knocked on the blue door.

The door was opened a mere two inches and a very nervous voice said, 'What do you want?'

Glen carefully slipped his warrant card through the small gap and said, 'Mr Burgess. We're from the CID. It would be extremely helpful if we could talk to you about the telephone call you made to the police earlier. We've respected your wishes and not come in uniform. Can we come in for five minutes?'

There was a long pause, before the door opened and Gerald Burgess said, 'You'd better come inside. I don't mind talking to you, but I'm telling you now, so there's no misunderstanding, I won't make a written statement and I won't go to court and give evidence.'

Once inside the neat semi-detached house, Glen could see just how afraid the old man was. He said gently, 'Mr Burgess, my name's DC Lorimar and this is DC Holden; we're from the Major Crime Investigation Unit. Let me reassure you that if you don't want to make a statement, nobody's going to force you.'

The old man nodded and said, 'Come through, and I'll tell you what I saw.'

The two detectives followed the old man into the living room. There was a comfortable two-piece sofa, and an armchair that was obviously where the man spent most of his time. He had arranged everything on a small coffee table at the side of the armchair. His spectacles, the television listings magazine and the newspaper were all placed where he could easily reach them. A plate containing a half-eaten slice of toast and an empty mug were also on the table. The gas fire was on, and the room was toasty.

Glen sat down next to Ray and said, 'What exactly did you see, Mr Burgess?'

The old man leaned forward in his chair and said, 'To start with it was more what I heard than what I saw.'

'Go on.'

'I was in bed, you see. I was wide awake but still in bed. I live on my own now, ever since my wife died last year, but I still sleep in the main bedroom at the front of the house. Anyway, I was in bed when I heard the most horrendous noise. It sounded like a car was being driven at speed, but in the wrong gear. The engine was straining and banging.' He paused. 'It was that bad, I got out of bed to see what the hell was going on.'

As the old man paused again, Glen coaxed him gently. 'What could you see, Mr Burgess?'

'I looked out of the window, through the net curtains. I never draw the main curtains anymore. I like the light from the streetlights to shine into my bedroom. Now I'm on my own, I'm not keen on the dark. Anyway, the car had broken down right outside the house and I could hear the driver trying to start it. I could also hear raised voices coming from inside the car.'

'Could you see who was in it?'

'Not at that time.'

Ray said, 'Did you hear any names being used?'

'No. All I could hear was raised voices, but I couldn't make out what they were saying.'

Glen said, 'When you called the police you mentioned that you'd seen three people running away.'

'That's right. After a couple of minutes, three of the car doors flew open and three youths ran away.'

'Which way did they run?'

'They went straight across the road into the estate.'

'Bull Farm estate?'

The old man nodded.

'Can you describe any of these youths?'

'The streetlighting is good, and I did get a proper look at them, but they were all wearing dark clothing and all three had those black beanie hats on. So, although I saw them, I couldn't really give you a good description. I'm sorry.'

'Don't worry, Mr Burgess. Take your time and have a good think. Is there anything about any of the three youths that stood out?'

The old man paused for a long time, before saying, 'The only one whose face I got a real look at was the driver. He did stand out – because he was so much smaller than the other two. I was shocked; he looked like a kid. I mean, he looked about ten or twelve years old.'

'Anything else?'

'That's it, I'm afraid.'

'That's great. You've been a huge help and thank you for talking to us.'

'I'm sorry about the statement business, but since my wife passed, all I want to do is keep myself to myself. Sometimes, I don't see or speak to anybody for weeks. And you hear such awful stories about the elderly being picked on by these gangs of youths.'

'Don't you have any family or neighbours who could pop in?'

'Not really. I never see my neighbours and my son lives in Scotland now, so it's hard for him to get down here to see me as much as he would like.'

Glen could see how lonely the old man was, so he reached into his jacket pocket and handed him a card that contained his name and contact number. 'These are my details. I want you to feel free to contact me any time if anyone or anything is bothering you. Okay?'

The old man put his spectacles on and read the card aloud. 'Detective Constable Glen Lorimar.'

As the two detectives stood to leave, Gerald Burgess stood and said, 'Thank you, Detective Lorimar, that means a lot. This way, gents. I'll show you both out.'

As the two detectives left the house, Ray waited for the old man to close the door before saying, 'Shouldn't we have got a statement, Glen?'

'Possibly. But sometimes you get more information by not putting things down on paper. You could see how scared he was. If we had tried to take a written statement, he would have clammed up completely and told us nothing. It's all about judgement, Ray. Sometimes you need to go with the flow to get what you want. And now we know that one of these three car thieves is very young and very short.'

The younger detective grinned. 'Every day's a school day.'

Glen said, 'Let's split up, that way we'll cover the over-looking houses a lot quicker.'

Ray pointed towards the large recovery vehicle that was now reversing towards the RS Cosworth and said, 'At least the vehicle examiners have turned up.'

Glen walked over to the recovery vehicle and spoke to the driver. 'DC Lorimar, MCIU. Can you take the car straight to the forensic bay at headquarters? They're expecting you. You can book it in, in my name, reference it under the Lionel Wickes murder investigation.'

'No problem.'

55

2.20 p.m., 16 February 1991
The Red Lion, Haymarket Street, Leicester

As soon as the two men sat down in the quiet booth with a beer, the first thing Mark Bradbury did was to make it clear to Mike Hermitage that he wanted him to represent him and to be his legal advisor, thereby invoking the client-solicitor privilege.

Mike could see by his old university friend's worried demeanour that he had a serious problem and had readily agreed to help him.

The solicitor had then listened with growing incredulity as Mark recounted how he had recently discovered that he had been adopted at birth. How he had traced his birth mother to a nursing home in West Bridgford and had subsequently learned he had a twin brother.

Mike sat back in his chair as Mark described how he had

since discovered that his twin brother was currently on remand in HMP Lincoln for murder.

He took a sip of his pint and said, 'That's an awful lot of personal information to discover over a short time, mate, but I don't see why you need my services.'

'It's about my brother. I think he's innocent of the murder he's been charged with.'

Mike cautioned his friend, saying, 'It must have been emotional, meeting your brother for the first time, especially under such harrowing circumstances. You're bound to want to think the best of him, but prisons up and down the country are full of supposedly innocent men, who are as guilty as sin. Why do you think he's innocent?'

Mark made eye contact with his friend and said evenly, 'I don't think he's innocent, I know he is.'

'How can you know that?'

'Because I'm sure I killed the man he's accused of murdering.'

Mike's shock must have shown on his face because Mark hurriedly said, 'I need to tell you what happened before you judge me, Mike.'

There was a note of irritation in the solicitor's voice when he said, 'And now I understand why you called me. You're thinking this conversation is covered by legal privilege, aren't you?'

'Well, isn't it?'

'This conversation is, but if you tell me information that leads me to think you're guilty of any crime, let alone one as serious as murder, there's no way I can represent you.'

Noting his friend's tone, Mark said, 'I'm sorry. I didn't know who to turn to and, yes, I did factor in the legal privilege angle, but please can you just hear me out and let me tell you what happened?' He paused before adding, 'Once I've told you everything, if you still want to walk out, I won't resent you for doing so.'

He was nervous as he saw his friend sit back, deep in thought. He had placed him in such a delicate situation and he didn't know how he was going to react.

Much to Mark's relief, Mike eventually said, 'Okay. Tell me exactly what happened.'

Mark took his time and recounted every detail he could remember of the knifepoint robbery, the way he had defended himself after suffering a serious injury from his assailant's knife and how one punch had been sufficient to knock the man to the floor.

Mike interrupted. 'And once you knocked this man to the floor,' he said, 'what did you do next?'

'He dropped the knife as he fell, and it landed at my feet. I picked it up and ran off.'

'This is important, Mark. Are you sure you didn't follow up that single punch with any more force?'

'No. I just ran as fast as I could, and his accomplice ran in the opposite direction.'

'There were two of them?'

'Yes. I saw the other one first, but I'm sure he was acting as the knifeman's lookout.'

'Did this man join in the attack on you?'

'No, he didn't.'

'Okay. So, after you knocked your attacker down, did you check on him?'

'What do you mean?'

'Could you see if he was badly injured?'

'No, I couldn't see that. I know he went down hard, but that's all I know. I just picked up his knife and ran away. It all happened so quickly. All I wanted to do was get out of there.'

'You said you picked the knife up. Where's that now?'

'Once I knew they weren't following me, I dropped it down a drain.'

There was a heavy silence as Mike processed everything he had been told.

After careful deliberation, Mark broke that silence. 'I know it's a mess. I felt I had no choice but to fight back. The bloke had already sliced my hand open, what was I supposed to do?'

'You could have run when you were first confronted.'

'I couldn't. One was in front of me and the other behind me. I couldn't run, and I wasn't going to just stand there and let them take my wallet either.'

Mike listened carefully and then said, 'The question is, what do we do about it?'

Mark shrugged and nervously sipped his beer.

Mike said, 'I do know a detective on the Nottingham MCIU. I could talk to him about the case to gauge what the strength of the evidence is against your brother – before we commit to any course of action that puts you in the frame. For all you know, this Randall Clements bloke could have got up and walked away after you punched him. He could have then gone on to try and mug someone else that night, and that was when he was killed. If that did happen there's a possibility it was your brother who killed him. We need to see what the evidence is first. Trust me, Mark, people don't get charged with murder without the police having good evidence.'

'How do you know this detective? Can you trust him?'

'I don't know him very well at all. I've only met him on a

few social occasions through his wife. Sally Wills is a barrister who my firm has employed to defend several of our clients. I've always got on well with her, and whenever I've spoken to her husband, he seems very approachable. I think I could talk to him.' He continued. 'I can see by your face that you're not sold on this idea, but I think this is the right way to go. We need to establish exactly why the police are so convinced your brother's guilty of this murder.'

'I'll be guided by you,' Mark reassured his friend. 'Thanks for this, Mike.'

'Let's see how it goes. For now, leave it with me and don't do anything unless I tell you to. Okay?'

Mark knew he had to put his trust in Mike's judgement – what choice did he have? And so, he simply nodded his reply.

56

3.30 p.m., 16 February 1991
MCIU Offices, Mansfield, Nottinghamshire

Glen Lorimar knocked once on Danny's door before walking in. 'Have you got five minutes, boss? I wanted to update you on the progress with the stolen vehicles enquiry.'

Danny sat back in his chair, put the report he was reading down, rubbed his eyes and said, 'Of course, Glen. What's happening?'

'Thanks to our research, we found twelve vehicles had been stolen within one mile of the scene – all on the night Lionel Wickes was killed. Up until this morning, we'd located eleven out of the twelve. We now have that twelfth vehicle.'

'Good work. Is there anything to report evidentially?'

'From the previous eleven vehicles, unfortunately not.

No forensics, and no arrests have been made in connection with any of those vehicles. Some of them have been back with their owners for quite a time, so forensic examination was never viable.'

'That's a shame, but it sounds like you've got something positive to tell me about the twelfth car.'

Glen allowed himself the fleetest hint of a smile before saying, 'The twelfth vehicle was a Ford Sierra RS Cosworth. It was stolen just four streets away from where Lionel Wickes died. It was the nearest vehicle to the murder scene and the one we've wanted to track down the most.'

'And we've only recovered it now?' Danny raised an eyebrow. 'How come it's taken so long to locate?'

'I can't answer that for sure, but the only reason I can think of is that it's possibly been stashed somewhere.'

'A criminal pool car?'

'The RS Cosworth is a high-powered, high-performance car and a prime target for joyriders. It could be a case of joyriders keeping it hidden and taking it in turns to drive.'

'Does that happen?'

Glen nodded. 'I've spoken to a lot of traffic patrol officers during this enquiry. They tell me that when these idiots get hold of a high-powered car, like the RS Cosworth, one of the games they like to play is to taunt the police. Inviting a pursuit and then trying to outrun the cops. The traffic officers are left in a no-win situation and are often ordered by the control room to abort the chase. It becomes too dangerous for other road users for them to continue. You know what it's like.'

'Damned if they do, and damned if they don't.'

'Exactly.'

'Where was this Cosworth recovered?'

'Chesterfield Road, Mansfield. Near the Rufford Arms crossroads. We've got a reluctant witness who saw three youths running away from the vehicle, after it had broken down.'

'Reluctant?'

'The witness is an elderly gentleman who lives alone and is extremely nervous of reprisals. He was happy to talk to us about what he saw but won't make a witness statement or attend court.'

Danny grimaced. 'I understand his reasons, but they sadden me. When people feel that afraid, I feel we're somehow failing them.'

Glen nodded. 'I know exactly what you mean, it's very frustrating. But he did tell us something that could be a huge help in identifying the offenders.'

'Go on.'

'He described the driver as being very short in stature and very young. He described him as looking somewhere between ten and twelve years of age.'

'A juvenile? That could narrow the search significantly. Sounds promising. Where's the car now?'

'In the forensic bay at headquarters. The vehicle examiners recovered it early this morning. It's currently the subject of a full forensic examination.'

There was a knock on the door and Danny shouted, 'Come in.'

Ray Holden stepped inside and said, 'I've just had a call from Tim Donnelly – they've found a fingerprint inside the car.'

Danny said, 'Good enough for court?'

'Yes.' Ray grinned. 'He said it was found on the rear-view mirror, looks like a thumb print and is very clear. The lift has been forwarded to the fingerprint bureau to see if they can find a match.'

Glen asked him, 'Have you given Tim the description of the driver? It could help to speed up the search if they know where to look.'

Ray nodded. 'I did. I'd already pulled a list of known juvenile car thieves in the Mansfield area, so I've sent him that. Hopefully, they'll be able to find a match.'

'This is good work, gents,' Danny said. 'Keep me informed of any updates. We need to move the Wickes inquiry forward if we can.'

57

8.30 p.m., 16 February 1991
Di Santo's Restaurant, High Pavement, Nottingham

S ue Flint and Rachel Moore had enjoyed the evening. The Italian food and red wine had been delicious, and the baby talk had been both entertaining and informative.

The bill had been paid and the two women were relaxing with a coffee before their taxis arrived.

'Thank you so much for this, Sue,' Rachel said, turning to the older woman with a smile. 'It's really helped to put my mind at rest. Understanding the pitfalls you and Danny faced in those early days with Hayley will help me and Jack enormously.'

Sue replied, 'Anytime you need a chat, just pick up the phone. I'm sure you'll both be fine.'

'With a little help from our friends and Jack's family I'm sure we will.'

Sue was thoughtful for a second and then added, 'Would you mind if I asked you something?'

'Of course not.'

'It's a little delicate and if you don't feel able to answer, I'll understand.'

'Sounds worrying, what's up?'

'I was wondering how my husband's been, since he came back to work?'

'He's been fine,' Rachel said thoughtfully. 'I haven't noticed any change in him at all. Are you worried about him?'

'Not worried as such. It's just that when he's with me, I know how he always puts a brave face on things. That business with the gun in Durham, it really shook him up. He badly needed that time away from work.'

'Can I speak freely, Sue?'

'Of course. I wouldn't mention anything you share with me to Danny.'

'Before that happened in Durham, a few of us at work, Rob Buxton, Andy Wills and I, had spoken about how exhausted Danny looked. Rob advised him to take time off on several occasions. We could see he wasn't his normal self and was struggling a little. But we all know what your husband's like, he needs to see a job through, so he refused to take any time off.' She paused and then added, 'But the good news is, since he's been back, he seems back to his old self. Please don't say anything, but I heard him and Rob talking about a holiday he's booked for you all, later this year. Seems to me that he's finally got the message that a break from work, now and then, can be a good idea.'

Sue smiled warmly. 'Thanks for being so honest and open, Rachel. I appreciate it. You've really put my mind at rest.'

A waiter approached their table and said, 'Ladies, your taxis are here.'

As they stood, Sue said, 'Thank you, Rachel. And good luck with everything. I know you and Jack will be fine. I can't wait to go shopping and choose a new dress for your wedding.'

Rachel groaned. 'Don't mention the W word, there's an endless stack of things to organise.'

As the two women embraced, Sue chuckled in sympathy. 'Stay in touch,' she urged, 'and let's do this again soon.'

58

A ndy Wills parked and made his way to the main
coffee bar in the services. He had been intrigued
by the phone call from Mike Hermitage. The
solicitor had informed him that he may have important
information about the murder of Randall Clements but that
he didn't want to go down official channels to start with.

Andy had pressed him for answers, but the solicitor was
reticent to speak on the phone and pushed instead for a
face-to-face meeting. Although it was Andy's day off today,
he wanted to hear what Mike had to say, so had arranged to
meet him here; the M1 services being equidistant for
both men.

He saw Mike Hermitage sitting alone at a table, already

nursing a coffee. He waved in acknowledgement, before getting himself a coffee and making his way over.

The solicitor stood to greet him and the two men shook hands.

Mike said, 'Thanks for coming, Andy. I'm sorry for all the cloak-and-dagger stuff, but this is an extremely delicate situation for me.'

Andy said, 'I take it this conversation's off the record then?'

Mike nodded. 'All that I'm about to tell you is covered by solicitor-client legal privilege, so yes, it's effectively off the record.'

'Okay. You mentioned you had information concerning the Randall Clements murder investigation. Are you aware that we've charged someone with that offence, that he is currently on remand awaiting trial?'

'And that's where you may have a problem. I genuinely believe you may have charged the wrong man.'

'Why do you think that?' Andy said, the shock clear in his voice. 'The evidence we have is compelling.'

'Let's just say, I've good reason to believe that the person in custody isn't responsible for that man's death.'

Andy suddenly realised what was happening. 'Your client's confessed to the murder, hasn't he?' He paused. 'If that's the case you can't possibly represent him, so any legal privilege is void. Who's your client, Mike?'

The solicitor held a hand up and said, 'Slow down, Andy. My client has given me enough detail to convince me that on the night this happened, he was acting in self-defence. He had been the target of an attempted robbery at knifepoint. I'm convinced that if he were charged and the case was taken to trial, he would stand an excellent chance of having all charges against him dropped; that's why I feel able to represent him. I'm convinced he acted in self-defence because he was left with no other option.'

He paused waiting for Andy to understand his reasoning. 'If I had made this an official approach, it would seriously muddy the waters around your case. It may even cause enough doubt for a jury to acquit the man you've already charged.'

'How so?'

'Because it would throw sufficient doubt on your case, that's how.'

Andy shook his head. 'When I said our evidence is strong, I meant it. We found blood at the murder scene that matches our offender. It's a DNA match that's good enough for court. We also have other evidence that puts him at the scene and that he received a knife wound prior to him striking the fatal blow.'

Mike smiled. 'The only mention of a knife in all the reports I've seen was that of a possible sighting of a man running near the scene carrying what could have been a knife. There's never been any mention of a robbery.'

'Your point being?'

'My client has informed me he was the man seen running away carrying the knife. He also received a serious wound to his hand as he defended himself against the knife attack.'

'That's all well and good, Mike, but we have the offender's DNA and that doesn't lie.'

'This is where it gets complicated, which is why I needed this meeting to be off the record. It's possible that the man you have in custody is closely related to my client.'

'That's impossible. Our suspect has no close family: he was adopted.'

'What do you know about that adoption?'

'Nothing. We've no information at all on it.'

'My client was also adopted at birth and has good reason to believe that the man you have in custody is his twin brother. Which in turn could have all sorts of implications for the strength of your DNA evidence.'

Andy was stunned. He had heard that DNA profiles could be shared by twins in certain circumstances.

As if reading his thoughts, Mike said, 'Ever since my client approached me, I've spent hours researching the science of DNA profiles. The consensus of current scientific opinion is that if the twins are monozygotic, formed when one egg is fertilised by one sperm and becomes a single embryo before dividing in two, they will have the same DNA profile.'

Andy was deep in thought. 'I need to consult my boss about all this,' he said. 'Thanks for talking to me, Mike. The last thing any of us want is to put an innocent man in prison.'

'Exactly.' Mike nodded. 'If, when you've talked to your supervisor, he wants to meet me, I'm fine with that. Obviously, I can't sit on this information indefinitely either. If I've got good reason to believe you have the wrong man locked up, at some stage I'll need to act on that information.'

'I'll talk to DCI Flint and get back to you.'

As the two men shook hands before parting, Andy said, 'Bloody hell, Mike. What a can of worms.'

'My thoughts exactly,' Mike replied. 'It's good to see you again, Andy. I look forward to hearing from you, and hopefully DCI Flint, soon.'

59

'Have you got a minute, boss?' Andy said as he knocked on the door to Danny's office.

Danny waved him in and said, 'Grab a seat. I thought you were off today. What are you doing here?'

'This wouldn't keep. I've just had an off-the-record meeting with a solicitor who believes he has a client who's responsible for the murder of Randall Clements, and that we have the wrong man locked up.'

Danny immediately thought back to his own misgivings about the guilt or otherwise of Craig Stevens and said, 'Well, you obviously believe there's some merit in his claims, or you wouldn't be here. What exactly has he told you?'

Andy explained everything he'd been told by Mike Hermitage. When he had finished, Danny placed his pen carefully on his notepad and said, 'So what you're telling me is that even though we have DNA evidence, it still won't be enough to convict Craig Stevens, because he has a long-lost twin brother, who possibly has an identical DNA profile, and who has confessed to the murder claiming he was acting in self-defence.'

Andy nodded. 'That's it, in a nutshell. Yes.'

'And how long before this solicitor goes public with this information?'

'I think that will depend on how we proceed, boss. My gut feeling is that he would like to keep his client out of our hands for as long as possible and wants us to reinvestigate the murder officially first.'

'Bloody hell.' Danny rubbed his eyes. 'Slater's going to love this. I need advice from our lawyers before I do anything. Call this solicitor and tell him we're taking legal advice and once we've got that we'll be in touch.'

'Okay, boss.'

60

3.30 p.m., 18 February 1991
Nottingham Crown Court, Canal Street, Nottingham

Danny was relieved to see the barrister Audrey Barker striding towards him, her black robes flowing behind her. She had a reputation for being extremely knowledgeable when it came to complex cases where identification was an issue.

Danny said, 'Thanks for seeing me so quickly.'

She said brusquely, 'I've literally got twenty minutes before I'm due back in court for the judge's summing up. What's the problem?'

Danny quickly outlined what he'd been told, before handing her a folder that contained a written report of the information that had been hastily prepared by Andy Wills.

She flicked through the report and said, 'On first glance, I think this will seriously impact your case against Craig

Stevens. If this turns out to be true, and he does have a monozygotic identical twin somewhere, then the identification evidence would be thrown into doubt and he, quite rightly, should be acquitted.' She looked up at him, her hazel eyes clear and intelligent. 'I'll need time to study this report properly. It's certainly an interesting one, chief inspector. I'll call you tonight when I have a definitive answer.'

Danny handed the barrister a card with his home telephone number. 'It doesn't matter how late it is,' he urged. 'I'd like you to call me at home, please. I need to get this straightened out as soon as possible. If we've put an innocent man in prison, we need to act fast to rectify the situation.'

'Indeed, chief inspector. No such worries for the distraction burglar I've been prosecuting today, guilty as sin. I'm hoping the jury agree with me and that he's sent down for a long time. He's been targeting the elderly, with the old Water Board ploy, nasty little sod.'

61

9.30 p.m., 18 February 1991
Mansfield, Nottinghamshire

Danny and Sue were relaxing at home. Hayley was asleep and the television was off.

Danny put his book down and said, 'How did your chat with Rachel go?'

'The food at Di Santo's is wonderful – we'll have to go ourselves one night. And we had a nice time and a good chat.'

'That's good. Was it baby talk all night?'

Before Sue had a chance to answer the telephone rang out. Danny snatched it up on the second ring. 'Hello, Danny Flint.'

'Sorry, it's late, chief inspector.'

Danny recognised the voice of Audrey Barker and said,

'No problem. I'm glad you called. Have you any thoughts on how we should proceed?'

The barrister replied curtly, 'Short answer, with great care. This is a legal minefield. In my opinion, the claims by this man on their own would probably not be enough to dismiss the murder charge against Craig Stevens. The DNA evidence coupled with all the strong circumstantial evidence would still be compelling.' She took in a deep breath before continuing. 'I think your best option would be to try and prove that this so-called twin brother's account is the truth, and that he was indeed responsible for Randall Clements' death.'

As the barrister paused, Danny wondered just how he was going to achieve that near-impossible task.

Audrey Barker had more to say. 'I know it's a tall order, but if you can do that, and the circumstances are as he told his solicitor, that he was attacked and was defending himself against a knifepoint robbery, then I can see him being acquitted. Even if a jury found him guilty of manslaughter, I still think there's every chance he wouldn't receive a custodial sentence.'

Danny sighed; this really was a mess. 'So, what you're advising me to do is to reinvestigate this murder, but to run the inquiry in such a way as to prove this other man's version is the truth?'

'I don't see any other way. The only other point I need to stress is that you really need to do these enquiries as quickly as you can. As soon as Craig Stevens' defence team get any wind of this, they will push for an immediate acquittal – and you could end up with nothing.'

Again, she paused as if further ordering her thoughts before adding, 'Always bearing in mind that there's a good chance this is all rubbish, and that Craig Stevens is guilty. Be careful: that won't matter; once the waters have been muddied sufficiently, Stevens could walk.'

Danny was lost for words. He was stunned by what the barrister was telling him, and what she was suggesting he do to remedy the situation.

Breaking that silence, Audrey cautioned, 'As the officer in charge of this investigation you are walking a legal tightrope, Danny, without the proverbial safety net. Just on that score, I'd prefer it if you kept my name out of any future conversations about this case. If you'd given me the name of the twin brother, I'd have been duty bound to disclose it to Stevens' defence team. So, what I'm telling you is: this conversation never happened. Okay?'

'I understand the predicament I've inadvertently placed you in and I'm sorry. Thank you for your advice.'

'Crack on, Danny. You won't have long to sort this before everything gets out into the open. If you haven't sorted it by the time it comes out, you could find yourself in a world of legal pain.'

Danny put the phone down and Sue asked, 'Is everything all right? You look worried.'

'It's just a work problem,' he said shortly. 'One that I need to get sorted.'

Deep in thought, Danny walked into the kitchen and made himself a coffee. He knew he would need to talk to Mark Slater first thing tomorrow and hopefully the chief superintendent would give the green light for the inquiry to be reinvestigated. He was worried as he knew he was going to have to be very selective about what information he disclosed to the senior officer.

For the first time since he had returned to work, Danny

could feel a massive tension building inside him. He tried to calm himself down, but still the muscles in his neck twitched as he sipped his coffee.

62

10.00 a.m., 19 February 1991
Police Headquarters, Nottinghamshire

Danny had thought long and hard about what he was going to say to Mark Slater.

As he walked from the car park to Slater's office, he prayed that the chief superintendent would agree to his request. If he didn't, he would need to think again and quickly.

He knocked once and waited for Slater to invite him in.

No shout came; instead the door was opened by Mark Slater who said bluntly, 'Good morning, Danny. Your call this morning was a surprise. What's so urgent?'

'I need to speak with you about the Randall Clements investigation.'

As the two men walked into the office and sat down, Slater said, 'I thought that investigation was done and dusted. You've charged a man with murder, what's the problem?'

Danny chose his words carefully. 'The problem is I think we may have overlooked something.'

'I don't understand.'

'Yesterday, I received an anonymous tip-off that Craig Stevens wasn't responsible for the murder of Randall Clements and that we had the wrong man behind bars.'

'An anonymous tip-off!' Slater scoffed. 'Jesus Christ, Danny, you can't be serious.'

'This informant stated that Clements was killed by a man who was defending himself after becoming the target for a knifepoint robbery.'

'How does your informant know that person wasn't Stevens?'

'Because he told me he was responsible for the punch that had killed Clements.'

'I'm not buying this at all. Sounds like a load of bollocks probably cooked up between Stevens and one of his dodgy mates to try and get him off the hook.'

'I thought that initially, but the caller gave details that only the killer would know. I don't think it would do any harm to quietly reopen the investigation and have a closer look at Clements, just to see if there's any truth in the informant's account. We already know that Clements has previous convictions for street robberies, where weapons were used. The last thing the force needs is for this informant's account to be true, and we do nothing. Then everything comes out years later, by which time an innocent man has been rotting in jail for God knows how long.'

Slater leaned back in his chair and steepled his fingers. After a long pause he said, 'I'm still not convinced. We have

DNA from Stevens at the murder scene: in my book that trumps any anonymous tip-off. As far as I'm concerned, Craig Stevens is guilty as charged.'

'There's one other thing the informant said that might change your mind about that DNA evidence being so strong. He claimed to be Craig Stevens' long-lost twin brother, which can in certain cases lead to an identical DNA profile.'

'If it's his brother, we must know who he is. Arrest him,' Slater snapped, clicking his fingers in frustration, 'and get this sorted.'

'It's not that simple. Both men were adopted at birth, and we've no idea when or where this happened. Craig Stevens has no knowledge of his adoption, and during our investigation of him we've been unable to find any details.' He paused to allow Slater to process that bombshell. 'I can't just sit on this information and do nothing. I either disclose this anonymous confession to Stevens' defence team, which is going to seriously muddy the waters of any trial, or we do as I suggest and quietly reopen the investigation. In my opinion we've no choice. We must prove all over again that we've got the right man in prison.'

Slater said nothing.

Danny pressed on. 'If I'm being honest, I've had reservations about Stevens' guilt since I saw his reaction during the interviews. We should also factor in that some of the circumstantial evidence we're relying on is sketchy at best.'

His final roll of the dice to convince Slater was to play on the chief superintendent's own career ambitions. 'The last thing any of us need, is to be involved in a serious miscarriage of justice simply for the sake of spending a little time reinvestigating these claims.'

Danny wasn't sure which part of his argument had won

the day, but Slater reluctantly nodded and said, 'Okay. But this is the deal. I'm not totally convinced by any of this, and you still have the unsolved murder of Lionel Wickes to investigate. We can't afford to tie up countless resources investigating something that will, in all probability, turn out to be a wild-goose chase. You can allocate two detectives to investigate these possibly spurious anonymous claims, while the rest of the MCIU concentrates on bringing the killer, or killers, of Lionel Wickes to justice. Is that understood?'

It wasn't what Danny had wanted. He had wanted to throw the full weight of the MCIU into investigating the Randall Clements murder again, but he could see that Slater had made his mind up.

'Understood, sir.'

Danny stood to leave and, as he reached the door, Slater said, 'Don't waste too much time on this, Danny. It's important you bring the Wickes investigation to a conclusion, and soon. The chief constable is starting to come under serious pressure from councillors responsible for the Meadows area.' He fixed Danny with a look that meant business.

'I'll keep you informed on any progress, sir.'

'You will.' Slater tapped hard on his desk, stressing his point. 'I don't need to remind you that this elderly man was killed right outside his own home, defending his property. The press is having a field day, saying the police aren't interested because of the location, that we are failing the Meadows community. Every day the murderer remains undetected that failure looks more and more apparent to the public. We need a result, Danny.'

63

12.30 p.m., 19 February 1991
MCIU Offices, Mansfield, Nottinghamshire

As Danny walked in, he scanned the main briefing room for Andy Wills and Jane Pope. When he saw them sitting at their desks he said, 'Andy, Jane. I need to speak with you both now, please.'

The two detectives followed Danny into his office.

Danny sat down and said, 'Andy, you already know what this is about and I'm relying on you to bring Jane fully up to speed. I need you both to drop what you were doing and concentrate solely on reinvestigating the murder of Randall Clements. I want you to thoroughly research Clements and find out who his associates were, who he's previously committed crimes with. We need to find out everything we can about this man. I'm aware that Glen's already done quite a bit of research into Clements. Speak with him and read all the intelligence and files he got from the robbery squad.'

'No disrespect to Jane,' Andy said, 'but wouldn't it be easier to pair me up with Glen to work on this?'

'Glen's moved on to the Lionel Wickes investigation and is doing some crucial work that could be about to bear fruit, so I don't want him to stop what he's currently doing. I can only afford two detectives to work on this, so it's going to mean long hours and a lot of hard work for you two. Does that cause either of you any problems?'

Jane was the first to answer. 'Not for me, boss.'

Andy shook his head. 'No problem.'

'Good. Andy, you'll understand that speed is of the essence during this investigation. I need you to keep me informed of progress. Any questions?'

Andy said, 'I'm sure Jane has a ton of questions.' He glanced at his colleague and said, 'I'll brief you fully, as soon as we're back in the office.'

Jane nodded.

He then looked at Danny. 'Have you any objection to me approaching Mike Hermitage to work with us? I think we might be able to get closer to his client, and hopefully identify the man who started all this. We're going to need every scrap of information the solicitor has been told if we're ever going to find out exactly what happened that night.'

'That's a good idea but be careful what you tell him.'

'I'll contact Hermitage and tell him that we're reopening the investigation and want to prove that the version of events given to him by his client is what happened. I want to see if he'll be open to us meeting with his client and talking to him in person.'

Danny shrugged. 'I think Mike Hermitage might need a lot of convincing to allow that.'

'With a man already charged and awaiting trial in prison,' Andy went on, 'I don't see that I've any grounds to arrest his client on suspicion of what's an already solved murder. I just hope he sees it that way. If I can convince him that the easiest way to find something that could help us prove his client's version of events is to obtain a first-hand account from him, that's going to be a huge help.'

'Good luck with that. Remember, Andy, time is of the essence.'

64

R ay Holden was pleased to see Glen Lorimar walk into the main briefing room.

As Glen was taking his overcoat off, Ray said, 'We've had a report come through from the fingerprint bureau. They've got a match for the thumb print found in the Cossie.'

Glen smiled. 'No way. Is it good enough for court?'

'Absolutely.'

'Who's the offender?'

'Jamie Mullins.

'Do we know who his associates are?'

'I'm still researching that, but I've found one older youth who looks very interesting.'

'Go on. No, wait. Is the boss in yet?'

'Arrived five minutes ago. I wanted to wait for you before I told him.'

'Good man,' Glen said with a grin. 'Come on, let's go and give him the news.'

Danny was checking the overnight arrest sheets from across the force when Glen and Ray walked into his office. He looked up. 'You're both smiling. Have you got some good news for me, gents?'

Ray said, 'The fingerprint found inside the RS Cosworth has been identified. The offender's a young lad called Jamie Mullins. He's fourteen years old and lives with his parents on the Bellamy Road estate in Mansfield. He's got previous cautions for car theft, theft and burglary. Numerous cautions, but only one conviction. He recently appeared before the juvenile court and received a three-month suspended sentence for a shed burglary.'

Glen said, 'Ray's been checking out his associates. It's still a work in progress, but he's already found one associate who looks like he could be a strong suspect.'

Danny turned to the young detective and said, 'Go on, Ray.'

'Mullins is known to be running with a nineteen-year-old youth who's recently been released from a young offender institution, after serving two years of a three-year sentence for assault. As well as being violent, this lad's a prolific car thief with links to Nottingham city centre.'

'Name?'

'Reginald Glover, known as Reggie. There's no current address listed for him, but his parents live on the Oak Tree Lane estate in Mansfield.'

'This is good work, Ray. Carry on with the research and let's find out if either Mullins or Glover have any other associates who could fit the profile. I want you to establish everything we know about this pair. I've often wondered if there was more than one offender that night.'

'Will do, boss.'

Danny looked at Glen. 'It could also explain why it took so long for the vehicle to be located. They may have hidden it because of the circumstances leading up to its theft. They'd know that we might connect the two car thefts.' He paused, deep in thought. 'When you've done all the research you can, I want you to get current locations for anyone you think could be a suspect in the original theft of the RS Cosworth. Once you've got that, Glen, I want you to prepare an operational order for coordinated arrests. I want this group, however many there are, in custody sooner rather than later. We need to be proactive and move this forward. Great work, both of you.'

'Will do, boss,' Glen said. 'I'll come and see you with an operational order before going off duty tonight.'

'Excellent. I want the arrests planned for the morning of the twenty-second, at the latest.'

65

9.15 a.m., 21 February 1991
Swanson Road, Leicester

It had taken two lengthy telephone calls and a long meeting at Mike Hermitage's office to convince him to allow Andy Wills and Jane Pope to meet his client in person. And that conviction only happened when Andy said that the one real chance they had of finding that crucial nugget of information was to speak with the man, face to face. It was quite possible, Andy had explained, that his client might not realise the importance of the small details.

Reluctantly, the solicitor had agreed, after persuading Andy to treat his client as a possible witness in the first instance. Both men knew it was a promise that meant nothing, but both men also realised something was needed to break the deadlock.

Andy had no intention of arresting the man, but he was

keen to identify him. That way, if an arrest became necessary later, he would be able to locate the suspect.

It had been arranged for the meeting to be held at Mike Hermitage's offices in the centre of Leicester.

The client was already waiting when Andy and Jane followed Mike Hermitage into the conference room.

Andy studied the man. He was wearing a charcoal grey suit, white shirt and burgundy tie, tied in a classic Windsor knot. This smart appearance wasn't what Andy had been expecting at all.

However, the most striking thing about the man was how closely he resembled Craig Stevens. Any doubts about the two men being identical twins instantly evaporated.

'First things first,' Andy said. 'I have no plans to arrest you at this moment in time and you will be treated as a witness, but if you tell me anything I think is a blatant lie, that stance will change.' The man nodded and Andy continued. 'I'm going to need you to give me your full name.'

'Mark Bradbury.'

The man was visibly nervous, but his voice as he answered was confident, and self-assured.

'Your solicitor has already given me a basic outline of the information you have. Can you take your time and tell me exactly what happened in Nottingham city centre on the night of the ninth of January?'

Mark Bradbury fiddled with the gold cufflinks on his shirt and said quietly, 'I had been at a conference in Nottingham. I had a few drinks in the hotel bar and then decided to go for a walk to get some fresh air.'

'Were you drunk?'

'Not at all. I'd literally had two pints of lager.'

'Where did you go?'

'I don't know Nottingham very well, but I remember walking across the main square and down some back streets.'

'Did you visit any other licensed premises while you were out? Any pubs or clubs?'

'No. I glanced in a couple of late bars, but they looked really rough, so I didn't bother and decided to make my way back to the hotel.'

'What happened then?'

'I wasn't sure exactly where I was, but I remember walking by the side of a churchyard. I did see one building I recognised, though.'

'What was that?'

'The Shire Hall.'

'Okay.'

Mark Bradbury remained silent as if trying to organise his memories. 'The first thing I saw that looked a bit strange was a man leaning against the railings that surrounded the churchyard.'

'Why strange?'

'Strange is probably the wrong word,' Mark said. 'He looked a bit suspicious. He was just hanging around. I kept watching him as I walked by.'

'Did he say anything to you?'

'No. But as soon as I turned away from him, I was confronted by a second man who was holding a knife. He stepped towards me and demanded money.'

'Then what happened?'

'Instinctively, I stepped back to keep a distance between me and the knife, but then I remembered the second man who was behind me.'

'Did he get involved in the robbery?'

'Not physically, but he was involved all right. I'm certain he was acting as the knifeman's lookout.'

'Why do you think that?'

'Because when I glanced back, he was still standing there calmly smoking a cigarette. Even though he could see what was happening.'

'Could you have run away at that point?'

'I thought about it, but there was no way I could get away. You've got to understand this all happened very quickly. When I refused to hand over my wallet, the man with the knife tried to stab me. I managed to grab the blade and push it away from my stomach but cut my hand as I did so. The second time he lunged at me with the knife, I stepped to the side and punched the man once on the cheek.'

'And what happened?'

'The man went down and, as he fell, he dropped the knife, so I picked it up and ran.'

'How did he fall?'

Mark was thoughtful for a few seconds before saying, 'He twisted as he fell and landed on his back.'

'Can you remember which way you ran?'

'I don't know the names of any streets, but I remember crossing a main road and a car narrowly missing me. Then I came to a square.'

'What did you do with the knife you picked up?'

'I dumped that down a drain. My hand was injured quite badly and was bleeding a lot by then. I wrapped it in my handkerchief and walked back to the hotel.'

'Did you tell anybody what had happened?'

'No.'

'Why not?'

'I didn't want the incident to affect my chances of

changing my career – something I've been working on for a while. My hand was injured but nothing had been stolen; I thought it best to move on as though nothing had happened.'

'What career change?'

'I am hoping to join the security services.'

Andy paused before saying, 'What did the second man do, once you knocked the knifeman down?'

'He ran away, but in the opposite direction.'

'He didn't attack you, or try to help the other man?'

'No, he just ran.'

'What did this first man look like?'

'It was quite dark, but I did get a good look at him. He was quite short, stocky and had his hair in cornrow plaits. He wore a dark-coloured Adidas tracksuit and Nike trainers.'

'You say you got a good look at him. Do you think you would recognise him if you saw him again?'

'In a line-up you mean?'

'Either a line-up, or a photo?'

'Possibly. I stared at him as I walked past. I didn't take my eyes off him, as I immediately didn't quite trust what he was doing there.'

'And the knifeman?'

'He was much taller and looked like he worked out. He was a lot bigger than me. His teeth flashed like he had a gold tooth and his hair was in long dreadlocks. I think he had some kind of hat on, but I'm not sure.'

'What about his clothing?'

Mark sat deep in thought and then said, 'I'm sorry. I don't recall what he was wearing. I remember his face, and I remember the knife, but that's it.'

'Why did you punch the man?'

'Because I was terrified. Once I saw the knife, I thought he was going to kill me. I wanted to get out of there in one piece.'

'And how many times did you punch him?'

'Like I said before, just once. As soon as he went down, I ran for my life and didn't stop until I was sure they weren't following me.'

'Is there anything else you can remember about this incident?'

'No.' Mark shook his head, reflecting on the evening. 'I wish I could be more help.'

'And why have you decided to come forward now?'

'I've only just found out what happened – to the knife-man, I mean. I believe I was somehow involved in that man's death and wanted to tell the truth. What's going to happen now?'

'I'm going to take some more personal details from you, then I'll need to talk in private with your solicitor about how we proceed from here.'

66

2.00 p.m., 21 February 1991
MCIU Offices, Mansfield, Nottinghamshire

Andy and Jane were sat in a report writing room, at Mansfield police station. Spread out on two desks in front of them were all the exhibits from the Randall Clements murder investigation.

Jane said, 'There's nothing startling here, sarge. Yes, Randall Clements was wearing a baseball cap, but there's nothing else to confirm what Mark Bradbury told us.'

Andy said, 'Pass me the exhibits log.'

Jane handed him the booklet and said, 'What are you looking for?'

'Items that have already been submitted for forensic examination. They won't be here, but there will be a record of them in the log.'

Andy flicked through the pages until he said, 'Yes! Here it

is. A cigarette butt was recovered at the scene and has been sent for DNA profiling.'

'Which might back up what Bradbury said about the second man smoking.' Jane smiled. 'So, is there any update on the forensic examination?'

Andy shook his head. 'It just says negative at the side of the entry. There's no mention if the examination yielded a DNA profile or not.' He paused, put the log down and said, 'Come on. Let's get this lot signed back into the store. We need a conversation with Tim Donnelly. We need to establish exactly what that "negative" means.'

67

4.00 p.m., 21 February 1991
Robbery Squad, Central Police Station, Nottingham

The telephone conversation with Tim Donnelly had been very enlightening. A DNA profile had indeed been established from the cigarette butt found at the scene. The bad news and the reason for the 'negative' entry in the exhibits log was that the profile raised didn't match either Randall Clements, or Craig Stevens.

Andy knew that he needed to somehow identify this second man involved in the robbery. The best way to do this was to start researching robbery offences in the city that had been committed just before and just after the death of Randall Clements.

Which was why he had contacted Detective Sergeant Fraser Jones and arranged to meet him at the robbery squad office.

DS Jones helped the two MCIU detectives retrieve all the relevant files needed to research the outstanding offences.

After two hours of painstaking work, Andy and Jane had established that in the relevant time frame, there had been over a dozen robbery offences committed in the area around Shire Hall. Only one of those offences reported the use of a knife. The problem was that that offence hadn't been reported to the police until 24 January, two full weeks after Clements' death.

DS Jones said, 'Is that one going to be relevant? It's a long time after your man was killed.'

Andy replied, 'We both know there are any number of reasons why the offence might not have been reported at the time. I'll take it with the others. It might be relevant.'

'No problem. You can take whatever files you need, but make sure you sign them out and get them back to us when you've finished with them.'

'Of course. A quick question about Clements. Has he always used weapons to commit robberies?'

'Not at all. Clements was a big guy, physically quite intimidating. It was only recently that he started carrying a knife all the time. It was always fists and feet before that.'

As Jane gathered up the robbery files, Andy said, 'We'll take them all and work through them properly back at the MCIU. We could have missed something rushing through them today.'

'No problem. If you two need anything else, you know where to find me.'

68

4.00 p.m., 21 February 1991
Police Headquarters, Nottinghamshire

D anny and Rob had driven to headquarters to push for an update from Tim Donnelly. It had been almost two weeks since blood had been found on the front wing of the vehicle owned by Lionel Wickes.

The blood samples that had been recovered following the luminol procedure had been immediately sent to the Forensic Science Service to try and establish a DNA profile.

Danny knocked on Tim Donnelly's door. The scenes of crime supervisor looked tired and motioned for the detectives to sit down. 'Just shift some of that paperwork, there's a seat under there somewhere.'

Danny sat down and said, 'Everything all right? You look shattered.'

'Not enough hours in the day, but you know what that feels like. What can I do for you?'

Danny didn't want to pile more pressure on, so he said, 'We were at headquarters for something else anyway, and I just wondered if you'd had an update from the FSS about the blood found on Lionel Wickes' car.'

A puzzled expression appeared on Tim's face.

Danny said, 'The blood from the luminol tests?'

It was as if a light bulb had been switched on inside Tim's head. He started shuffling papers on his desk muttering, 'I've got the report here somewhere. You're on my to-do list today.' He grabbed a report and said, 'Here it is. DNA profile raised successfully. That's the good news. The even better news is that I'd asked them to check it against the DNA profile of Lionel Wickes and it's come back negative. No match.'

'That's great. It means we could now have a DNA profile of the killer.'

'Theoretically speaking, yes.'

Rob said, 'How soon could you do a luminol procedure on the interior of the Ford Cosworth we recovered the other day?'

'Do you think the two offences are connected?' Tim asked.

'It's possible. The Cosworth was stolen four streets away, on the same night. If we can find blood inside that car, it could prove it was stolen by the same person who attempted to steal Lionel Wickes' vehicle.'

'And we already have a fingerprint identification for the Cosworth?'

'Yes.'

Tim grabbed his diary. 'The earliest I could arrange for a

full luminol examination of the RS Cosworth would be in a week's time.'

Danny grimaced. 'No chance of it any sooner? We're hoping to arrest the lads identified from the fingerprints in the next couple of days.'

Tim flicked the pages of the diary and shook his head. 'I'm sorry, boss, there's no way. I'm literally snowed under here.'

Danny could see the stress levels the man was under and said, 'Okay. Book it in as soon as you can, Tim.'

As Tim wrote the request in his diary, he said, 'In the meantime, if you let me have a list of any suspects you have, I can check to see if we've DNA profiles for them.'

'Perfect,' Rob said. 'Will do. Thanks, Tim.'

69

5.00 p.m., 21 February 1991
33 Church Lane, Linby, Nottinghamshire

Andy pointed to the stone cottage and said, 'That's it.'

Jane indicated and slowed the CID car to a stop. 'There's a light on, so somebody's home.'

The two detectives had decided to speak to the victim of the knifepoint robbery that had apparently happened two weeks after the death of Randall Clements.

Simon Cathcart had walked into the central police station in the middle of the day to make the report. Andy knew that most robbery offences were committed during the hours of darkness, so it was possible this crime had happened earlier than the date listed – because, for whatever reason, Cathcart had delayed reporting.

Andy rang the doorbell and after a short delay the door

was answered by a man in his mid-twenties, wearing a t-shirt and jeans.

Andy said, 'My name's DS Wills and this is DC Pope. I'm looking for Simon Cathcart.'

A worried expression crossed the man's face. 'That's me. Is anything wrong? Has something happened to my mum?'

Jane Pope held up both hands and said softly, 'Nothing's wrong. We need to ask you a few questions about the robbery you reported to the police last month.'

'Have you caught someone?'

'No. But we do need to ask you a few questions. May we come in?'

'Yes, but I haven't got long.'

As the two detectives followed him into the house, Cathcart said, 'My partner doesn't know about what happened that night, and I'd like to keep it that way. He's going to be home in the next half an hour.'

'This won't take long,' Andy said as he sat down. 'You said, what happened that night. The report we have suggests the offence occurred during the daytime.'

'I knew this would happen.' Simon Cathcart put his head in his hands. 'Look, I wasn't exactly truthful when I made the report. I wasn't going to bother, as I hadn't been hurt, but when the bastard tried to use my bank card, I decided to report it.'

'When did the robbery happen?'

'On the fifth of January.'

'You told the police that it happened near the Broadmarsh bus station, is that part of the report correct?'

Cathcart shook his head. 'No. It happened in the churchyard near the Shire Hall. If my partner finds out I was there he'll go mad.'

Jane said, 'What's the issue with the park?'

There was a long delay. 'I was there to meet someone.'

'And that someone wasn't your partner?'

'Exactly. I don't make a habit of it, but he'd been a pig to me all week and I was feeling miffed.'

Andy tried to placate the man. 'That's none of our business, Simon. We just need to know exactly what happened that night – please?'

'There were two men. One stood by watching, while the other one stuck a knife in my face and threatened to stab me if I didn't give him money. I was terrified, so I handed over my wallet and they both ran off.'

'On the original report you stated you were unable to provide a description as the lone offender wore a ski mask. I take it that bit isn't true either?'

He slowly shook his head. 'Neither of the men wore a mask. Both were black. The one with the knife was big, had dreadlocks and a gold tooth; the other man was short and quite fat. His hair was a lot shorter than the other man.'

'You've described how the bigger man threatened you with a knife, so what did this second man do?'

'He just stood there, watching. He didn't get involved in the robbery, but he was there, and afterwards they ran off together.' Simon looked around, anxiously. 'Is this going to take much longer? Only my boyfriend will be home any minute.'

Andy stood up. 'No. We're done. Do you think you would recognise either of these men again?'

'I don't think so – well, maybe the knifeman at a push.'

As he and Jane stepped back outside the house, Andy said, 'My advice, and it's entirely up to you if you take it or not, would be to tell your partner the truth about what happened that night. It will be better coming from you. We will need to return for a full written statement from you.'

Simon Cathcart nodded. 'Of course, you're right. I'll tell him tonight; God help me when I do.'

As the two detectives got back in the car, Jane said, 'Definitely sounds like a Randall Clements type of offence.'

'And it also gives massive credence to Mark Bradbury's story of two men being involved. The key to all this is going to be identifying the second man. He's the only person who knows exactly what happened that night – and, more importantly, who killed Clements.'

Jane glanced back at the house. 'There's going to be some strife in that house tonight.'

70

6.00 p.m., 21 February 1991
MCIU Offices, Mansfield, Nottinghamshire

Glen Lorimar and Ray Holden were sitting in Danny's office. They were presenting the operational order they had prepared for the arrest of the car thieves believed to have stolen the RS Cosworth.

DI Buxton and DS Moore were also in the office.

Danny said to Glen, 'And you're satisfied that these three youths are the ones seen running from the vehicle when it was abandoned on Chesterfield Road?'

Glen said, 'We know Jamie Mullins was definitely in the vehicle and, from all the intelligence reports and sightings we've gathered, we know the two other youths named in the order are his main associates.'

'Tell me about Paul Rowland?'

'Rowland is another juvenile. A very similar record to

Mullins. They only live a few doors apart and have been friends all the way through school. By all accounts where you find one, you'll find the other.'

'Okay.' Danny nodded. 'And Reggie Glover?'

'Glover is older than the other two and from what we've learned he calls the shots. He's very much the leader of their little group and physically a bit of a handful. He will always resist arrest and is extremely violent. He has warning markers on the PNC for carrying weapons.'

'Seems a strange combination. Why would someone like Reggie Glover surround himself with young lads?'

Ray said, 'Maybe he likes the way they look up to him. Likes being the top dog.'

'I suppose that's possible. What have you organised for the arrests?'

Glen said, 'We've now housed all three. The two young lads live on Willoughby Court, Bellamy Road estate with their parents and Glover is staying with a mate at Taylors Close, Ravensdale.'

'What do we know about the mate?'

'The house is owned by Liam Kominski. Drug addict, part-time dealer and petty thief. He allows anybody and everybody to doss at his house. The council are trying to get him evicted for antisocial behaviour. There could be any number of people at that address tomorrow morning. It could be interesting, putting that door in.'

'Have you got warrants?'

'Yes. Ray swore them out at the magistrates' court this afternoon.'

Danny looked at Ray. 'Any problems?'

'None, sir.'

'Good. Who have you designated for the arrest teams?'

'That's why I haven't been in to brief you before now, boss. I've been waiting for a phone call from Chief Inspector Chambers at the Special Ops Unit. He's giving us a section tomorrow morning to effect the arrest of Reggie Glover. They will also assist with any searches we need doing following the arrests.'

'Excellent. And the other two arrest teams?'

Rob Buxton said, 'Rachel and I will arrest Rowland, and Glen and Ray will detain Jamie Mullins.'

'What time's the briefing tomorrow morning?'

'Briefing will be at five thirty,' Glen said, 'and looking to make the arrests at six.'

'Are you carrying out the briefing, Glen?'

'Yes, sir.'

'I'll make sure I'm here for it. This is good work, both of you.'

Glen and Ray exited, leaving the supervisors alone in the office. Rob said, 'This is why I love the MCIU. We don't even have to be here; the lads and lasses just get on with the job and get things done.'

'Very true.' Danny smiled. 'But don't let them hear you say that, or we'll all be out of a job. I'll see you bright and breezy tomorrow morning.'

71

6.00 a.m., 22 February 1991
16 Taylors Close, Ravensdale, Mansfield, Nottinghamshire

T he four Special Ops officers stood in silence at the back door of 16 Taylors Close, Ravensdale. One of the men was holding the red metal enforcer – used to open doors by force. He was poised ready to smash the lock off the door.

Sergeant Graham Turner glanced once more at his watch before whispering, 'Now.'

PC Tom Naylor swung the enforcer back in a wide arc before smashing it into the mortice lock that secured the door. It only took one hefty blow for the flimsy door to be breached. The other two officers standing by immediately raced inside followed by Sergeant Turner.

Tom Naylor dropped the enforcer and raced in behind his sergeant. Other Special Operations Unit officers streamed from the van that was parked out of sight of the house. These officers raced to the front and the back doors, thus effectively securing the property.

Within thirty seconds of the door being forced the officers had secured the perimeter and had somebody in every room. The only two people found inside the house were in the main bedroom. They were quickly identified as the householder Liam Kominski and his girlfriend, Lauren Sharpe.

Graham Turner spoke to Kominski, 'Is there anybody else in the house?'

'There's no one else here, man. Who's going to pay for my fucking door?'

Turner barked orders to the officers. 'I want this place turned upside down. Glover will be hiding in here somewhere.'

The officers carried out a systematic search of the property, until the only space left was the loft.

Tom Naylor said, 'There's the print of a training shoe on the banister rail, sarge. I reckon he's climbed up there.'

'You know the drill, Tom. Grab a Dragon light and get up there.'

As other officers brought up a set of step ladders and the powerful Dragon torch from the van, Tom secured his NATO helmet and readied himself to enter and search the loft.

It was always the worst space in a house to search, as there was only one way into a loft, and that was head first through the narrow hatch. If a suspect wanted to cause the searching officer harm, the loft space offered them the perfect opportunity to do so.

The briefing had made it clear that Glover would not hesitate to use extreme violence to avoid arrest.

Once everything was ready, Graham looked at an understandably nervous Tom Naylor and said, 'Once that hatch opens, get up and in as fast as you can. Once you're through the hatch, I'll be right behind you. If he's up there, between us we'll be able to restrain him. You know the drill, Tom. Move carefully, stay on the rafters, and get away from the hatch as quick as you can.'

Tom nodded, climbed to the top of the step ladder and placed his hand gently on the underside of the hatch. He tensed the muscles in his arm and pushed slowly, trying to gauge if there was any resistance. The hatch moved easily.

He took a final deep breath then shoved open the loft hatch, climbing the last few steps of the ladder as he did so. Within seconds, he was through the hatch and squatting on a roof joist. The only light came from the hallway below. As his eyes adjusted to the gloom, he thought he saw movement in the corner of the loft.

He flicked on the Dragon torch and the space was instantly flooded with an intense, bright white light. He heard Graham Turner climbing the step ladder behind him, at the same time as he saw Reggie Glover moving towards him. Glover was stooped over and squinted against the powerful torchlight, now blinding him.

To his horror, Tom could see Glover was carrying a large carving knife in one hand and a wicked-looking claw hammer in the other.

Tom drew his baton and tried to move to one side. He desperately wanted to put space between himself and Glover and clear the entrance to the hatch.

Thinking that Graham Turner would be right behind him – there to back him up – Tom took the initiative and moved towards Glover.

Glover instantly raised the hammer and brought it down in a long arc aimed directly towards Tom's head. With only a split second to react, Tom raised the Dragon torch and blocked the blow from the hammer. The force of it sent the heavy torch spinning from his grasp.

Now the powerful torch beam made crazy patterns as it spun through the air. Tom reacted to the threat and aimed a blow with his baton towards the legs of his attacker. He heard Glover cry out, as the heavy baton connected with his right shin.

Glover fell onto one knee but swung the hammer again. This time the weapon narrowly missed connecting with Tom's head.

The force and momentum he generated swinging the hammer with such violent intent caused Glover to overbalance completely. He fell on his side, directly in front of Tom. As he fell, he dropped the large, bladed knife between the rafters, freeing his hand to grab one of the rafters.

Tom seized his opportunity and grabbed Glover's other wrist, attempting to wrestle the claw hammer from his grasp. The two men now began to struggle violently on top of the rafters. Tom put his foot down to gain some leverage and was horrified to feel his foot miss the rafter and burst through the plasterboard of the ceiling below.

Now that his leg was effectively stuck, Tom struggled to contain his violent attacker. He could see Glover reaching for the dropped knife.

Just as Glover's hand closed around the handle of the weapon, Tom saw Graham Turner come into view and strike Glover's wrist with his baton. The blow caused the man to drop the knife for a second time.

After a brief struggle Graham and Tom finally managed

to gain the upper hand and placed a still-struggling Glover in handcuffs. Even when he was handcuffed, Glover continued to lash out with his feet and head, snarling loudly in fury.

More officers climbed into the loft and helped to secure Glover's legs, placing his ankles in plasticuffs. Then, once secured, the violent offender was manhandled through the narrow loft hatch and down the step ladders.

Only when Glover had been removed from the loft space was Graham able to help Tom extricate his leg from the ceiling.

Graham looked at Tom. 'Are you okay?'

'Yeah. He had a couple of good swings at me with the hammer, but luckily missed both times.'

'Grab the torch, we need to locate and recover the weapons.'

After a quick search, the claw hammer and the knife were recovered and both officers headed down to stand at the foot of the step ladder on the landing.

As the adrenaline receded from his body, Tom felt a throbbing pain in his right leg and rolled his trouser leg up. His leg was bleeding badly. There was a three-inch gash that ran from just above his ankle to halfway up his shin, the blood soaking into his sock. It had obviously happened when his foot had gone through the ceiling.

Graham took one look at the badly damaged leg and said, 'Hospital, now. That will need cleaning properly and probably a couple of stitches. Sorry I took so long to get up there.'

Tom gave an unsteady smile. 'I must admit, once my leg was stuck, I was struggling to hold him – and when I saw him reaching for the knife again, I did start to panic a little.'

'I bet. I would've been up there a lot quicker, but I slipped on the top step. I nearly fell down the fucking ladders.'

'I'd have been in the shit if you had.'

'You did well up there; it's never an easy situation. There's another van on its way, which will take the three prisoners back to the nick, while we stay and search the house. I'll make sure they drop you at the hospital first.'

Tom grinned, more himself now. 'Cheers, sarge. I'll give you a shout when the nurses have done with me.'

Graham gave him a knowing look and said, 'Yeah, you do that and make sure you don't take all day.'

72

7.30 a.m., 22 February 1991
MCIU Offices, Mansfield, Nottinghamshire

T he briefing room at the MCIU was a hive of activity and there was a general hum as detectives chatted about the individual raids they had carried out.

Danny was pleased that the three main suspects, Jamie Mullins, Paul Rowland and Reggie Glover were all now in custody awaiting questioning. There would be a lengthy delay before that could happen, as detectives awaited the arrival of solicitors and appropriate adults to sit in on the two juveniles' interviews.

The parents of both Mullins and Rowland had declined to attend the police station, leaving it for the police to provide protection for the youngsters, via the appropriate adult scheme.

Sergeant Graham Turner walked into the briefing room and made straight for Danny. 'Morning, boss. I wanted to give you an update on 16 Taylors Close. The search has been completed, and we've made a couple of interesting seizures.'

Danny said, 'Sounds promising, Graham. What have you got?'

'We recovered a large bag of greyish powder from the freezer compartment of the fridge in the kitchen. A preliminary test has indicated the powder is amphetamine.'

'How large?'

'It weighs around ten ounces.'

'Enough for possession with intent to supply then?'

'I would say so, coupled with the large quantity of deal bags and scales we've also recovered.'

'Good work, Graham.'

'There's more. Between the mattress and the bed where we found Kominski and Sharpe this morning there was a hoard of cannabis resin already in deal bags and over three thousand pounds in used notes. It's obvious that Kominski and Sharpe have been dealing for some time.'

'How many deal bags?'

'Thirty-six.'

'This is great news and totally justifies the force used to execute the warrant. Speaking of force, how's your officer?'

'PC Naylor's at the hospital being treated for a badly cut shin. The last update he gave me, he was waiting for the doctor to put stitches into the wound. He'll need a couple of days off work, but he'll be fine.'

'How did it happen?'

'He was struggling with Glover, who was hiding in the loft. Glover used a claw hammer and knife to try and avoid arrest. During the struggle to disarm Glover, Tom's foot slipped off one of the rafters and crashed through the ceiling, cutting his shin.'

'Have you recovered the weapons?'

Turner nodded. 'We have.'

'As soon as Tom is feeling up to it, I'll need his witness statement. I intend to charge Glover with assault and with offensive weapon charges.'

'I'll make sure you have all our statements within the hour, boss.'

'Good work today. Please thank your officers on my behalf.'

Danny turned to Rob. 'Any news on when we'll be able to start the interviews?'

'Jag and Sam Blake will be interviewing Kominski and Sharpe about the drugs seizures shortly as neither have requested legal advice. They were only waiting on the search logs from the unit lads.'

'What about Glover?'

'His solicitor has indicated she'll be here by nine o'clock, at the latest. Rachel and I will be interviewing Glover; hopefully we'll have all the Unit officers' statements before then.'

'Okay, and what of the two juveniles?'

'Glen and Ray will be doing the interviews with Jamie Mullins and Paul Rowland.'

Danny looked at Glen. 'Any reason why you want to do both the interviews?'

Glen said, 'Ray's an experienced interviewer already and I just think it will help if we know exactly what each one is saying first hand. There's every chance we'll be able to turn either one, or both youngsters, and obtain a full account.'

'Anticipated time for the interviews?'

'Bit of a delay getting the appropriate adults here. Realistically, I think we'll be looking more towards ten o'clock.'

'Okay. Regular updates, please.'

73

After the hectic start to the day, Danny was alone in his office reflecting on the events of the morning, wondering if he was about to get a very welcome breakthrough in the Lionel Wickes murder investigation.

There was a knock on his door and Andy Wills walked in. 'I know you're busy this morning, but have you got a minute for a quick update on Craig Stevens?'

Danny indicated for his sergeant to take a seat and said, 'Any progress?'

Andy nodded. 'We saw Mike Hermitage yesterday at his office in Leicester. He introduced us to his client, a guy called Mark Bradbury. The first thing you need to know about Bradbury is that physically he's a dead ringer for Stevens.'

'What, as in identical?'

'Not quite. But it doesn't take a wild stretch to think they could be brothers.'

'Right. And was Bradbury willing to talk to you?'

'Yes,' Andy confirmed. 'I had reassured Mike Hermitage we weren't there to arrest his client, so Bradbury was happy to talk to us. He was understandably very nervous about how things would develop, but he gave us a full account of what happened that night.'

'Did he tell you anything significant?'

'The main thing was that in his account there were two offenders trying to rob him. He described a man fitting the description of Clements as threatening him with a knife and a second man acting as a lookout. He also said that his hand was badly cut when he grabbed the knife blade as he tried to protect himself.'

Danny knew there was more but waited patiently, waiting for Andy to continue.

Andy said, 'This is where it got tricky for me.'

'Go on.'

'Bradbury admitted punching the knifeman once, as he feared being seriously injured and felt he had no choice but to defend himself. By rights I should have arrested him at that point.'

'Don't worry, Andy.' Danny nodded his understanding. 'I will take any flak coming our way. You were acting under my direct orders.'

Andy breathed out in relief.

Danny said, 'Did Bradbury follow up that initial assault?'

'No. He stated that the punch knocked the man down and, as he fell, he dropped the knife. Bradbury claims he picked up the knife and ran off immediately.'

'What did the second attacker do?'

'According to Bradbury, he heard him running the other way.'

'Did Bradbury indicate that he thought his attacker was seriously injured?'

'No. He just ran.'

'Which could also explain the sighting we have of a man running with a knife.'

'My thoughts exactly, boss. He did say that he was nearly hit by a car as he ran across a road.'

'At least we now know we were right to look at the failed robbery angle.'

'Just on that,' Andy intercepted. 'Jane and I visited a victim of a knifepoint robbery last night. It had previously slipped through the net because it wasn't reported until two weeks after Clements was killed. Simon Cathcart told us he'd been robbed in the same location as Bradbury. He also described two offenders being involved. The description of the man carrying the knife fits Randall Clements.'

'That was also a knifepoint robbery?'

'Yes.'

'That's too much of a coincidence and I don't do coincidences. It gives massive credence to the version of events Bradbury gave you earlier – yes?'

'Exactly.'

'Any reason why Cathcart didn't report the offence at the time?'

'Personal reasons. Apparently, it's a cruising area frequented by gay men. That's why Cathcart was there – but he's in a long-term relationship.'

'Okay. I get that, so why report it at all?'

'The offender – not Clements, from the timing – tried to use his stolen bank card.'

'Okay, so any idea who this second offender could be?'

'Not at the moment, but we're going back to the robbery squad today to see if we can find anything else out.'

'The attempted use of the bank card could be a good place to start. Identifying this second man could be the key to this whole investigation.'

'When I started this inquiry,' Andy said, 'I wasn't convinced at all. I thought Craig Stevens was as guilty as sin, but after speaking to Mark Bradbury and Simon Cathcart yesterday, I'm beginning to think we may have an innocent man locked up.'

'Keep digging and keep me informed, Andy. Sounds like you and Jane are on the right track.'

74

After completing the introductions of everyone present in the interview room, Rachel repeated the caution to Reggie Glover.

She paused, waiting to see if his solicitor would interject with a prepared statement. The solicitor remained silent, so Rachel said, 'You were arrested earlier this morning on suspicion of stealing a motor vehicle, police assault and offensive weapons offences. Do you understand why you're here?'

'I didn't assault any copper,' Glover sneered. 'He fell through the ceiling.'

'We'll talk about your arrest later. Why don't you tell me about the stolen RS Cosworth?'

'I don't know what you're on about.'

'When you were detained this morning, other officers were arresting Paul Rowland and Jamie Mullins for the same offence. Are those names familiar to you?'

Again, Glover scowled at Rachel. 'Yeah, I know them. I know lots of people.'

'Is it fair to say you spend a lot of time with Rowland and Mullins?'

'What if I do?'

'We have a witness who saw three people abandon the stolen RS Cosworth on Chesterfield Road six days ago. We recovered that vehicle and carried out a forensic examination.'

'So what.'

'As a result of that examination, we know that Jamie Mullins had been driving that vehicle immediately prior to it being abandoned.'

'That's Jamie, not me.'

'We'll be interviewing both boys this morning. How confident are you that they won't say you were there with them?'

Glover simply shrugged, ignoring the question.

Rachel continued. 'That RS Cosworth was stolen from the Meadows estate in Nottingham on the same night as a man was murdered by car thieves. Tell me what happened when the Cosworth was stolen?'

Glover's scowl turned to shock and he shouted, 'That's bullshit! I don't know anything about that car being stolen from Nottingham. And I don't know anything about any murder.'

'But you do know something?'

Glover turned to his solicitor and whispered, 'I need to talk to you.'

'My client has requested a further consultation,' the solicitor said. 'Can we take a break?'

Rachel replied, 'No problem. We'll continue this when you've had your conversation.'

The two detectives left the solicitor alone with her client and waited in the custody area. After fifteen minutes she emerged from the interview room and said, 'My client's ready to give you an explanation now.'

Rob murmured under his breath, 'I wasn't expecting that. I thought he would be answering no comment to everything.'

Once inside the interview room, Rachel said, 'Your solicitor has indicated that you want to give us an explanation.'

'Not an explanation. I just don't want you lot fitting me up for a murder. Yes, I've been in the Cosworth. We all have. But we found it abandoned in the car park at King's Mill Res. It was unlocked and had already been boosted. There was even a screwdriver still wedged in the ignition.'

'When was this?'

'It was over a month ago, the middle of January sometime. I can't remember the date.'

'Tell me what happened?'

'We were just out and about, having a mooch around when we saw the car. Mullo saw it first and tried the door.'

'Who's Mullo?'

'Jamie Mullins.'

'He tried the door, then what?'

'He shouted us over. I looked inside and that's when I saw the screwdriver hanging out the ignition casing. The casing had already been smashed off. It was obviously nicked.'

'What did you do?'

Glover shrugged and said, 'What do you think? I turned the screwdriver and when it fired up, we took it for a spin up the motorway.'

'All three of you in the car?'

'Yep, I drove that night, but we've all had a go since then.'

'If that was back in the middle of January, where's the car been all this time?'

'We hid it in a lock-up on the estate. We took it out every now and then for a jolly.'

'What happened the night it was abandoned?'

'Mullo was driving and he's fucking useless. He blew the engine up with his shit driving. It conked out, so we left it where it was.'

'Why have you decided to tell us about this now?'

'Don't get me wrong, I ain't no grass. I'm only telling you because none of us had anything to do with any murder, or nicking that motor from Nottingham, and I want my solicitor to be here when I tell you that, so you lot can't fit me up.'

Rob said, 'On the night you found the car at King's Mill, did you see anybody else with the vehicle, or nearby?'

'I didn't see a soul that night. I do know that car park is often used to dump nicked motors though.'

'Do you know anybody who has left stolen cars there before?'

'Fuck off. I've just told you I ain't no grass. I'm not saying anything else about it.'

Rachel said, 'Why did you resist arrest this morning?'

'Because I hate coppers, that's why. It always takes two or three of you lot to best me, and I don't give a fuck.'

'Do you deny being in possession of a hammer and a knife when you were arrested this morning?'

'That copper was lucky. He knew I had him when his leg

went through the ceiling. It's a good job his mate was there to save his skinny arse.'

'And did you have the weapons?'

'Yeah. You lot have your truncheons, so why shouldn't I protect myself?'

Rob said, 'A quantity of controlled drugs was recovered from the address where you were detained. Do you know anything about those?'

'You must be thick, mate. I've just told you I ain't a grass. No comment.'

Rob continued to question Glover, but he now answered every question with 'no comment'.

Eventually, Rob said, 'I've no further questions. Is there anything else you want to say?'

Glover grinned. 'Yeah, no fucking comment.'

75

10.30 a.m., 22 February 1991
Robbery Squad, Central Police Station, Nottingham

Detective Sergeant Fraser Jones said, 'Are you two back already?'

Andy Wills said, 'Afraid so. We called in on Simon Cathcart yesterday and it's as I suspected: the offence happened a lot sooner than he said and in the same location where Randall Clements died. Cathcart gave us a description of the offender that could easily be Randall Clements.'

DS Jones said, 'I think the best thing for you to do is talk to the detective who was dealing with the Cathcart robbery.'

'That would be great. I saw on the file it's DC Amanda Jennings, but I've not heard her name before.'

'Amanda's doing an attachment here from Newark CID. She's just nipped out but will be back shortly. Grab a coffee while you wait.'

Andy and Jane had just sat down with their coffees when a young woman wearing jeans and a baggy sweatshirt walked into the office and saw them sitting at her desk.

She said, 'Can I help you?'

Jane said, 'I'm DC Pope and this is DS Wills, we're from the MCIU. Are you Amanda?'

The young woman looked slightly flustered and said, 'Yeah. Is something wrong?'

Andy said, 'We just need to have a chat with you about the Simon Cathcart robbery.'

Amanda sat down and said, 'Okay. What do you want to know?'

'What did you make of his robbery report?'

'My honest feelings?'

Andy nodded. 'Of course.'

'I thought he was lying through his teeth, but I couldn't get him to open up.'

'Lying about what?'

'The whole thing. Well, not entirely the whole thing. I do believe he was robbed, but the details he gave me were all rubbish, I'm sure of it.' She paused. 'I don't think he would have reported it at all, if it wasn't for the bank card business.'

Jane said, 'What do you mean?'

'He seemed more bothered that some toerag had tried to use his card, than he was about being robbed at knifepoint. It was all a bit bizarre.'

Andy said, 'We spoke to Cathcart last night as part of the investigation into the death of Randall Clements, and your instincts were right. He did lie to you about where and when that robbery happened.'

Amanda shook her head and muttered, 'The lying shit.' She took a deep breath and said, 'Sorry for swearing, but I've been looking at a series of robberies that have all happened within a two-hundred-yard radius of the Shire Hall. I always fancied Randall Clements to be involved in those robberies. I never put the Cathcart incident in that series because of the date he said it had happened. Did the robbery happen before Randall Clements died?'

Andy nodded. 'Yes, it did.'

'Bloody hell. Have I cocked up by not notifying the MCIU about my suspicions?'

'Not at all. To a certain extent, we all must accept what we're being told by victims.'

'I guess,' Amanda said, still looking frustrated. 'But why are you still investigating the Clements murder? I thought somebody had been charged for that.'

'We're just making the final enquiries ready for the court file. Did anything ever come of the bank card use?'

'I went to the shop in question. The suspect had tried to buy food and drink. A lot of it, but the card declined and they ran off.'

'Any description?'

'Better than that, there was CCTV in the shop. I haven't been able to identify the man who tried to use the bank card, that's why it's still undetected. One thing's for sure, it wasn't Randall Clements; he was dead by then.'

Jane said, 'You said you always fancied Clements for that series of robberies around the Shire Hall – why was that?'

'I had no real evidence as such to connect him to them, just a gut feeling. Unfortunately, the description given by some of the victims was sketchy at best, so there was never enough to nick him.'

'Did you have anything else besides your own suspicions?'

'Only confirmation from an informant who told me it was Clements. But I don't trust the word of that informant enough to go out on a limb for. He's got a raging drug habit and has, in the past, given me a load of shit info for the price of a deal bag. Like I said, he's not somebody I would ever trust.'

'What exactly did he tell you?'

'Just that it was Randall Clements doing the knife jobs in the city.'

Andy said, 'Would you have any objections if we spoke to your informant?'

Amanda shrugged. 'I've no objections, but I'm warning you he's not a reliable source. I can give you a recent photo, plus a list of locations where you're likely to find him. His name's Clifton Scarlett.'

'Thanks, that's great. One other thing, do you still have the CCTV from the shop?'

'No. I had to return the tape back to them, but I did take a couple of stills of the offender before I did.'

'Perfect. Could we take a copy of the photo?'

'No problem, they're still in my locker. I'll get them for you.'

She returned moments later with photographs of the man using the card, and a recent photograph of her informant, Clifton Scarlett.

Andy passed the photo of Clifton Scarlett to Jane who said, 'He shouldn't be too hard to spot, that gangly, beanpole build.'

'Let's hope so.'

Amanda still had a worried expression on her face. 'Am I in the shit for not giving all this information about Clements to the MCIU earlier?'

Andy said, 'Not at all. Thanks for all your help.'

'Just be careful with Scarlett, sarge. That man's a liability.'

76

12.30 p.m., 22 February 1991
Mansfield Police Station, Nottinghamshire

The interview with Paul Rowland had been disappointing. He had steadfastly answered 'no comment' to every question Glen and Ray put to him. After three quarters of an hour of continuous questioning, the detectives stopped the interview and returned the youngster to his cell.

As they waited for Jamie Mullins' solicitor to let them know his client was ready to be interviewed, Glen said, 'I'm going to change tack on this interview. I'm telling Mullins from the outset that Glover's already told us everything. I think Rowland was scared stiff of being seen as a grass by Glover.'

Ray shrugged. 'The kid probably won't believe you, whatever you tell him, Glen.'

'If I give him just enough detail to let him know that somebody's talked, he might start talking to us.'

'It's worth a try.'

Ten minutes later and the two detectives sat opposite the schoolboy. He was flanked by his solicitor and an appropriate adult. He had a couldn't-care-less expression writ large across his face as he leaned back in his chair with his arms folded across his chest.

Glen said, 'I want to talk to you about the RS Cosworth you abandoned on Chesterfield Road.'

Mullins made eye contact with the detective and said, 'No comment.'

'When you were arrested this morning, we also arrested Paul Rowland and Reggie Glover. Both have now been interviewed and have told us what they know about the Cosworth.'

'No comment.'

'Do you want to tell me where you've been keeping the Cosworth since it was stolen?'

'No comment.'

'Talk to me about the lock-up garage on the estate where you've kept the car so you could take it for a jolly every now and then?'

Silence filled the room.

Glen stared at the youngster. 'I'm not lying to you, Jamie. We've found your fingerprints inside the vehicle, and Reggie has already told me everything. How you're such a shit driver that you blew the Cosworth's engine and that's why you had to abandon it.'

Mullins blurted out, 'It wasn't my driving.'

Glen waited, holding the silence. He knew that now the youngster had said something he would continue to talk.

After a lengthy pause, Mullins continued. 'That night was the first time I'd driven the car, so it wasn't my driving.'

Glen said, 'Who drove it on the first night you got it?'

'Reggie. He always gets first crack at everything.'

'Where did you steal the car?'

'We didn't steal it, we found it.'

'Where?'

'Near the res. It had been dumped.'

'When you say the res, do you mean King's Mill Reservoir in Mansfield?'

'Yeah, the res.'

'How do you know the car had been dumped?'

'Because the doors were open, the ignition casing had been smashed off and there was a screwdriver wedged in the ignition.'

'Can you remember when that was?'

'January the tenth.'

'How can you remember the date?'

'It was the morning after I'd been expelled from school for fighting.'

'Where did you go in the car on that first night?'

Mullins shrugged. 'I don't know. I do remember going on the motorway. I was shitting myself. The car was like a rocket.'

'Tell me about the lock-up?'

'That's Reggie's. We got a padlock and locked the car away, so we could use it later.'

'Where is it?'

'On the Ladybrook estate. I think it belongs to Reggie's dad.'

'Have you all driven the car?'

'We've all had a go, yeah.'

'When you found the car, was anybody with it?'

'No.'

'Did you see anybody hanging round the area?'

Mullins shook his head. 'Nobody.'

'Do you know who stole the car in the first place?'

'No.'

'Had Reggie stolen it before he showed it to you?'

'No. He was shocked when we found it. He was happy, but I could tell he was shocked too.'

'Have you ever been to Nottingham, Jamie?'

'Not since I was a little kid. I went on a school trip to see the castle.'

'I've no further questions for you currently. Is there anything you want to ask me?'

Mullins looked down at his hands. 'What's going to happen now?'

77

4.00 p.m., 22 February 1991
MCIU Offices, Mansfield, Nottinghamshire

Danny sat down in the briefing room and said, 'How did you get on with Rowland? Did he say anything other than "no comment" in his second interview?'

Glen shook his head and said, 'No. It didn't matter what I tried or how many times I gave him hints that the other two have already dropped him in it, he wasn't having any of it. He's been well schooled by his old man.'

'Ah yes, the pillar of the community that is Jack Rowland. Is he actually out of prison now?'

'He's out. He's just finished a five-year stretch for burglary.'

'Okay. So, young Rowland isn't cooperating, but we've still got enough evidence to charge.'

'We have. I was thinking it might be better to bail him and Mullins in the first instance. We still haven't had the result of the luminol examination on the RS Cosworth. It could be that shows something else.'

Danny glanced at Rob Buxton. 'Any news when that's getting done?'

'I spoke to Tim Donnelly yesterday and he assured me it would be carried out within the next week.'

Danny was thoughtful. 'If we bail the two youngsters, what do we do with Glover?'

Rob said, 'There's no reason why we can't bail Glover on the vehicle theft charge, but charge and remand him in custody for the offensive weapons and police assault offence.'

'That sounds like a plan. I know if we bail him, he'll be in the wind and we'll struggle to find him.'

Glen added, 'Plus, he's a nutter and bloody dangerous.'

'Talk to the custody sergeant and see if he agrees with that course of action. How did Jag and Sam get on interviewing Kominski and Sharpe for the drugs offences?'

Rob said, 'Liam Kominski has coughed everything. He's kept the love of his life out of it – and she denied all knowledge of the drugs anyway.'

'Do you think that's right? That she didn't know about the drugs?'

'Lauren Sharpe is like her name; she doesn't miss a trick. She would have known about the drugs and the money, but we can't prove she did. And with his admissions, there's not much point in pushing it.'

'So, she gets a walk-out and Kominski gets a charge for possession with intent to supply?'

'That's it.'

'Is there enough to remand him in custody?'

'That's a decision for the custody sergeant. Jag is pushing for a remand because of the quantities involved. It may be we have to bail him pending the forensic testing of the drugs seized.' Danny paused. 'The bottom line is, it's been a good day's work, but it doesn't take us any closer to finding the killer of Lionel Wickes.'

Rob nodded his agreement. 'Not unless the luminol testing of the Cosworth tells us something different.'

78

4.30 p.m., 22 February 1991
Trent Embankment, Nottingham

I t had been a long, frustrating day for Andy Wills and Jane Pope. They had spent it searching the city for the robbery squad's informant, Clifton Scarlett.

Jane Pope's earlier prediction that with his beanpole height and long skinny frame he would be easy to locate had proved both optimistic and very premature.

As they walked down the steps from the Trent Bridge onto the embankment, Andy said, 'How many other places to look after this one?'

Jane glanced at the piece of paper she was holding and said, 'This is the fifth place on the list; there's only the squat in Radford after this one.'

'Well, it's a nice afternoon. Let's hope our man Scarlett fancied some fresh air.'

Jane suddenly pointed and said, 'Over there on the bench, is that him?'

As the two detectives ducked back behind the wall, Andy peered over and could see a tall skinny man sitting on a bench at the side of the river. He said, 'I think we just got lucky, that's him all right and it looks like he's fast asleep.' As he weighed up the situation, Andy said, 'I'll wait here and give you time to get round and approach him from the other direction. Once I see you walking along the embankment towards him, I'll make my way in from this side. That way, if he runs, we've got him covered.'

Jane smiled. 'Unless he decides to go for a swim.'

Andy chuckled. 'If he goes in the river today, I won't be going in after him. That water will be bloody freezing.'

Ten minutes later and Andy could see Jane walking towards Clifton Scarlett from the opposite direction. The informant seemed to have woken from his slumbers, but was still sitting on the bench, staring out across the river.

Andy started to walk towards the man and got to within thirty yards of the bench. Scarlett suddenly turned and looked straight at him. Without a second's hesitation, the man was on his feet and running in the opposite direction, straight towards Jane Pope.

As Scarlett ran alongside Jane, she brought him down with a perfectly timed rugby tackle. She was sat astride the informant, putting him in handcuffs when a breathless Andy reached them. 'Bloody hell, Jane. Where did you learn to tackle like that?'

As she hauled the lanky Scarlett to his feet, she said, 'I've got four rugby mad brothers. I've played rugby all my life.'

Groaning loudly, Clifton Scarlett said, 'I hope you guys are cops, or I must be in some deep shit.'

79

4.45 p.m., 22 February 1991
Trent Embankment, Nottingham

ndy Wills and Jane Pope sat either side of Clifton Scarlett on the same bench he'd been sitting on prior to being detained. They had taken the handcuffs off the man and had showed him their identification.

Andy said, 'Why did you run?'

'That's simple. I owe money all over the place. That's why I come out here, to keep myself out the limelight, so to speak. I was just enjoying the peace and tranquillity when I saw you. I took one look at that fancy suit and knew you were a cop, or worse. In my position you need to run first and ask who's chasing later.' He paused for breath and said, 'Why are detectives after me anyway? I've got no warrants on my head.'

'We need to talk to you about Randall Clements.'

'That brother's dead, man.'

'You told DC Jennings on the robbery squad that Clements was responsible for several knifepoint robberies in the city. Was that genuine information?'

Scarlett feigned a hurt expression and said, 'That girl always disrespects me. All my information is diamond, brother. I don't give out any rubbish, it's bad for my rep.'

Andy took out the photograph DC Jennings had given him and said, 'The credit card being used by this man was stolen during one of those robberies. He's not Randall Clements, so who is it?'

'Blood! That ain't Clements, that man's Trevor Winstanley, soon to be Councillor Winstanley. He and Clements were thick as thieves, until the man passed over.'

Jane said, 'Are you sure this man's Trevor Winstanley?'

'That's definitely him, one hundred per cent.'

Andy said, 'Why would a man running for election to the local council be out on the rob with a villain like Clements?'

'Nah. You've got it all wrong. Trev would only be with Clem to try and get him to change his ways, that's what he does. He's very big on law and order, on helping the poor. He's a good guy.'

'That big on law and order, he was trying to use a stolen credit card.'

'If you check at that shop, I bet the man was using the card to buy food. He runs a kitchen for the homeless, and he's always after donations. He would see that plastic and think of it as a donation for a good cause.'

'Yeah, very charitable. You'll be telling me he's a regular Robin Hood next.'

'Them's your words, brother. But yeah, he's got a bit of that dude's vibe going on.'

'Why wouldn't Clements use the card, if he stole it?'

'I don't want to appear disrespectful to the dear departed, but Clem was always a bit thick, if you know what I'm saying. He only ever wanted cash. He probably wouldn't know how to kite a card.'

'But Winstanley does. He sounds a real pillar of the community.'

'I'm telling you, detective. Trev's a good guy and will get elected to the council for sure. The people on the Meadows estate are full of love and respect for that man.'

Andy said, 'We've got choices to make here, Clifton. I could take you in to the police station and carry out a full strip search for drugs, or I can let you walk right now.'

'That's no choice, brother. I'm not carrying, and I've been respectful and cooperative.'

'But if I let you go, how do I know I can trust you not to go blabbing to Winstanley?'

Despite his words to the contrary, Andy could see the panic on Scarlett's face and knew that he was holding drugs of some kind. There was a level of fear in Scarlett's voice as he said, 'I know of Winstanley, but I don't know him as a brother. He means nothing to me, man. Trust me, if you let me loose, I ain't saying a single word to that man.'

Andy held the silence long enough for the panic to reappear on Scarlett's face, then said, 'All right, Clifton, get going. And don't forget – we found you once, and if you talk to Winstanley, we can find you again.'

As he walked away, the skinny informant smiled. 'I ain't saying a word, man. I don't want to be tackled to the ground by your chick again.'

'Did he just call me your chick, sarge?'

Andy couldn't help but laugh. 'He did, Jane, but don't let it go to your head.'

80

9.00 a.m., 23 February 1991
MCIU Offices, Mansfield, Nottinghamshire

Andy and Jane sat opposite Danny in his office updating him on their progress of the day before.

Danny said, 'So, what do we know about Trevor Winstanley?'

Jane replied, 'I spent most of yesterday evening researching him and, from what I've gathered so far, he really is the pillar of the community that Clifton Scarlett described. He has no criminal record, not even a caution. He runs a soup kitchen for the homeless and has also started a food bank that operates from the local community centre. He does a lot of work with local youths, trying to steer them away from crime and onto the right path.'

'So, why was he spending time with a lowlife like Randall Clements?'

Andy said, 'I think he has a bit of a saviour complex. As far as he's concerned there are no lost causes. Clements isn't the only hardened criminal he likes to spend time with by all accounts.'

'All that good work contradicts sharply with using a stolen bank card.'

Jane said, 'We checked with the shop owner. Clifton was right – the stuff he was trying to buy was large quantities of tinned food, bread and milk.'

'Couldn't the shop keeper identify him?'

'No. Winstanley's not stupid. He was trying the card at a shop in Arnold, well away from the Meadows where everyone knows him.'

'What about his home life?'

'He's single and lives alone in a two-bedroom flat on Eugene Gardens in the heart of the Meadows estate.'

'What does he do for income?'

'He works in a hardware store near Castle Marina and also makes a bit of cash on the side as a DJ.'

'And is it true that he's running for election?'

'He certainly is. He's standing as an independent and hopes to be the new councillor for the Meadows area. From what I learned yesterday he's almost a shoo-in to be elected. He's using the appalling crime record on the estate as his platform, promising huge changes to the way the estate will be policed and the amount of money the council spends to improve the area. It seems the people who live in and around the estate genuinely love the guy.'

'At the moment, all we have is the cigarette butt found at the scene,' Danny mused, 'and the fact that Mark Bradbury described the second mugger as smoking in the area it was recovered. Plus, the word of a flaky informant and the CCTV image of him attempting to use the stolen bank card from a separate robbery offence.'

Andy said, 'That's enough, surely. Do you want us to bring him in for questioning?'

Danny sat quietly, deep in thought, tapping his Biro on the pad in front of him.

Eventually he said, 'I don't think it will do us any good to bring him in yet. The strongest evidence we have linking him to Clements and the robberies is the attempted use of the stolen bank card. If he says he found the card, we're no further forward. We have the DNA profile on the cigarette butt from the scene, but if he doesn't cooperate and volunteer a sample for us to profile, again we're no further forward.' He took a deep breath and added, 'And there's no way we can rely on the testimony of Clifton Scarlett.' He paused. 'I just don't see Winstanley wanting to do, or say, anything that could jeopardise his chances of winning this council election. We need something else to put the pressure on him before we speak to him, which will preferably be before the election. When is that?'

Jane said, 'Voting day is fifteenth March.'

Andy said, 'What are you thinking, boss?'

'I'm thinking that we have the DNA profile from the cigarette butt found at the scene of Clements' murder. We know that profile doesn't fit either Clements or Craig Stevens, so there's a good chance it was from the second mugger. I want you to follow Trevor Winstanley and obtain something we can get a DNA profile from. I need to be one hundred per cent sure he was at the scene of that robbery before we confront him. That's the only chance we have of forcing him to cooperate with us, and finally getting to the truth of what really happened that night.'

'That's going to be no easy task, boss. Winstanley's a home boy. Apart from going to work every day, he doesn't stray far from the Meadows. We're going to stick out like a sore thumb on that estate.'

'It's our only chance, Andy. Dress down and act as a couple who are new to the area. I'm sure an opportunity will present itself, so hopefully you won't have to spend too long following him around. Are you both up for it?'

Jane nodded enthusiastically. 'Definitely.'

Andy spoke with an element of caution in his voice. 'I think we'll need somebody else watching our backs while we're on that estate.'

Danny said, 'I'll speak to Sam Blake. I believe he still has family who live on the estate. He can keep an eye on you while you're watching Winstanley and if anything looks like trouble, he can sort out backup for you both.'

'That's good enough for me, boss.'

'I'll brief Sam and you can get started this afternoon. Good luck.'

81

10.30 a.m., 23 February 1991
MCIU Offices, Mansfield, Nottinghamshire

Danny held the phone in one hand and flicked through his notepad with the other until he found the telephone number he was seeking.

He dialled and the phone was answered on the second ring. 'Hello, Mike Hermitage. Can I help you?'

'It's DCI Flint. I wanted to update you on the progress we've made. We think we may have identified the second man, as described by your client, who was there on the night Randall Clements attempted to rob him.'

'That's great news,' Hermitage replied. 'Are you going to arrest him?'

'Unfortunately, it's not that simple. We currently only have the word of an unreliable informant and some sketchy evidence. My detectives are working hard to sure up that evidence, so that we're in a strong enough position to arrest and question him.'

'What you're telling me isn't really progress at all, is it, chief inspector? It sounds to me like you're no further forward.'

'I disagree. Everything we've learned so far vindicates what we're doing and strengthens my belief that we may have the wrong person in prison. I can't and won't allow that to happen. I'm asking for a bit more patience from you and your client. I know it would be easy for him to give himself up right now and take his chances. I think that would be a huge mistake.'

'How so?'

'Because the DNA evidence we already have against Craig Stevens is so strong. There's every chance that even your client's confession wouldn't be enough for Stevens to be released.'

'I hear what you're saying, chief inspector, but my client is understandably nervous. He's convinced that any day detectives are going to raid his home and arrest him, thereby taking away any credit he would undoubtably get for handing himself in.'

'Off the record. Let me assure you that's not going to happen. I've no plans to arrest your client. When we get the additional evidence we need from the second mugger, I will contact you and arrange to meet you and your client at your office. Hopefully, that assurance will ease your client's worries enough for him not to do anything rash.'

'I'll talk to him, but I can't promise anything. My client's an intelligent, articulate man who can assess a situation for himself. He knows his own mind.'

'Tell him to be patient and I'll be in touch again soon.'

'Hopefully, with better news.'

Danny terminated the call.

Sitting alone in his office, he was troubled. He knew this whole investigation could go badly wrong. He also knew that if it did the criticism that would come his way could easily spell the end of his career.

82

7.30 p.m., 27 February 1991
The Meadows, Nottingham

I t was the evening of the fourth day that the two
detectives had been following Trevor Winstanley.

During those four days they had begun to understand the daily routine of their suspect. He would be up and
out by eight o'clock every morning. At which time he then
walked from his flat to the hardware store on Castle Marina
where he worked, stopping to buy a newspaper and a take-
away coffee on the way.

His lunch break, between one o'clock and one thirty, was
spent within the canteen of the store where he worked.

He finished work at four o'clock in the afternoon and
walked straight home. He spent two hours at home before
coming back out on the streets to push leaflets through

doors. At eight o'clock he would spend an hour at the soup kitchen he helped to run, chatting and joking with the homeless, before going back to his flat alone.

Andy and Jane had been able to observe Winstanley from a distance and had encountered no problems on the estate thus far. They strolled around hand in hand, dressed in jeans and sweatshirts and didn't look too out of place.

Only once had Andy been forced to duck into an alleyway to avoid a man he recognised, and who would have undoubtably recognised him too.

One thing they had both noticed was the genuine love and respect that Trevor Winstanley was held in. People, of all ages, who lived in the Meadows liked and admired the man.

This evening was warm for the time of year and after spending an hour with kids kicking a ball about on the local five-a-side court, Trevor Winstanley was heading back towards the soup kitchen.

He suddenly made a change from his daily routine and ducked into the Spinning Jenny public house.

Andy said, 'Fancy a drink, Jane?'

Jane laughed. 'Don't mind if I do.'

The two detectives were still chuckling when they walked inside the pub, where they looked across and saw Winstanley at the bar ordering a pint of lager shandy.

Andy stood beside him and ordered two drinks, while Jane sat down at a nearby table.

It was still early in the evening and, apart from a group of four elderly West Indian men playing a very loud game of calypso dominoes, the pub was empty.

Having got his pint, Winstanley sat alone at a table three along from where Jane had sat. He took a long drink from his glass, took an election poster from inside his jacket and returned to the bar, leaving his pint glass unattended.

While Andy was paying for his drinks, he heard Winstanley say to the barmaid, 'I was ready for that, Barbra. I've been playing five-a-side football with the kids and I'm sweating bullets here. Do you mind if I put this poster up in the pub?'

'Not at all. Put it where you want, love. You've got my vote, Trev.'

'Thanks, Babs, I appreciate that.'

As Winstanley used tape to stick the poster to the door of the pub, Andy joined Jane at the table.

The two detectives engaged in natural conversation as they sipped their drinks and casually observed Winstanley.

Andy, who had his back to Winstanley, whispered, 'If we get the chance we should take the pint pot, when he's finished with it.'

Jane said, 'Even better, he's just lit a cigarette. It will be a lot easier to take that, and it will provide a stronger DNA sample.'

'Is there an ashtray on the table?'

'Yeah, and it's empty.'

'Brilliant. I think this could be our best chance. Let me know when he's nearly finished his beer. If he doesn't look like he's having a second pint, I'll follow him outside while you grab the butt from the ashtray. You happy with that?'

'No problem.'

Five minutes later, Winstanley drained the last of the lager shandy from his glass. As he placed his empty glass on the bar he said to the barmaid, 'I'm off, Babs. Thanks for that, I needed it.'

'No problem, darling. Take care of yourself.'

Andy drained his own glass and followed Winstanley outside.

Jane slipped a glove on. She placed the gloved hand in her pocket and carried their two empty glasses to the bar with the other. She put the glasses on the bar and said, 'Thanks, love.'

As soon as the barmaid turned round to put the dirty glasses in the sink, Jane stepped over to the table where Winstanley had been sitting and with her gloved hand deftly picked the cigarette butt from the ashtray.

Without waiting to see if anyone had seen what she'd done she turned and stepped outside the pub.

She could see Andy fifty yards away and walked briskly to try and catch him up. As she walked, she slipped the cigarette butt into an exhibit bag and stuffed it deep inside her jacket pocket.

Suddenly, she became aware of a presence immediately behind her. Before she could react, she felt a rough hand clamp across her mouth and a strong arm snake around her neck. Someone with real strength was now pulling her backwards and her feet were almost off the ground. The hand clamped over her mouth stank of stale beer, tobacco and urine.

She bucked and struggled but couldn't break the man's grip.

Her windpipe was being compressed by the arm around her neck, and she started to feel light-headed as her exertions made her desperate to suck more air into her lungs.

As she was dragged backwards into a dark alleyway, she felt warm breath in her ear as the man whispered, 'Stop struggling, or I'll properly fuck you up.'

With his arm still tight around her neck, the man snatched his hand away from her mouth and began fumbling at the front of her jeans.

She gasped for air as the hold on her neck tightened even more. She managed to rasp, 'I'm a police officer, get the fuck off me.'

'That's nice,' the same whispered voice said with real menace. 'I've never fucked a cop before.'

The grip around her neck tightened again and she felt the man's hand on the zipper of her jeans.

Just as that zip was starting to be pulled down, she felt the man's grip around her neck jerk away and she felt the body weight that had been pressing her into the wall fall away.

She spun around, gasping for air, and could see her attacker on the floor being punched repeatedly by another man.

As soon as those punches had incapacitated her attacker, the man turned to face her and said, 'Are you okay, Jane?'

She felt tears of relief as she recognised the man who had pulled her attacker off her.

DC Sam Blake had obviously been watching her as she left the pub alone and had spotted the imminent danger she was in.

As he hauled the would-be rapist off the floor and pinned him to a wall, he handcuffed him and said, 'I've got this, Jane. Backup's on the way. Get going and catch Andy up, quick as you can. I'll see you later at the Meadows nick.'

'You sure you've got him?'

'Yeah, no problem. Get going, you've still got a job to do.'

Sam's sharp words snapped her back to work mode and

although her throat and neck were sore and her legs felt like jelly, she realised that what he'd said was right.

She took a couple of deep breaths. 'Thanks, Sam,' she said. 'I owe you.'

83

9.00 a.m., 28 February 1991
Police Headquarters, Nottinghamshire

Danny and Andy were at the Scenes of Crime
Department waiting patiently for Tim Donnelly
to arrive.

Danny said, 'Have you spoken to Jane this morning?'

Andy replied, 'Yeah, I spoke to her as soon as I came on duty.'

'How is she?'

'Shook up. She's a tough cookie, but what happened last night was bloody scary. Thank God, Sam was there. I dread to think what would have happened if he hadn't spotted the danger to her.'

'I'm sorry, Andy. That was a good call, by you, to insist on backup while you were on that bloody estate. That was something I should have thought of myself. I phoned Jane

last night when the control room told me what had
happened. She said the local CID have been investigating a
series of nasty sexual assaults all within the vicinity of the
Spinning Jenny pub. It looks like they've got their man now,
thanks to some great work by Sam Blake.'

'He really stepped up last night, that's for sure.'

'I'm going to talk to the chief when I get back to the
office. What they both did last night was above and beyond.
They deserve some recognition for their courage.'

'When will Jane be back at work?'

'The doctor has signed her off for a fortnight, and I've
told her to make sure she takes all fourteen days. Physically,
it's nothing more than bruising to her throat, but I'm worried
about the psychological effects of an attack like that. We
need to keep a careful eye on her, between now and her
coming back to work.'

'I'll make sure I stay in touch with her, boss.'

Tim Donnelly was now walking along the corridor
towards them. He frowned when he saw the two detectives
waiting and said, 'Not very often I get a welcome committee.
This looks ominous.'

Danny followed Tim into his office and said, 'I need
something submitting to the Forensic Science Service
urgently. It must go today.'

As Tim took his coat off, he said, 'What have you got?'

'It's a cigarette butt that was recovered last night. I need
the FSS to examine it and, as soon as possible, raise a DNA
profile from it.'

'That's not a quick ask, boss. It will be submitted today
but there are no guarantees when it will get looked at by the
lab.'

'If the lab can raise a profile from it, I'll also need it to be compared immediately with the DNA profile we already have from the cigarette butt found at the scene of the Randall Clements murder.'

'Okay. Can I ask what this is all about?'

'As you know I've always suspected that Randall Clements may have died after an intended robbery victim fought back. I've also always thought there could have been a second offender involved in that robbery. If the two DNA profiles from the cigarette butts are a match, then we will have identified that second offender.'

Tim was puzzled. 'I don't see how this will help to convict Craig Stevens for murder.'

'I can't explain everything now, Tim. But this isn't just about Craig Stevens.'

'I don't understand.'

'It will only become relevant if the two DNA profiles match. How soon can you get a result if it's submitted today?'

'The current working parameters for new submissions are between two and three weeks.'

'If at all possible, I need this result before fifteenth March.'

'I'll make sure it goes first thing today and will stress the urgency. The lab tends to work at its own pace, and it will depend entirely on their current workload.'

'Thanks, Tim. I'm counting on you.'

As he took the exhibit bag containing the cigarette butt from Andy, Tim said, 'I can't promise, but I'll see what I can do.'

84

2.50 p.m., 5 March 1991
Mansfield Registry Office, Mansfield, Nottinghamshire

Rachel's big day had arrived.

After weeks of planning, she was finally waiting outside the registry office. Danny was sitting in the back of the limousine next to her. He could see her scanning the area outside the registry office.

'I'm sorry, Rachel. It doesn't look like Joe's going to get here.'

'Five more minutes,' she said as she glanced at her watch. 'I know he received the letter I sent.'

'No problem. We can wait.'

Danny had been hopeful when the ceasefire was announced at the end of February that by some miracle Rachel's brother Joe would be able to get home from the war, in time for his sister's wedding.

When Rachel had phoned the night before to say that she hadn't heard from her brother, he could hear the emotion in her voice.

He glanced quickly at his watch, reached over and squeezed her hand. 'It's time, Rachel. Jack will be inside waiting for his beautiful bride.'

She nodded and opened the car door.

As Danny got out the other side of the sleek black car, he looked up just in time to see a taxi skidding to a halt in front of the limousine. Before the taxi had even stopped moving the back door was being opened and Danny saw Joe emerging, resplendent in his dress uniform.

Rachel ran to greet her brother. Joe said, 'I'm so sorry I couldn't get word to you. My train only arrived in Nottingham forty minutes ago. This taxi driver has broken every speed limit to get me here on time, bless him.'

'I'll let you off this time,' Rachel said, wiping away a tear. 'I'm so pleased you made it.'

Danny walked over, shook Joe's hand and grinned. 'You're looking very tanned. Have you been away?'

'Got back late last night. Let's just say it's been an interesting few months.'

'Pleased you're home safe and pleased you made it today. I'm going to let you and your sister catch your breath, while I take my place inside with Sue. Good to see you Joe.'

Then Danny turned to Rachel and said, 'You look absolutely stunning. Enjoy this special moment.'

85

3.00 p.m., 10 March 1991
Oadby, Leicestershire

Mark Bradbury was unshaven and looked as if he hadn't slept for a week. He held his head in both hands and said, 'That's what you told me over a week ago. This is taking the police too long to sort out.'

Mike Hermitage had driven straight to Bradbury's home after his client had intimated he was going to the police station to hand himself in for the murder of Randall Clements. Now he watched as Mark paced nervously around his lounge, listening as he explained the current situation.

He knew he would need to tell his client more than he wanted him to know at this time, just to stop him doing something rash.

Mark said, 'You don't understand, Mike. I can't leave my

brother to rot in prison for something he didn't do. I should go to the police, tell them everything I know and let them arrest me. At least that way my brother will get out of that awful place.'

The solicitor held both hands up, trying to placate his client as he chose his words carefully. 'If you want my honest opinion, Mark, I think that would be a huge mistake. There's every chance that all that would achieve is for you both to be locked up. You need to understand that the evidence the police have against your brother is way too strong. A verbal confession from you will not be enough to get him released. You need to be patient and let the police do their job.'

'I don't know. If I don't give myself up officially this could go badly wrong for me. I was only defending myself that night, but a jury might not believe that if I take too long to come forward. Every day I delay makes me look that bit more guilty.'

'You're going to have to trust me. The detectives dealing with your brother's case already know what's happening, so any unnecessary delays on this are down to them and not you. DCI Flint will be the person responsible for any criticism that comes later. He's the man running the investigation. It's his choice to delay using the information you've provided. No blame will ever be levelled at you for not coming forward earlier. I'll make it clear to the courts, and, more importantly, the public that you cooperated with the police from an early stage, and that it was Flint's decision to sit on that information and leave an innocent man in prison.'

Bradbury was thoughtful. 'Is that what you genuinely think, Mike?'

'Yes, it is. You need to be patient. I promise you it won't be for much longer. All the police are waiting for is the result of a single forensic test. If the result of that test is a positive one, things will move quickly. Please, be patient.'

Bradbury nodded slowly. 'Okay, Mike. I'll try. But if we haven't heard anything by this time next week, I will go to the police station.'

86

3.00 p.m., 13 March 1991
MCIU Offices, Mansfield, Nottinghamshire

T im Donnelly knocked once and walked into Danny Flint's office. 'I've come straight here, boss. I know you said you needed these results before the fifteenth of March.'

Danny held his breath and then saw the face of the scenes of crime supervisor break out into a wide grin. 'The two DNA profiles are a perfect match. The DNA from the cigarette you submitted is a perfect match for the DNA from the cigarette butt recovered from the murder scene.'

Danny walked to his door, looked in the main briefing room and could only see Fran Jefferies. 'Fran. Have you seen Andy today?'

'He's been in the office most of the day. He's literally just left.'

'Did he say where he was going?'

'The robbery squad at central, I think.'

'Get onto the control room, please. I want him back here sharpish.'

'Will do.'

Danny stepped back inside and said, 'This is great news, Tim.'

'Does it mean we'll be charging a second offender for the Clements murder?'

'No. If anything I'm hoping it means we'll lose the conviction we could have had.'

Tim looked puzzled. 'I don't understand.'

'I promise I'll explain everything, Tim. Just not now. It's very complicated, but I believe Craig Stevens is an innocent man and the last thing I want to be involved in is a miscarriage of justice.'

'But we have his DNA at the scene.'

Danny grinned. 'Contrary to popular belief around this place, DNA isn't infallible.'

There was a knock on the door and Fran Jefferies said, 'The control room have just phoned. They've contacted DS Wills, and he'll be back here in ten minutes.'

'Thanks, Fran.'

Danny turned to Tim and said, 'And thank you, Tim, for getting this done so promptly.'

'I'm happy to help,' the scenes of crime man said, with a puzzled expression on his face. 'Even though I've still got no idea what's going on.'

87

3.20 p.m., 13 March 1991
MCIU Offices, Mansfield, Nottinghamshire

'Something wrong, boss?' a slightly worried Andy asked as he walked into Danny's office.

Danny grinned. 'Just the opposite. I've had Tim Donnelly here with the results of the DNA test. The profile raised from the cigarette butt you saw Trevor Winstanley leave at the pub is identical to the profile found on the cigarette butt recovered from the Randall Clements murder scene.'

'That's incredible news. We can definitely put him at the scene of the attempted robbery of Mark Bradbury now.'

'Exactly.'

'And his attempted use of the stolen bank card ties him to the Simon Cathcart robbery. Do I fetch him in now, boss?'

Danny was thoughtful. 'Not straight away. I want you to

go back to the Meadows and establish what Winstanley's got planned for the rest of today and tomorrow. We need to pick our moment carefully.'

'Will do. So, a watching brief for now?'

Danny nodded. 'I need to work out the best way to use this information. I'm going to need Winstanley's full cooperation. The court will require nothing less than a full written statement of the events of that night to even consider releasing Craig Stevens. The problem is, with this election looming, I just don't see him wanting to talk to us.'

'Maybe we can use that to our advantage and talk to him tomorrow, on the very eve of the election?'

'What are you thinking, Andy?'

'The thought of not being elected that close to the vote is bound to put massive pressure on him. I think that could be the best time to get his full cooperation. We've amassed a lot of evidence about his involvement in at least two knifepoint robberies, where it's only by the grace of God that neither of the victims were seriously injured or killed.'

Danny said, 'But somebody has died as a result of those robberies, Randall Clements.'

'That's true. None of that's a good look for a prospective councillor on the eve of an election. He can protest all he likes that his reason for being there was to try and talk Clements out of committing a criminal act. The facts are that he was there, on at least two occasions, and both times the robberies still happened.'

'And you're thinking the public will see and hear all that and think of that old adage, "there's no smoke without fire"?' Danny was thoughtful. 'Okay. This is what I want you to do. Get hold of his full itinerary for tomorrow. Then we'll pick a time and location where we can get him on his own and talk to him.'

'I'm on it, boss.'

Left alone with his thoughts, Danny reflected on the decisions he had made, and the actions he had taken, since the information from Mark Bradbury first came to light. He had never bent the rules so much in his entire police career as he had on this one single inquiry.

He was struck by the paradox of the entire bizarre situation. He was bending those rules to prove a man was innocent, not guilty as charged.

88

4.00 p.m., 14 March 1991
52 Eugene Gardens, The Meadows, Nottingham

ndy knocked loudly on the door and waited. He turned to Danny and said, 'There's movement inside.'

The door was opened by Trevor Winstanley.

Danny said, 'Trevor Winstanley. I'm Detective Chief Inspector Flint and this is Detective Sergeant Andy Wills. We need to talk to you about the murder of Randall Clements.'

Winstanley folded his arms across his chest, blocking the door and said, 'Now's not a good time, chief inspector. I'm due at the community centre in an hour. It's the final hustings before tomorrow's elections.'

'Your choice. We can either talk here, or I'll arrest you on suspicion of robbery and take you to the police station.'

The tone in Danny's voice left no doubt about what would happen if Winstanley refused.

Still, the would-be councillor wasn't intimidated. He remained standing in the doorway and said, 'I don't see how you can arrest me for robbery, detective.'

'Believe me, I wouldn't be here if I didn't have the evidence. Do you want to continue this discussion here, or at the police station?'

Winstanley finally relented, sucked air through his teeth and said, 'You'd better come in, and I'll listen to what nonsense you've got to say.'

The two detectives followed him inside the flat. All three men remained standing in the lounge and Winstanley said, 'You said you want to talk to me about Randall's death?'

Danny said, 'I know you were with him on the night he died. I need you to tell me exactly what happened.'

'How do you expect me to believe a word you say? I've been nowhere near that man, especially not on the night he died. This is ridiculous.'

'I have an eyewitness who describes how two men tried to rob him at knifepoint. The description of one of the men fits Randall Clements and the other description fits you.'

Scoffing loudly, Winstanley said, 'There are hundreds of brothers who look like me, detective. Does your witness know me personally?'

'I also have forensic evidence linking you to the scene of the murder. Trust me when I tell you that evidence is irrefutable. Now, you either cooperate and start talking to me here, or I will continue this at the police station. That will mean you won't be present at the hustings this evening, or for the election tomorrow. Personally, I'd prefer to talk to you here because I need your cooperation. I know you are the only person who knows exactly what happened on the night Randall Clements died.'

Winstanley sat down, deep in thought. Eventually he held up both hands and said quietly, 'Sit down, please. Okay, I was there that night, but I wasn't there to rob anybody.' He paused before continuing, 'Randall Clements was a troubled man. He struggled with addiction and never had any opportunities in life. In my heart I believed that deep down he was a good man. I heard he was out and about in the town centre that night, intending to rob some poor soul, so I went to look for him. I wanted to offer him the hand of friendship and try to talk him out of doing something stupid.'

'Thank you. I appreciate you telling me that, Trevor. Where did you find him?'

'Before I talk to you, chief inspector, I want to get one thing straight. I'll tell you what happened, but I won't be making any statements, or getting involved in any court cases. The people on this estate trust me, and if they thought I was a police informant that trust would disappear overnight.'

Danny nodded. 'I understand. Where did you find Clements?'

There was real reluctance in Winstanley's voice as he said, 'He always hung around near the Shire Hall. I found him sitting in the churchyard next to St Mary's church.'

He paused and then continued. 'I spoke with him for about thirty minutes, and I thought I was getting somewhere, but then a man walked around the corner towards the churchyard. It was as if a switch had been turned on inside Clements. Ignoring everything we had spoken about, he was instantly on his feet and moved into position to rob the man.'

'What did you do?'

'What could I do? There was no way I could stop him physically. You must understand what Randall was like. He was a violent man with a vicious streak a yard wide. If I'd physically got in his way he would have been just as likely to stick his blade in me.'

Andy said, 'Why didn't you shout a warning to the man approaching?'

'There wasn't time. The man kept his eyes on me as he walked towards me. Randall approached him from behind.'

Danny said, 'If you knew Clements was going to rob the man, why did you stay?'

'I've asked myself that question so many times, detective. I think I wanted to make sure nobody got seriously hurt. Randall was prone to cruelty for no reason other than it made him feel good. That's the viciousness I mentioned. It was maybe naïve of me, but I thought if I stayed things wouldn't get too out of hand.'

'What happened?'

'Randall had a knife. He threatened the man with it, and demanded he hand over his wallet. I was shocked when the man refused.'

'What did Clements do then?'

Winstanley shook his head. 'I couldn't believe what I was seeing. He tried to stab that poor man.'

There was a pause and Danny remained silent, knowing there was more to come.

'Randall lunged at him with the knife and cut the man.'

'How?'

'I think the man tried to grab the knife and the blade sliced his hand. Randall went for him again, but this time the man defended himself. He stepped sideways and punched Randall once, knocking him down.'

'Then what?'

'Randall went down hard, and he stayed down. The man picked up the knife and ran.'

'Did you check on Clements?'

'No. I knew Randall would be plenty irate and I didn't want to incur his wrath, so I ran in the opposite direction.' There was a long pause before Winstanley added, 'And that still troubles me, detective. I consider myself as much to blame for Randall's death as that guy who was simply defending himself. I was too scared to check on him after he went down. I knew the other man was cut badly; there was a lot of blood on the ground. The whole thing was a mess.'

Danny said, 'I believe the only reason you were there that night was to try and prevent a robbery. I do need you to make a full witness statement about what happened though.'

'No way! I told you before we started that I wouldn't make a statement!' Winstanley paused, trying to compose himself before saying through gritted teeth, 'I have cooperated with you and told you what I know. I stand to be elected as councillor for this estate at tomorrow's election. I can't afford to be linked to a thief like Randall Clements.'

Danny made full eye contact with Winstanley and said firmly, 'Whether you can afford to be linked with him, or not, is immaterial to me. The fact is I can put you at the scene of two knifepoint robberies together with Randall Clements. Now the voters may believe your story that you were only there to try and talk Clements out of committing an offence on one occasion, but two occasions would be pushing it.'

Winstanley stood up and roared, 'What are you talking about, two robberies?'

Andy opened his briefcase and took out the photo of Winstanley trying to use the stolen bank card to buy food. He said, 'This is you, isn't it?'

Winstanley snatched the photograph, staring hard at the clear image before saying, 'Yeah, it's me. So what?'

'The "so what" is that you were attempting to use a bank card that was stolen during a knifepoint robbery near the Shire Hall. And guess what, the victim described how two men were involved, just like the robbery when Clements died.'

A defiant Winstanley said, 'You can't force me to make a statement about that night.'

Danny said, 'You're right, I can't. I also can't afford to turn a blind eye to serious offences of robbery, attempting to obtain goods by deception and handling stolen goods. But I do have a choice in the way I deal with those offences.'

'What choice?'

'I can arrest you for all those offences and take you to the police station right now, and no doubt charge you with some or all of them.' He paused for effect before saying, 'Or I can believe your version of events and that you were in no way involved in the robberies and were there simply to try and prevent the offences happening.'

'I don't understand.'

'The problems for you are the deception offence and the handling stolen goods offence. You attempted to use that credit card to obtain goods, knowing it to be stolen. There's no way I can ignore that or give you the benefit of the doubt. I should arrest you right now and take you to the police station, effectively ruining your political career before it's even got started.'

'Is there an alternative?'

'If you agree to make this statement, I could choose to deal with those offences by way of a formal police caution.'

'What does a caution entail? Will you need to arrest me tonight?'

'You don't have any previous criminal convictions and are of previously good character. The deception offence wasn't completed, so there's mitigation there. I could also delay administering the caution until after the election if you cooperate with me tonight. You would still have a criminal record, but it wouldn't be out in the public domain – and the votes would already be in by the time I see you at the police station.'

A deflated Winstanley sat down heavily and said, 'Okay, okay. Why is this statement so important to you, chief inspector? I thought you already had someone for Randall's murder?'

'You're right,' Danny said. 'A man is currently in Lincoln prison charged with Clements' murder. The problem is, I don't think he did it. Your statement would help to prove that, and hopefully prevent an innocent man spending the next twelve to eighteen years of his life in prison for something he didn't do.' Danny looked firmly at Winstanley. 'Use that to your advantage, Trevor. When people question why you cooperated with the police, you can tell them it was to keep an innocent man out of prison. Surely that would go down well with your voters.'

There was a long pause before Winstanley said, 'And if I make a statement about what happened that night, will you still need to talk to me about the stolen bank card? I was only trying to buy food to feed the homeless – and at the end of the day I didn't use it.'

Danny could now clearly see the politician in front of him, as Winstanley angled for a deal that would benefit him. 'As I said before, if you make the statement, I will make the decision that a caution is an appropriate way to deal with your offending. I take it you've no plans for doing anything similar in the future?'

Winstanley shook his head. 'Definitely not.'

'Will you make the statement?'

'I'll make the statement. How long will it take?'

Andy opened the briefcase again, took out several sheets of statement paper and said, 'Not long at all.'

89

11.30 a.m., 15 March 1991
Mansfield Police Station, Nottinghamshire

Solicitor Mike Hermitage and his client Mark Bradbury had arrived at Mansfield police station at nine o'clock that morning as arranged.

Danny had contacted the solicitor as soon as he had obtained the witness statement from Trevor Winstanley that corroborated Mark Bradbury's account of Randall Clements' death.

Upon his arrival at the police station Danny had arrested Bradbury for manslaughter. After being booked into the custody area, Bradbury and his solicitor had been taken directly into an interview room.

Danny and Rob Buxton had undertaken the interview. There had been no surprises, and Mark Bradbury had repeated what he had already told the police through his solicitor: that he had been attacked at knifepoint and that there were two men present. He had suffered a stab wound to his hand and was forced to defend himself when the knifeman had lunged at him again. That self-defence had consisted of a single punch that had knocked the attacker with the knife to the ground. He described how his attacker had dropped the knife as he fell.

Bradbury told the detectives how he ran away, as soon as he had the opportunity, and had not followed up the initial punch with any further assaults. He also gave an account of picking up his attacker's knife before he ran, subsequently dropping the blade down a drain.

He showed the detectives the vivid red scar on the palm of his hand, a scar caused by the knife wielded by his attacker.

At the conclusion of the interview, Bradbury had been placed in a cell, and Danny spoke to Mike Hermitage. 'Your client will be charged with manslaughter. He's admitted punching Clements and how it was that punch which knocked him down. The post-mortem evidence shows that Clements died because of his head striking a kerb edge as he fell. It will be for a jury to decide the culpability of your client. He has a good argument of self-defence, but at the end of the day a man died. If the blood sample he has provided for a DNA profile is a match for the profile obtained at the murder scene it will only help his case.'

Mike Hermitage said, 'We both know that Randall Clements died because of his own criminal enterprise. If he hadn't set out with a knife to rob an innocent passerby that night, he'd still be alive today.'

Danny sighed and said, 'You won't get an argument from

me, Mike, but the law has to be seen to take its course, and your client will be charged and put before the court.'

'Will you oppose a bail application?'

'We won't be bailing him from the police station, but we won't oppose any bail application at his first court hearing. The court will no doubt want to put some stringent conditions on his bail, but I don't think there's any chance of him being remanded in custody.'

'I truly hope not, chief inspector.'

90

11.00 a.m., 29 March 1991
Nottingham Crown Court, Nottingham

Craig Stevens didn't really understand what was happening. He had been rushed out of his cell that morning, loaded into the prison van with all his property and transported to the Crown Court at Nottingham.

Still in a mild state of shock, he was now standing in the dock at the Crown Court, facing a judge. There was no jury inside the court, and he struggled to hear his barrister who was talking in hushed tones to the judge.

Suddenly, the judge called out his name. 'Craig Stevens. Will you stand, please?' Craig immediately stood up and the judge addressed him directly. 'Do you fully understand what's happening this morning, Mr Stevens?'

Craig shook his head. 'Not really, Your Honour.'

'In that case, let me enlighten you. Fresh evidence has come to light that throws considerable doubts on one of the charges that has been made against you. In respect of the murder charge, the Crown now intends to offer no evidence at all against you.'

'What does that mean, Your Honour?'

'What it means, Mr Stevens, is that because of the amount of time you have already spent in custody on remand I won't be imposing an additional custodial sentence for the assault on your wife. You are now free to leave this court. Step down from the dock and speak with your barrister, Mr Davidson. He will endeavour to explain to you exactly what's going to happen next. Thank you.'

The prison officer standing next to Craig in the dock immediately unbolted the dock door and whispered, 'Go on then, scarper.'

Craig stepped out of the dock smartly and was met by his barrister who said, 'Follow me, Mr Stevens. Let's go somewhere we can talk.'

As he followed his barrister out of the courtroom, Craig said, 'Is that it then, can I go home now?'

'We need to have a quick chat first, and you'll need to get your property from the holding cells here at court. Once you've done that, you can go home. You are a free man, Mr Stevens.'

91

3.00 p.m., 29 March 1991
20 Western Avenue, Mansfield, Nottinghamshire

C raig Stevens only had enough money to catch the bus from Nottingham back to Mansfield. The bus had driven into the bus station on the edge of town and Craig had been forced to walk the last mile home, in the pouring rain.

He was soaking wet by the time he arrived back at his house on Western Avenue. His wet hands sticking to the cheap polyester material of his suit, he fumbled in his trouser pocket for his front door key. After a struggle, he extricated the key and slipped it into the Yale lock. As the front door opened, he shouted, 'Tricia!'

His shout echoed strangely around the house. There was no reply, so he shouted again and flicked the light switch on in the hallway.

There was still no reply, and the light didn't come on.

Glancing up, he could see there was no bulb in the light fitting and no lamp shade.

As he walked along the hallway, his heavy shoes clumped on bare floorboards and he muttered under his breath, 'What the fuck?'

He pushed open the door that led into the lounge and was shocked to see the room was empty. Every piece of furniture had been removed, all the carpet taken up, the light fittings and curtains removed. The room had been totally cleared out.

In a state of growing alarm, and with his anger rising steadily, he walked slowly around the house. Every room he checked was a repeat vision of the lounge. The house had been stripped of all furniture, fixtures and fittings.

There wasn't a chair to sit on, a bed to sleep in, a table to eat off, or a TV to watch.

He leaned against the wall and roared, 'You conniving fucking bitch!'

Leaving the front door open behind him, he stomped back outside into the rain and walked down his neighbour's drive and banged on the front door.

His neighbour was a big man and wasn't easily intimidated. He looked down at Craig and said, 'What's all the noise about, Stevens?'

'Where's my fucking wife?'

The neighbour stepped down from his front step, shoved Stevens hard in the chest, forcing him away from his front door, and said, 'Watch your mouth, Stevens. My kids are inside.'

Not wanting a confrontation, Craig held both hands up and said, 'Sorry, sorry. Have you seen Tricia?'

'Tricia left a couple of weeks ago. A lorry came and was loaded up, haven't seen her since. We thought you'd moved out.'

'Did she say anything to your wife? Do you know where she's gone?'

'Haven't got a clue. She never spoke to my wife. Now, are we done? I'm getting wet through standing here talking to you. Go home.'

Craig let out a maniacal laugh. 'Go home! That's a fucking joke! There's fuck all inside the house. She's taken everything and gone.'

The neighbour knew full well that Stevens was a drunk who regularly abused his wife. In fact, he'd called the police on numerous occasions, after hearing violent domestic disputes from next door.

He smiled and thought, *Good for her.*

He took a step closer to Stevens and said, 'I've warned you once about your mouth, Stevens. Go home now, before I throw you off my property.'

Muttering obscenities under his breath, Craig turned and stomped back round to his empty house. He walked inside and slammed the door behind him.

There was one thing he hadn't checked. He walked into the kitchen and saw the wall-mounted telephone was still in place. He picked up the receiver and for the first time since he had got off the bus, he had something to smile about. There was still a dialling tone. The telephone hadn't been cut off.

He reached inside his jacket and pulled out his saturated wallet. Inside was a damp business card with his solicitor's contact details. He dialled the number and waited.

He said, 'Can I make an appointment to see Martin

Anderson tomorrow, please. It is quite urgent.' There was a pause and then he said, 'Yes, of course. My name's Craig Stevens. I want to talk to him about suing the police for unlawful imprisonment. He dealt with my case at court.' Another pause, then Craig said, 'Tomorrow at eleven o'clock. Thank you.'

He replaced the phone and thought who else he could call who might be able to lend him a few quid, just until he got back on his feet.

As he dialled, his thoughts turned to his absent wife.

God help her if I ever find out where she's gone.

92

3.30 p.m., 31 March 1991
MCIU Offices, Mansfield, Nottinghamshire

Detective Chief Superintendent Slater had a face like thunder when he walked into the MCIU offices. He saw Danny talking to Rob Buxton and said, 'Chief inspector, we need to talk in your office – now.'

Danny followed him inside, closed the door and sat down behind his desk. Slater remained standing, pacing up and down.

At last, he stopped pacing and snarled, 'I can't believe what you've done, Danny. How you've bent every rule going, just to prove some cock-and-bull theory.'

Danny remained calm and said, 'With respect, sir. It wasn't some cock-and-bull theory. It was the truth. Craig Stevens wasn't responsible for the death of Randall Clements, Mark Bradbury was.'

'You do realise that Craig Stevens has already instructed his legal team to sue the force for wrongful arrest and imprisonment. He stands to make a fortune and the chief is far from happy about the prospect of paying him out. The budget is already stretched without having to find thousands of pounds in litigation costs. Exactly when did you know that Stevens was innocent? How long did you keep him in prison, knowing he was an innocent man?'

Danny said, 'If you take a moment and sit down, sir, I can explain.'

He waited for Mark Slater to sit down and then said, 'I was never totally sure, until the day before we detained Mark Bradbury. Without the witness statement from Trevor Winstanley to corroborate what Bradbury had told his solicitor, it was always a case of one man's word against the strong DNA evidence we already had against Stevens.'

Having sat down Slater had calmed down a little; his voice was measured as he said, 'Just out of curiosity, I take it you've now obtained a DNA sample from Mark Bradbury?'

'Yes, we have, and as soon as we knew it was a match for the blood found at the scene, and to Craig Stevens, arrangements were made with the prison authorities to get Stevens in front of the first available court. We ensured Craig Stevens was released from custody at the earliest opportunity. There was an argument from one lawyer that Stevens should remain in custody until after Bradbury's trial, but it was decided that was the wrong course of action. There was already enough doubt for the charge of murder to be dropped, so he should be released immediately. The bottom line is this: I'm satisfied it was Mark Bradbury's blood found at the murder scene, and not Craig Stevens'.'

'Do you think the court will convict Mark Bradbury of manslaughter?'

'I never try and second-guess a jury's decision, but I think there's a very real chance that Bradbury will be acquitted. He had already been stabbed by Clements as he tried to rob him, and he reacted purely in self-defence. He was obviously in genuine fear for his life when he punched Clements.'

'So, you think he'll get off?'

'Winstanley's evidence will be crucial, but if he repeats what he's already said in his witness statement I'd be amazed if any jury would convict Bradbury.'

'Which will mean that, although we know who killed Clements, there'll be no conviction.'

'I think so.'

'And after the car thieves lead turned out to be another dead end, you're no closer to finding the killer of Lionel Wickes. Not your best few weeks' work, Danny.'

Danny could feel his anger rising and fought hard to control it. 'If I've stopped an innocent man from spending years in prison for something he didn't do, I would say that's definitely some of my best work, sir.' He took a long, steadying breath before continuing. 'And everyone on the MCIU is fully committed to bringing the killer, or killers, of Lionel Wickes to justice. That's not going to change just because we've had a setback.'

Before walking out, Slater stood up and growled, 'Keep me informed of any developments.'

Danny leaned back in his chair and muttered to himself, 'Well, Danny boy, that went well.'

93

10.00 a.m., 30 June 1991
Nottingham Crown Court, Nottingham

M ark Bradbury watched nervously from the dock as the twelve members of the jury filed back into the packed courtroom.

His defence team had constantly tried to reassure him that the trial was going well, that they fully expected the jury to be sympathetic to his plea of self-defence.

He could barely bring himself to look through the toughened Perspex that surrounded the dock, as he heard the judge ask the jury if they had reached a verdict.

The jury foreman, a middle-aged man wearing a dark suit and tie, stood and addressed the judge directly. 'We have, Your Honour.'

The clerk to the court then stood and read out the

manslaughter charge ending with the phrase, 'And how do you find the defendant?'

Mark held his breath.

After a long pause he heard the man say, 'Not guilty.'

He felt his eyes water with relief. He realised this nightmare was almost over.

He blinked hard as he heard the judge order him to stand before saying, 'Mark Bradbury. This court has found you not guilty on the charge of manslaughter, and you are free to go. You may leave the dock.'

On shaky legs, he stepped out of the dock and shook hands with his solicitor. 'Thank you so much, Mike.'

Mike Hermitage glanced towards the two detectives sitting in the public gallery and said, 'It's DCI Flint and DS Wills you should be thanking. If they hadn't persevered and found the second man at the robbery scene, this could all have turned out very differently. It was Councillor Winstanley's evidence that you had only acted in self-defence that finally swayed the jury.'

Mark held up his hand in acknowledgement towards the two detectives, who were looking down from the gallery. He mouthed a silent thank you.

Mike Hermitage said, 'And now you can get on with the rest of your life. Are you still planning that career change?'

'I don't know if that's going to be possible after all the publicity that's surrounded this trial. My application is still with the security service. Time will tell.'

'Well, you're free to go. What have you got planned for the rest of the day? A quiet celebration somewhere, perhaps?'

'Firstly, I need to go and let someone know that I'm okay.

I'll speak with you later, Mike. Thanks again for all your help.'

The two men shook hands for a final time and Mark walked out of the courtroom. He stood on the front steps of the Crown Court building and took a deep breath of cool air.

The nightmare was truly over.

He smiled and stepped down to the kerb edge, where he hailed a passing taxi.

Climbing in, he said, 'Briar Lodge Nursing Home at West Bridgford, please.'

As the taxi driver pulled away from the kerb, he said, 'Visiting someone special?'

'Very special,' Mark said as he leaned back in the car seat. 'My mother.'

94

10.00 a.m., 14 July 1991
The Sir John Cockle public house, Mansfield,
Nottinghamshire

It had been two weeks since Mark Bradbury had walked free from court. He had contacted Craig Stevens and arranged to meet him at the Sir John Cockle public house in Mansfield.

He was keen to try and get to know his brother and had promised their mother that the next time he visited her, he would bring his brother along as well. When Mark had given her the news that he had finally tracked down her other son, she had been overjoyed and had expressed her wish to see them both.

Mark was keen to find out more of what Craig's childhood had been like.

As he parked in the pub car park, he cursed the heavy

traffic. By the time he walked inside the pub, he was more than forty minutes late. He spotted Craig sitting alone in a booth and also noticed several empty pint glasses already on the table in front of him.

As Mark approached, Craig looked up at him and slurred, 'You finally made it then, brother dear.'

'Yeah. Sorry I'm late; the traffic on the motorway was a nightmare. Can I get you another drink?'

'Pint of Stella would be good. You've got some catching up to do. I've been here over an hour already.'

Mark could see and hear that Craig was already quite drunk, but he walked to the bar and ordered two pints.

As the brothers sipped their beers, they talked about their respective childhoods. As Mark described in detail how wonderful his adoptive parents had been and how they had given him the best possible start in life, he noticed a definite change in his brother's demeanour.

A truculent Craig started to pick fault with everything Mark said.

To get off the subject and change the mood a little, Mark decided to talk about something they could both relate to. 'I know what I was doing in Nottingham on that fateful night, but why were you in the city?'

'No special reason. I just prefer the pubs down there. Mansfield's a dump and not many of the pub landlords like me.'

Mark could tell that Craig was being deliberately obstructive now; he was barely talking. Mark persevered and said, 'The cuts on our hands were always crucial evidence for the police. Mine was cut by Randall Clements' knife, but how on earth did you cut your hand so badly that the cops thought it was a knife wound?'

'If you must know,' Craig slurred, 'I cut my hand climbing over my own garden gates. That stupid bitch I was married to deliberately lied to the cops to drop me even deeper in the shit. God help her if I ever get my hands on her.'

Mark flinched at the venom in his brother's voice. 'Where's she gone?'

'She's left me. When I got home from prison, I found her gone and everything taken out of the house. Not one stick of furniture left, the bitch.'

'Do you know where she went?'

Craig slowly shook his head. 'Nah. But if I had to guess, I'd say she's fucked off back to Ireland.' He paused before raising his voice and saying loudly, 'I swear if I ever set eyes on that whore again, I'll stick a knife straight through her fucking windpipe.'

Mark was really shocked now by his brother's drunken outburst and the level of rage and spite in his voice.

He was about to say something to try and calm his brother down, when Craig blurted out, 'You weren't the only one in a fight that night.'

Mark said, 'What fight? What are you talking about?'

'That night. I got pissed and somehow ended up in that shithole, the Meadows estate. It's dangerous down there and I needed to get away and get back to Mansfield, so I decided to nick a car.'

'Is that why you were fighting?'

'If you'd shut your face for two fucking seconds, I'll tell you why.'

He took another slug of the strong lager, belched and said, 'I must have made too much noise, because suddenly I'm confronted by this old fucker who must have owned the car. Anyway, we ended up scrapping on the street.' Warming to his theme, Craig took another drink before continuing. 'The scrap was getting noisy, the old man was shouting at me, I could see lights coming on in other houses, so I whacked him.'

'What do you mean you whacked him? What with?'

'I was holding a scaffold pipe that I'd been using to nick the car, so I cracked him over the head with that.'

'Jesus Christ, Craig. Why did you hit an old man with a metal bar?'

'Because he was besting me. Yeah, he was an old fucker, but he must have been a boxer or something when he was younger. He punched me in the face about half a dozen times and I'm telling you, brother dear, I was seeing stars. I had no choice; he was giving me a proper beating.'

Mark fought to keep his voice level as he asked, 'What happened after you hit him?'

'I dropped the bar and legged it. I nicked another car a few streets away and drove back to Mansfield before the place was flooded with cops.'

Disgusted at his brother's blasé attitude to violence and his sheer lack of compassion or respect for other people and their property, Mark came to the shocking realisation that he had nothing in common, apart from DNA, with the man sitting in front of him.

Deciding he wanted nothing more to do with his brother, he stood up to leave.

As he stood, the disgust must have been clear on his face, because Craig pointed an accusing finger at him and snarled, 'Don't you dare look at me like that. I've had to fight for everything all my fucking life. I wasn't adopted into the same privileged life you were, brother dear. I've been dirt poor and had to struggle all my fucking life.'

Realising that this was the truth, Mark tried one more time. 'I just don't understand why you didn't tell the police about trying to steal the car. Surely getting done for car theft has to be better than being in the frame for murder?'

'You don't get it, do you? The cops weren't interested in anything I had to say. They had what they thought was my DNA at a murder scene. Every one of them was convinced I'd done it. All I could do was keep denying it. I wasn't about to drop myself even deeper in the shit by telling them I'd been involved in a scrap somewhere else, as I tried to nick a motor. How thick are you? You don't live in the real world, mate.'

Craig finished the pint in front of him and said, 'Anyway, everything's turned out all right, hasn't it? My solicitor says I stand to get a six-figure sum in compensation from the cops, just for spending a few weeks in the nick. I can cope with that.' He slammed the empty glass down. 'It's about time I had some good luck for a change.'

Mark was about to walk out, but he stopped, turned and said, 'What happened to the old man you hit?'

'Fuck knows,' Craig snarled. 'I didn't care then and I don't care now. Fuck him and fuck you, with all your questions and your judgemental looks. If you're leaving, fuck off and don't let the door hit you on the arse on the way out.'

Abandoning any notion of introducing his long-lost brother to their mother, Mark didn't say another word. He simply turned and walked out of the pub.

95

Mark Bradbury had taken a long time to calm down after his meeting with Craig Stevens. It had been nothing short of a disaster. He now realised he had nothing in common with his brother, but the more he thought about what his brother had told him at the pub, the more concerned he became.

There had been something about the circumstances Craig had described that sounded familiar. The attempted theft of the car on the Meadows estate and how he had beaten an old man with a metal bar – it all sounded an alarm bell deep within his brain.

A grim realisation dawned. He walked slowly upstairs and retrieved the cardboard box full of newspaper clippings he had amassed, when he first researched the murder of Randall Clements.

He walked back into the dining room and tipped the contents of the box onto the table. He quickly picked up various clippings and scanned them, before moving on to the next. Finally, he found the article he had been searching for.

It was an *Evening Post* report about the murder of a man called Lionel Wickes on the Meadows estate. The report stated that the old man had disturbed a car thief trying to steal his car and had confronted him. That confrontation had cost the man his life. He had died at the scene from a catastrophic head injury and the police had subsequently launched a murder inquiry.

Mark checked the date of the horrendous crime, which proved his suspicions correct. It was now clear to him that it was his brother, Craig, who had been responsible for the death of Lionel Wickes.

After placing all the other reports back in the cardboard box, Mark remained staring at that single *Evening Post* article.

He read the content of the report repeatedly, as if trying to convince himself one last time that he was mistaken.

Eventually, he placed the article in the box with the others and closed the lid.

It was now entirely clear in his own mind what needed to be done. He would see that course of action through in the morning.

96

10.00 a.m., 15 July 1991
MCIU Offices, Mansfield, Nottinghamshire

Danny answered the telephone in his office on the second ring and said, 'DCI Flint. Can I help you?'

'Sir, it's Sergeant McAllister on the front desk. There's a Mark Bradbury in reception, says he needs to speak with you urgently.'

'Okay. Give him a seat in one of the interview rooms, I'll be down shortly. Did he say what it was about?'

'Only that it concerned his brother.'

Danny replaced the phone, puffed out his cheeks and sat back, deep in thought. He was aware that Craig Stevens had filed a lawsuit against both the force and him personally, which meant that if Mark Bradbury wanted to discuss something about his brother that could put him in a very awkward position.

He slipped his jacket on, stepped into the main briefing room and spotted Rob Buxton. 'Are you busy, Rob?'

'Nothing that won't keep for a few minutes. What's the problem?'

'Mark Bradbury's at the front desk, says he wants to talk to me about his brother, Craig.'

'That could be awkward.'

'My thoughts exactly, but I can't just ignore him.'

'No, you can't. Come on, we'll both talk to him. That way I'll be present, can witness any conversation and back you up later, if needs be.'

'Thanks.' Danny nodded. 'Let's hear what he's got to say.'

Five minutes later and the two detectives were sitting opposite Mark Bradbury in the small interview room.

It was Bradbury who spoke first. 'I never had the chance to thank you and your team for everything you did before the trial, and for persuading Councillor Winstanley to give evidence. My solicitor told me without that things could have turned out very differently for me, so thank you.'

'No thanks necessary,' Danny said. 'Why are you here, Mark?'

'I met in a local pub with my brother yesterday. He was already quite drunk when I got there. He spoke to me about something that happened the same night Randall Clements attacked me.'

'Go on.'

'He told me how he'd tried to steal a car from the Meadows estate that night and had ended up in a fight with the old man who owned the car.'

As Mark Bradbury paused, Danny said, 'Did your brother say anything else about that fight?'

Mark nodded but remained silent.

Danny coaxed him, saying, 'I know it's difficult to talk to us about your brother, but this is important. A man died on the Meadows estate that night.'

There were tears in Mark's eyes as he blurted out, 'And I think it was my brother who killed him. He told me he hit the man on the head with a metal bar, because the old man was beating him with his fists. Is that even possible?'

Rob said, 'That's possible. Lionel Wickes, the man who died, had been an accomplished boxer in his youth.'

Mark sighed as he said, 'He told me everything, but I don't know how you're going to prove any of it. Even so, I needed to come and tell you what he told me.'

Danny said, 'Are you prepared to make a written statement?'

'If you think there's any truth in what he told me, then yes, I am. If he did that, it was wrong, more than wrong, and he shouldn't get away with it.'

'Wait here. We'll be back shortly.'

The two detectives stepped out of the room and Danny said, 'Bloody hell. I wasn't expecting that. Can you get his account documented? I've a couple of phone calls to make.'

Rob said, 'The aerosol blood samples?'

'Exactly. It might be one brother's word against the other, but we have a DNA profile of the possible offender, and we already have Craig Stevens' DNA profile. I know exactly how we're going to prove this one. Get Bradbury's statement before he changes his mind. He's already struggling to come to terms with informing on his brother.'

97

6.00 a.m., 19 July 1991
20 Western Avenue, Mansfield, Nottinghamshire

I t had taken three days for the Forensic Science Service to carry out a comparison of the DNA profile found in the aerosol blood samples recovered from Lionel Wickes' car and the DNA profile of Craig Stevens.

As soon as they had provided the report that the two samples were identical, Danny had completed the operational order to arrest Craig Stevens for the murder of Lionel Wickes.

Danny and Rob were now waiting in a CID car parked five doors down from Stevens' home address. Detectives had watched the house throughout the previous night and had confirmed that Stevens was at home and alone in the house.

Danny allowed himself a grim smile as he watched the

black-clad Special Operations Unit officers stealthily surround the house on Western Avenue.

As soon as the officers were all in position, the SOU supervisor, Sergeant Turner, gave the order for the front door to be breached. Danny watched as officers smashed the front door down and streamed into the house, hearing their shouts as they cleared each room.

His radio crackled into life, and he heard Turner's voice. 'Sergeant Turner to DCI Flint. Suspect has been detained and the house is now clear. You can come forward now, boss.'

Danny and Rob walked into the house, passing the front door that was now hanging by one hinge and finding Craig Stevens in handcuffs, sitting on the floor of the lounge.

Danny said, 'Craig Stevens. I'm arresting you for the murder of Lionel Wickes.'

Stevens immediately flew into a wild rage and screamed, 'Fuck off, Flint! This is another fit-up. You fuckers will try anything, so you don't have to pay me out. My lawyers are going to crucify you for this, you corrupt fucker!'

Danny turned to Rob and said, 'Get him out of here.'

As Rob led the handcuffed Stevens from the house, Danny could hear the detained man screaming yet more abuse and threats at the top of his voice.

Turner said, 'Not a big fan of yours, is he, sir?'

'You could say that. How long will a search take?'

'Not long at all. There's nothing here. The house is devoid of furniture. He was kipping in a sleeping bag, on a camp bed upstairs. There're a few tins of beans, empty beer cans, a couple of Pot Noodles, one saucepan and a bin bag full of damp clothes. That's it.'

Danny nodded as he walked through the house. 'Okay. Good job this morning. I'll see you back at the nick.'

Danny returned to the CID car, where Rob was waiting with Stevens on the backseat. The detained man had finally fallen quiet; he said nothing as Danny got in and started the car.

98

10.00 a.m., 19 July 1991
Mansfield Police Station, Nottinghamshire

Craig Stevens had been in a long consultation with his solicitor, and as Danny and Rob now walked into the interview room, both detectives suspected that Stevens would either make no comment to all questions, or that Martin Anderson would hand them a prepared statement.

Danny settled himself and said, 'You were arrested by me earlier today on suspicion of the murder of Lionel Wickes. Do you have anything to say about that allegation?'

All thoughts of a 'no comment' interview were banished as Stevens snarled, 'Fuck off, Flint. Everyone knows this is a fit-up. You've got nothing except my so-called brother's word. You can't prove a thing. This is just some sad attempt to get out of paying me the compensation I deserve for being locked up for something else I didn't do.'

In a level voice, Danny replied, 'I want to go through the evidence we have with you, so you're left in no doubt that this isn't some spurious accusation we've made up.'

With heavy sarcasm, Stevens said, 'I'm all ears.'

'Your brother, Mark Bradbury, has made a written statement to the police outlining a conversation he had with you in the Sir John Cockle pub five days ago. Do you recall that conversation?'

'Not really. I'd had a lot to drink. I was probably talking bollocks like I usually do when I've had a few too many.'

'Let me refresh your memory. Mark states that you gave an account of how you had tried to steal a car on the Meadows estate and that you had been confronted by the owner and became involved in a fight with him. Do you remember saying that?'

'No.'

'Mark also stated that during that fight the man, whose car you were trying to steal, was beating you.'

'That's bollocks. As if I'd let an old man beat me.'

'I never said the car owner was an old man.'

A heavy silence filled the room. Danny waited.

Eventually Stevens spluttered, 'I don't remember any of that conversation.'

'Mark stated that during that conversation you described hitting the man with a piece of scaffold pole around the head.'

'That's a lie. It was the old man who used the scaffold pipe on me. He cracked me across my back with it.'

'Did he have it with him when he came out of the house?'

'Yeah. He must have heard me around his car and came out to have a go.'

'Did the owner do anything else to you?'

'He smacked me in the mouth a few times. I hadn't done anything, and he was attacking me.'

'You said you were around his car. So, were you trying to steal it? Mark has informed us that you told him you needed the car to get back to Mansfield.'

'He's a fucking grass. I was just standing by the car, not stealing it, when that bloke came out and attacked me. First with the metal bar and then with his fists.'

'Where did he punch you?'

'In the face.'

'Where?'

'He split my mouth open. He kept punching me in the mouth. I could taste the blood.'

'Was he beating you?'

'Don't be daft.'

'Did you take the scaffold pole off him?'

Craig paused and then said, 'Only to stop him hitting me.'

'Did you then use it?'

There was an even longer pause and Martin Anderson looked at his client and shook his head.

Ignoring his solicitor, Stevens said, 'I tapped him once, so I could get away.'

'Tapped him?'

'Yeah. It was a gentle tap on the side of the head. Just enough to stop him having a go.'

'Then what did you do?'

'I ran away, before other people came out of their houses.'

'You didn't stop to check if the old man was all right?'

'I knew he'd be all right. It was only a gentle tap.'

Danny paused and then said, 'I know that the scaffold pole used to attack Lionel Wickes was taken from a skip three streets away from his house. I believe you took it from that skip, so you could use it to break the ignition mounting on a car and steal it. And that's what you were doing when Lionel Wickes tried to stop you.'

'Fuck off, Flint. I'm not falling for that one. How can you know where the scaffold pole came from?'

'Lionel Wickes never did have that scaffold pole in his possession, did he?'

'No comment.'

'But he was battering you with his fists, wasn't he, and you couldn't stand the thought of an old man giving you a good hiding, could you?'

'As if.'

'And that's why you hit him over the head with the scaffold pole, isn't it?'

'Prove it.'

'And it wasn't a gentle tap, was it? You hit him hard because you intended to kill him, didn't you? Because he had made you angry.'

'Fuck off.'

Danny turned to Rob and said, 'Have you any questions?'

'A couple.'

Rob looked at Stevens and said, 'How did you get back to Mansfield that night?'

'I found another car a couple of streets away.'

'Found or stole?'

'Okay. I'll admit that. I did take another car that night, but I didn't try and steal the old man's car. I was panicking after the fight and needed to get out of the estate. It's dangerous down there.'

'Where did you dump that car?'

'At King's Mill Reservoir car park.'

'Okay. I've nothing else,' Rob said.

'I've no further questions at this time,' Danny added. 'Is there anything you want to say?'

Stevens snarled, 'Nobody's going to be fooled by this, Flint. My solicitor knows you're trying to fit me up. I didn't kill anybody that night and, apart from my grass of a brother, you've got fuck all.'

2.00 p.m., 19 July 1991
Police Headquarters, Nottinghamshire

Danny sat in Mark Slater's office, updating him on both the arrest of Craig Stevens, and the subsequent murder charge.

'Let me get this straight,' Slater said. 'You've charged Stevens with the Lionel Wickes murder?'

Danny nodded. 'We have a DNA match that irrefutably links Craig Stevens to that murder. Mark Bradbury has made a statement against his brother in which he details a conversation between the two men, during which Stevens confessed to killing Lionel Wickes.'

'Tell me about the DNA evidence you have.'

'Earlier in the inquiry we carried out a luminol procedure on the Ford Fiesta owned by Wickes. That procedure revealed a lot of aerosol blood spray on the front wing of the car. Aerosol blood spray can occur when somebody has a cut mouth and is exhaling heavily. And in this case, there was enough blood for the Forensic Science Service to extract a full DNA profile.' He paused and then said, 'After Bradbury's statement, I ordered the DNA profile of Craig Stevens to be compared against the DNA profile of the blood recovered from the Ford Fiesta. It was a perfect match.'

'Excellent work.'

'We knew from the post-mortem that there was a possibility that Lionel Wickes had punched his attacker several times, as there was what could have been bruising to his knuckles.'

'Did Stevens say anything when he was interviewed?'

'Much more than he probably should have. He came up with some bullshit story about Wickes attacking him with the scaffold pole first. We already had a witness statement from the owner of the scaffolding firm, who had identified the murder weapon as an offcut of a scaffold pole that his firm had dumped in a skip, two or three streets away from the murder scene. As soon as he was caught out in that lie, instead of shutting down, he carried on talking. Much to the obvious frustration of his solicitor. Stevens admitted that Wickes had punched him in the mouth several times and that his mouth had been cut.'

Slater said, 'Which would explain the aerosol blood spray on the outside of the car. Did he admit hitting Wickes?'

'Bizarrely, yes he did. He said he tapped him once, just to stop him. Again, we know from the post-mortem exactly how much force had been used to strike the old man. The pathologist's report states that the force used was easily enough to kill, and that the offender would have known how hard he'd hit the man.'

Slater looked thoughtful. 'He won't be getting a walk-out this time.'

'No chance.'

'And I suppose that will be the end of the lawsuit?'

'That remains to be seen. Just because he's guilty as charged for this murder, he wasn't guilty of the Randall Clements murder, so technically he still has a case for wrongful imprisonment.'

'Let's just wait and see on that, shall we? I do have other news that concerns you and the MCIU, regarding staff changes.'

Danny didn't like the sound of the finality of Slater's comment, but he said neutrally, 'Changes?'

'A couple of promotions. With immediate effect, Tina Cartwright is being promoted to chief inspector and will be starting at Central Division next week.'

'In uniform?'

'Yes. I take it you were aware that she's on the accelerated promotion scheme?'

'I did know that, yes.'

'Well, this is the next step up for her. The chief constable notified her of the promotion yesterday.'

'Tina was always destined for the very top, but I'll be sorry to see her leave the MCIU,' Danny said. 'Any chance of promoting DS Wills to her position?' he asked. 'He was very close to getting the role before Tina was promoted.'

'Unfortunately not. DS Wills is also being promoted to detective inspector, but will be transferring to Special Branch, with effect from next week. He's due to see the chief later today.'

'Bloody hell, sir,' Danny exclaimed. 'I've already got DS Cooper on maternity leave, with DC Bailey acting sergeant.

It's going to leave the MCIU a bit stretched, supervisor-wise.'

'No, it won't, Danny. A replacement has already been selected to take up the vacancy of detective inspector.'

'So, I get no say in who's working on the department I have to manage?'

Slater ignored him and continued, 'I understood from the chief constable that DS Sara Lacey had already spent time working on the MCIU, and that you would approve her promotion. Is that not the case?'

Danny remembered Sara Lacey from the Joanna Preston murder inquiry. 'Sara's an extremely capable detective and supervisor,' he said, a little chastened. 'I would indeed be happy to welcome her back to the MCIU.'

With a note of gentle sarcasm in his voice, Slater said, 'I'm glad she meets your approval, chief inspector.' He paused, then added, 'The chief has also suggested that DC Jagvir Singh be promoted in post to DS, to replace DS Wills. He excelled at the last round of promotion boards and is long overdue for promotion. What are your thoughts on him being promoted in post?'

'That would be a good move for Jag, and for the MCIU. He's a great detective and very well respected on the unit. I think he could take that next step up easily.'

'That's all sorted then. I take it DS Cooper intends to come back to work full time after her maternity leave?'

'Rachel's made it clear that's her intention, sir.'

'Excellent. We both know that personnel are always changing. It's the nature of our job, Danny. People come and go.' Slater leaned forward, his elbows on the desk before him. 'Let me know when a trial date has been fixed for Craig Stevens. There's bound to be a lot of media interest in this case, purely because of his recent release from prison and the outstanding lawsuit against the force. I don't want the press speculating that this is in any way a witch hunt against this man. Any problems with the media, you direct them straight to me. Understood?'

'Understood, sir. I'm always pleased to pass the media over to you.'

EPILOGUE

3.00 p.m., 19 July 1991
Prison van, en route to HMP Lincoln, Greetwell Road,
Lincoln

Feeling cramped for space, Craig Stevens was hunched over in the back of the prison van.

He still couldn't quite believe that Flint had charged him with the murder of Lionel Wickes.

He was monumentally pissed off with his useless solicitor, who had instructed him to say nothing during his interview. As if that ever worked. Then, after he'd been charged, the solicitor had moaned at him saying the reason he'd been charged was because he'd talked too much. Put simply, he was fucked.

It wasn't what he wanted to hear from his own brief.

In frustration, he banged the back of his head hard

against the metal door of the prison van three times. He felt warm blood trickle down the back of his neck.

He'd genuinely thought that after he'd got the walk-out on the other murder charge, he'd got away with battering the old man.

That bastard Flint had been right all along.

The old man punching him in the mouth had made him angry, and he had hit him with the metal bar as hard as he could. He'd known as soon as he hit the man that he'd killed him.

Alone in the dark of the prison van, he thought about his wife.

He cursed the day he'd met her. She had deliberately set him up with the cops, lying about how he'd cut his hand. Without that blood sample the cops would never have had his DNA, and he would never have been in the frame for the Randall Clements murder, and he certainly wouldn't have been linked to the Lionel Wickes murder. All they would have had him for was the theft of that RS Cosworth he'd nicked from Nottingham.

It was all that bitch's fault.

Her, his own grassing brother, and that snide bastard Flint.

WE HOPE YOU ENJOYED THIS BOOK

If you could spend a moment to write an honest review on Amazon, no matter how short, we would be extremely grateful. They really do help readers discover new authors.

ALSO BY TREVOR NEGUS

EVIL IN MIND

(Book 1 in the DCI Flint series)

DEAD AND GONE

(Book 2 in the DCI Flint series)

A COLD GRAVE

(Book 3 in the DCI Flint series)

TAKEN TO DIE

(Book 4 in the DCI Flint series)

KILL FOR YOU

(Book 5 in the DCI Flint series)

ONE DEADLY LIE

(Book 6 in the DCI Flint series)

A SWEET REVENGE

(Book 7 in the DCI Flint series)

THE DEVIL'S BREATH

(Book 8 in the DCI Flint series)

I AM NUMBER FOUR

(Book 9 in the DCI Flint series)

TIED IN DEATH

(Book 10 in the DCI Flint series)

A FATAL OBSESSION

(Book 11 in the DCI Flint series)

THE FIRST CUT

(Book 12 in the DCI Flint series)

DCI DANNY FLINT BOX SET (Books 1 - 4)

Made in the USA
Columbia, SC
19 September 2024

42651529R00238